CW01402084

First published by Michael Q. Black 12/22/11

ISBN: 978-1-4681-2956-4

Last Dance of The Libertines:
A 21st Century Odyssey

By Michael Q. Black

1. The Govan Lion

I had about fifteen minutes before the airport shuttle was set to arrive. It was an unusually dim and cool start to the day on that 25th of July in 2011. The light was struggling to break through the white whispers of cloud that covered the sky. I fixed myself a bowl of cornflakes and sat next to the open kitchen window, enjoying the crunchy goodness as I took in the fresh morning air.

I could hear the foghorn in the distance, muffled by the sandstone buildings built around the shipyards. I'd grown up in these parts, just as men like Alex Ferguson and Jimmy Reid had. We were schooled by hard-bitten lessons learned from the Clyde's river of self-knowledge, then moulded into men of substance from iron girders of insoluble strength. This was the lion's den that I'd called home, where I'd been nursed to teenage-hood; that malleable age of sixteen. Everything was just as it was then. Endless rows of shutdown shop fronts, the smell of vinegar and salted fish from chip & chicken bars, and the piss-water pubs that fuelled this pickled powerhouse. Seven years in America hadn't changed the way I felt about this place. It defined me in more ways than one. But in a few short hours I'd be bound for the New World again, the good old US of A, for a final trip before the curtain call came. It was a country that promised everything to everyone and delivered nothing to most.

The Westinghouse American Dream – a passing fantasy, advertised in glorious red, white and blue Technicolor, while the Star-Spangled Banner played on repeat in the background. It was an illusion, a mirage designed to lure desert weary travellers, hungry for a sliver of something sweeter; a wee bite into a better life. I'd lost my taste for those apple-pie pipe-dreams after suffering from a nervous breakdown, due in part to a series of bad investments and a string of rotten relationships. I was lost, broke and desperate; a pilgrim in an unholy land; forced to return to the primordial ooze that birthed me: spiritually at least, if not physically. But now, four years after coming back, I was at the mercy of cruel emotional turmoil once more.

I was lucky in having a friend I could reach out to in such a time of need. Rabbi Avi Glassman had been my spiritual adviser during much of my time in the States. He'd worked his way up from next to nothing and faced every tribulation that life brought his way. His 'take-no-prisoners' attitude worked in his favour and it quickly made him a millionaire. He was a success story: a true son of America. But I was often amazed by his graciousness and friendship. His accomplishments hadn't come at the expense of either, and that was a rare thing. The Rabbi was footing the bill for my trip. I wasn't sure if it was because he believed it would help me, or whether he just wanted to see a friendly face in these uncertain and troubled times. Either way, I was grateful.

My life had always been undeniably odd. I couldn't definitively say whether it was good or bad. Extremes of both were manifest in equal proportion. There were spurts of intense good fortune followed by serious stints of bad luck. I was constantly in the unenviable position of having life simply happen *to* me. This led some to the conclusion that I was a bad seed and 'out of control'. Others said I was born to break barriers. But the only really astounding thing about me was my uncanny ability to choose and keep a select few excellent friends, without whom there would never have been any highs. This was certainly true in relation to the Rabbi. We'd shared many adventures together and here I was, ready to embark on yet another one.

I washed out the empty cereal bowl just as the phone rang. A woman's voice on the other end told me my transportation was waiting downstairs. I'd already packed everything the night before and left my suitcase near the front door in the narrow hallway. I picked up my keys from the table and put on my tri-colour Nike baseball jacket, which went nicely with my floral shirt and washed out jeans, just the thing for a summer holiday. Cliff Richard couldn't have done better in the style department. I dragged my luggage out to the car and the shuttle driver helped me load everything into the boot.

Getting to Glasgow Airport wasn't a problem. At 6.30am there was never any traffic on the roads. But there were several diversions on the motorway, and some exits were stacked with traffic cones. What should have been a ten minute journey turned into a twenty minute sight-seeing tour. On the upside, it gave me the opportunity to go through a mental checklist; passport check, itinerary check; watch, wallet, keys; check. The designated drop zone was jam-packed with people dropping off their loved ones, wishing them well and then tackling them like the Scotland Rugby squad, seconds away from a crucial touchdown. My driver popped open the trunk and lifted out my case. I paid him and gave him a tip, along with half a broken polo mint. Thankfully, the suitcase had wheels underneath, which made it considerably easier to pull all the way into the main terminal.

I scanned through the information screens to find out where I was supposed to check-in. It was impossible to tell. Flight numbers flashed up quicker than Premier League score tables and I spent most of my time re-reading useless data. Finally, after ending up close to cross-eyed, I rolled over to Continental Airlines Desk 23. I had a quick read through my travel itinerary, more out of nervousness than anything. I had to take two connecting flights in order to get to LA and the thought of this made me wince slightly. There were a thousand things that could go wrong in-between and lost luggage was but one of my concerns, though a serious one. The line at the desk was longer than anything St. Peter had to contend with. Up there, heavenly forces did most of the work. Down here, flight attendants were left to their own devices. This made them vulnerable to human error and potentially full of bile. Angry travellers often engaged in the daily sport of 'harangue the employee'. The customer, of course, was always right. I imagined that in their worst moments, the air crew had sick fantasies about decapitating passengers with starched pillows while they passed through the aisles. But for now they had to endure and smile sweetly at the hordes of venomous vertebrates.

I got to the front of the queue and found myself flustered by the stone-cold stares and subtle interrogation methods being employed by the sultry queen bee facing me. Had I packed my own bags? Was I carrying any sharp implements in my hand luggage? Where was I travelling to? I answered all of her questions, but not in any particular order, which confused her slightly, so I clarified my position before the armed policemen to my left drew their guns and shot me like a daredevil duck in hunting season. Since the thwarted bombing attempt, airport security had been stepped up and the Five-o were armed to the teeth; in case another crazy tried to ram a Land Rover into the building. All it would take for a real catastrophe was a cop with an itchy trigger finger, letting rip a hail of bullets into the chest of some unfortunate soul. This was more likely to happen than not. It was just a matter of time. They had a word for it - escalation. Arm the police and the villains will up the ante each time. I had an inside knowledge of such things. Criminals rarely gave a fuck about collateral damage. But then, neither did the 'good guys'. They'd all been raised on Arnie movies. Bang bang, kill the baddie, get the girl, pickup the loot before the end credits run.

After checking my documents, she issued me with tickets and boarding passes for each of my flights.

"Just go up the stairs and follow the signs to the gate marked on your boarding card," said the redhead in uniform. "Have a nice flight Mr Blotnik."

"Thank you kindly," I replied.

I did as she suggested and proceeded to the second floor, past the gift shops and up to the security check point. Once I made it beyond this point, I could relax. Or at least not be worried about missing my plane. I was always scared shitless of that. I'd set foot on every continent bar

Australia, but every time I flew anywhere, my nerves would tingle like Spider-man in a crack den. Everyone else took off their coats and shoes and I followed suit. Next came the fun of emptying my pockets and putting the contents into those large grey and black containers, rolling through the x-ray machine and out the other side. There was always the possibility that someone might steal your stuff, but it was best to stick to approved procedure if you wanted to make it to your plane in good time.

I passed through the metal detector and the bastard thing beeped more times than the BBC bleep censor. I was stiff from fear. The chief of security pointed at me and ordered me to step to the side. I did as he asked and watched him wave his wand all over my person before he patted me down. It reminded me of the scene in the Godfather where Al Pacino got frisked before going for his hidden gun in the bathroom. In that movie, the pig caught a bullet between the eyes. But this fellow had nothing to worry about. I was a domesticated lion who had no intention of ripping off his head and feasting on his rotting carcass. Just as fast as I'd been accosted from the crowd, I was given the all clear and allowed to continue on my way.

I had with me a pocket version of the Book of Revelation. I was comforted by the fire and brimstone ravings. You got the everlasting sense that things could always be worse. Between it and the Old Testament, there was enough to scare you for eight lifetimes; far worse than anything the Marquis de Sade penned in his lifetime. But I wondered if it had concerned the security people. It was not the average sort of light-reading material that people took with them on long journeys.

In order to get to the gate, we all had to pass through the duty free shop. This was a brilliant method of encouraging people to spend their cash and prop-up Scotland's finances. It was like Willy Wonka's Chocolate Factory; except with scotch and tobacco. Alcoholic chain-smoking teens on the streets of Govan, Castlemilk and other Glaswegian suburbs would literally kill to have access to the multi-pack deals strewn on every shelf. But in comparison to where I was going, they were too expensive for my liking, and stealing them was out. However, if you knew the right people in the right places, there was no end to a readily available supply of cheap whiskey and smokes in Los Angeles. It was fair to say in the old days, the Rabbi knew every nook and cranny of that city. He was bound to have a stash of every banned substance known to man in his crib. Then again, he was a father now and had likely become a responsible parent. Even so, it seemed a better idea to wait until I got there.

I sat in the lounge and read for a while. The time passed slowly. I had an hour spare before boarding time. I hadn't slept well the previous night and spent most of it awake, like a kid on Christmas Eve, waiting for Santa to fall down the chimney. I'd unpacked and repacked a dozen or so times, throwing in extra towels and beach sandals; then realising that both were already in there. This frenzied equivalent of a memory test under military stress conditions was followed by back to back Columbo episodes. They took my mind off the inescapable reality of the travel hell that was sure to present itself the next day.

Babies wailed incessantly as their mothers comforted them and tried to shut them up. I was tempted to swat them all like flies while yelling, 'You want something to cry about? I'll give you something to fucking cry about!' and then simply run away as the intellectual dwarfs that were their parents gave chase. But no, that would not have been right. The trauma of being cussed at would only make them into future hell-raising frog torturers; not that I had any first-hand experience of that kind of thing. The worst I'd ever done was to tie a toy mouse to a dog's tail. It spent most of that afternoon going round in circles. This provided a great deal of amusement to our gang of miscreants. After all, we'd skipped Math class to smoke dope on the green of a nearby golf course. It was only sensible that we did *something* to stimulate our minds. The sight of a German Shepard losing its marbles gave us a proper psychological case study for research purposes. Vincent, the resident philosopher in our group of teenage tearaways, commented on the similarity between this and the Ouroboros – the image of a snake eating its own tail, supposedly symbolizing the cycle of life. The rest of us nodded and smoked some more pot next to the 9th hole. The club secretary caught us and we were threatened with police involvement for trespassing. In the days prior to the ASBO, there were no deterrents for our shameless shenanigans.

The airport was getting busier. A young man was holding a toddler, presumably his son, up against the large window. The child clapped its hands and giggled in excitement as they both watched a plane take off into the sky. It brought a smile to my otherwise curmudgeonly face. I paced around the corridor and came upon a vending machine that dispensed candy bars at twice the recommended retail price. I had exchanged most of my money into dollars already and carried only ten pounds in Scottish notes, broken into two fives. I slid one into the robotic behemoth, but it didn't return any change. Instead it threw out five bars of Dairy Milk. I kicked it repeatedly as my rage boiled over. Out popped a fountain of coins, which I stuffed into my pockets, along with the chocolate bars. The flight to Newark was going to be a long one, and it was worth my while to stock up on energy reserves for the journey. Airplane food often left a lot to be desired and it always came in tiny portions that wouldn't satisfy the hunger of an ant. High doses of sugar were the only way to go. The dental consequences could be dealt with on my return.

Finally, the boarding call came for my flight. Old people and baby makers first, then the barren and childless youth. I fell firmly into the last category and had to wait while the sticky fingered spawn of legless mothers got priority. Having been exposed to shows like Trisha, I wondered how many of these brats were actually conceived at drunken New Year's parties. That helped explain the population problem in China. Their new year was always celebrated in style with sex, fireworks, and those weird paper lanterns that were often mistaken for UFO's.

I had my passport and ticket at the ready when a male member of staff asked for them. He flashed the barcode and microchip across a blue screen, which consequently turned green. It deemed me a responsible member of society, fit to fly. But the honour was fleeting and the fact that I was now on board the plane terrified me. I took my seat next to an overweight Mexican.

"Do you want the window seat?" he asked politely.

"No thanks," I replied. "I don't like thinking about how far off the ground we're gonna be."

I dug my nails into the armrests and my veins bulged from the pressure. People were still flowing in, like rats storming a peanut factory. I felt a lot better once we were taxiing down the runway. At thirty thousand feet, we could order refreshments and I planned to get completely smashed and anesthetized during the flight. That was the only way to combat the spectre of motion sickness. The plane took off and climbed further and further toward the stratosphere, until eventually the pilot hit that magic number that allowed us all to breathe a little easier. Of course, I still had to contend with the fact that we were soaring so high, we could tumble down to earth with all the grace of a falling football. This thought was foremost on my mind and not even the relaxed baritone sound of my Mexican friend's voice could alleviate my stress. He tried his best, offering platitudes and pretzels. But once the stewardess started carrying out the safety demonstration and pointed out all the emergency exits and the lifesaving devices, it cancelled out any positive changes in my condition. The card depicting a plane crashing and burning bodies did not help.

I was looking at the little monitor in the headrest in front of me when a female voice broke my concentration. This was no time to be disturbed by idle gibber jabber; I was in right in the middle of taking down these critical readings. Distance travelled, ETA to destination, and our present position. These were essential if we needed to radio for help. But what if we went down in the ocean? Who would find us then? There would be no chance of our surviving that kind of appalling situation. Giant manta rays would barb us to death and electric eels at the bottom of the seabed would swallow our tongues.

"Sir, can I get you anything? You seem a little... unsettled." said the voice.

I turned around and my saucer like eyes met with hers. It was one of the cabin crew.

"No. I'm perfectly fine. Just a frequent flier on holiday. But tell me, can you serve drinks yet?"

"I think we can. You look like you could use it. What would you like?" she asked.

2. A Bad Trip In A West Coast State

We were heading down Lincoln Boulevard when my associate spoke.

"Dude, you look like you've been mangled by a meat mincing machine!"

He wasn't far off the mark. Only a few hours earlier I had been at the mercy of three very large burger loving fat fuckers, in the gainful employ of their President and country. At first glance, they looked moderately respectable in their smart uniforms, but my psychic perceptions told me they were related to Freddy Kruger. Little did I know that I would soon be proved correct.

"Mr Blotnik?"

"Yes?"

"Mr Maxwell Qasim Blotnik?"

"Yes, that's me."

"You've been selected for a body cavity search, sir," said a man at the immigration check point. "Could you step over to the left? These gentlemen will escort you to the appropriate area."

I was quickly hauled into a private room and watched in horror as they donned the glove of evil. There was no doubt left as to the intentions of these hell-spawn. They talked quietly amongst themselves for a few short moments while I waited in a tiny, hermetically sealed room. I heard them laugh as one of their number grabbed me by the collar and threw my shell shocked body against a wall.

"We know all about *your* kind. We don't want them coming over. But we *do* know to treat you people right. We're going to help you get used to the way things are done here. Agent C?"

"Our computer and camera system selected you for screening. Your behaviour has raised concerns, and as required by the subsections of the P.A.T.R.I.O.T. Act, we will have to carry out the necessary checks," said agent C, grinning.

He made it sound like I'd won a prize at the carnival.

It was true, I had been acting jittery and was sweating like an Algerian camel's balls; this was because of my predilection for Southern Comfort; I was dehydrated. I was a nervous flier, I told them, but it did no good. In their eyes, I fit the profile of a Colombian drug baron; or perhaps a Tahitian terrorist who'd shoved a bomb up his ass to cause an explosion in his trousers. This dangerous assumption led them to the conclusion that I would enjoy the perverse experience that was to follow. I panicked in a moment of temporary sanity.

"Thus I clothe my naked villainy with old odd ends," I blurted.

Things were clearly bad if my subconscious had begun quoting Shakespeare. It was then that I realized that these Big Mac loving pig-men were intent on penetrating my outer core. And so, they explored my every orifice, all without adequate lubrication. I'd heard it said that even the devil used spit before ramming his pitchfork into some unfortunate sinner. I wondered how long the terrible torment would continue. In just under twenty hours of travel time by plane, train and auto mobile, I had been scanned, searched, fingerprinted and finger-fucked; by not one, but three massive mammoths. Regardless of the depths their depravity would now sink to, it was already past the point of decency.

This was America, the land of the free. But they had all been caught and caged, to *protect* them from harming themselves. Civil liberties pioneered by this home of the brave were being betrayed, shredded and shot out of the flint pistol that was once fired for freedom. In two-thousand and eleven, we were still seeing Martin Luther King Jr's dream in action. Three years after the change in the Whitehouse colour scheme, the whitewash continued to remain the same. The dream was in danger of becoming little more than a hallucination - a hangover from decades' worth of magic mushroom induced highs.

Even now, the corruption previously prevalent was thriving throughout every tier of every political establishment; and it overshadowed any sexual scandal involving Bill Clinton. In both Capitol Hill and Westminster, rent boys were being hired out to politicians and press packers alike, in exchange for lucrative oiled-up back room deals. These thoroughly abused young things - wealth and power - were too seductive for any of our self-serving representatives to turn down, and it didn't take long before servants of the state were following their masters' lead.

"Excuse the inconvenience, sir. Just follow the signs toward the exit. Your friend is waiting for you at arrivals. *Everything* checked out just fine," said Agent C, smiling with smug satisfaction.

Was he making some kind of veiled reference to our private session of 'find the drug filled condom'? I scowled at him as he and his accomplices threw me out of the search booth.

I grabbed my suitcase from the baggage claim and tried not to dwell on what had just transpired. My friend and spiritual adviser Rabbi Glassman was indeed waiting in the greeting area. I was glad to see him. He smiled at me in recognition. It was one of those scarce smiles that brought with it an innate feeling of reassurance and warmth that infectiously encompassed everyone fortunate enough to be in its path. It added to his natural film-star good looks and inherent charm. His set and permed hair gave him the appearance of a man who idled away his Sunday afternoons in misty steam rooms and expensive eateries. But this was far from the truth. The Rabbi was a workhorse. When he wasn't saving lost sheep, he was busy cranking out homemade movie projects that were aimed at Hollywood's elite. That was his ambition, to become a fully fledged avant-garde film-maker, among other things. He also harboured a secret desire to write a novel. I supposed that was one of the many reasons why he and I had become such close friends.

We exchanged pleasantries and made passing glances at the cosmetic surgery addicts to our left. The older of the two, a blonde - easily in her fifties, squealed in a high pitched shriek that almost burst my eardrums. I'd sat next to her on the final leg of my journey and found her to be as air-headed as a balloon. The Rabbi looked her up and down, checked the junk in her trunk and turned back to me. I hadn't seen him in over three years - not since that fateful night in New York - and here we were, just like old times exchanging glances and assessing the intricate work that went into breast implants, agreeing that it was a testament to the practical application of modern science.

We headed out to the car park where he'd parked his gas guzzling Mercedes SUV. He never purchased American cars and never bought small. It was his 'fuck you' to the concept of carbon taxation without representation. I understood his frustrations. Whilst I was all in favour of environmental awareness, high prices at the pumps, coupled with taxes that went into the pockets of corrupt financiers, did nothing to bring harmony to Mother Earth. People were still burning through oil as if it was sweet water flowing down from Mount Olympus. We were still waging wars for this finite substance that kept the wheels greased on the road to El Dorado, killing for plastic; illogically killing to produce the logical computer.

I basked in the warm Californian sun as we drove toward the Rabbi's fortified castle. Without warning he shouted, "God, it's good to see you again, bro!"

His eyes were firmly on the road ahead and the sudden return to his previous calm composure made me feel both relaxed and uneasy at the same time. There was no telling what the crazy bastard was likely to do when he got excitable. "There's a bottle of Bourbon in the back to take the edge off if you need it," he added.

"Thanks man. It's good to see you too. How's your kid?" I asked him, picking up the bottle resting on the back seat, just next to the baby booster. It worried me.

"I had a swig before coming into the airport," he said, reading my mind. "The kid's great. You know what they say. They grow up so fast. He'll soon be getting to that age where girls will start taking notice of him. He'll be fighting them off with sticks!"

There was almost a hint of fatherly pride in his voice. He paused before he said his next words. "Oh, Bella was asking for you."

Bella? The name rang a bell in the back of my mind, but I couldn't place the face. Then it hit me. That night in New York again.

"So what's with this girl that had you all whacked?" he asked.

"I don't know man. She's a weird one. She's got this way about her that makes my head cry havoc."

"Yeah? I met a girl like that this year. But the problem with American women is they look at the size of your wallet more than the size of your shoes."

"Why should that prove a problem for you? You've got a big wallet and take a size 12. So what's the issue?" I asked him, genuinely confused by the nature of his concern.

"Bro, haven't you been keeping up with the markets? Stuff is crashing everywhere. The God business isn't as good as it used to be. That's why I had to turn to making those films. But even that isn't raking it in like before. I'm getting freaked out a little. It's not just about the chiquitas. I got to think about my son's future too."

He was right. Things were changing for everyone. The economy we were all used to was built on infinite inflation and unregulated debt. It was doomed to failure the moment the idea was hatched in the mind of an economic sex-freak who'd found a way to fuck the public without adequate protection. Absolute power had been granted to bankers who cooked their books to make markets look as good as risk free Thai hookers sprawled across street corners, enticing passing clientele with their empty promises of happy endings. In the middle of this global cluster-fuck of corruption was my friend, getting rammed like everyone else who had nickels and dimes put away for rainy days. I had no such troubles; it was the upside of having nothing.

"Don't worry buddy. Things will get better." I said, knowing full well that the system of old was teetering on the edge of inevitable destruction.

"So the girl…" he was quick to change to subject.

"What? Oh yeah. Her. Well, she's a real hottie, a Rita Hayworth type. I was thinking about giving her my plant."

"You were gonna give her your plant?!" he said, sarcastically. "Shit, it must have been love!"

His words faded into the darkness as my eyelids got heavy and I began to drift off, deep into the nightmare of modern living. I woke just as he pulled up to his mansion on Admiral Avenue. The Marina Del Rey, a secluded sanctuary for those who could afford the safe shelter within its confines. The hired help took care of my belongings while the Rabbi and I took a stroll around the garden and pool area. To say it was beautiful would have been an understatement. It was magnificent; opulence incarnate - the stuff of dreams.

"I was going to keep it a secret, but throwing a pool party tonight. Sort of in your honour. I know how you hate surprises."

"I don't know what to say man. I'm touched. Though I do hate things being sprung on me," I replied.

As the evening air got cooler, we took refuge indoors. He showed me to the guest bedroom and I examined the area for roaches and other bugs, of which I had a paralysing phobia. I shot him a look of intense disapproval on seeing the floral bed sheets that matched my shirt.

"They were not my idea!" he said. "Mom did the sheets in here. You know she thinks of you as a second son. Nothing but the best for my brother from another mother!"

"I'm flattered," I said. "How is the old battleaxe?"

"She's great. She's here. You can say hi once you've freshened up. I'll be in the den. Got some stuff to finish up on the editing front."

He left the room and I rummaged around through my

case to locate the shaving kit-bag I'd neatly packed next to an unopened pack of sports socks. I crept toward the bathroom, unworn clothes in hand, hoping to wash off the stains marking my psyche from the earlier unpleasantness. Eventually, after getting lost and ending up in various broom cupboards and closets, I found the wash room. It was bigger than my entire flat in Scotland. I was awed by the spectacular sight I was faced with. The sheer dimensions were astonishing. There was a hot tub installed in the centre, with more knobs and controls than a NASA space shuttle. I spotted some clean towels on the shelf next to the door. Eight in total; four large bath-towels, two hand towels and two that were a size somewhere in between.

One hour and an orgy of bubbles later, I emerged from the tank like the Loch Ness Monster, growling with intense determination and excitement. I'd made it through all the inane bullshit that accompanied air travel and had gotten to the other side, not unscathed, but at least with most of my sanity intact. My mind had also been taken off the emotional upheavals that lead to this unplanned exodus. But I knew this sense of peacefulness was not going to last. I got dressed and made my way to the den where I was sure I'd find the Rabbi hard at work. Instead, I came upon his mother Golda, painting her fingernails with purple nail-varnish.

"Max-well!"

She always added that inflection to the end of my name.

"Avi went to go fetch a few things for his party tonight."

Momma Glassman gave me a bone-crunching hug and pinched and kissed my cheeks.

"It's so good to see you! It has been too long," she added. "How are you? What have you been doing with yourself? Why have you been away so long?"

I didn't have the heart to tell her the truth. Being poverty stricken and without a pot to piss in is not something you can boast about as a prodigal son. I remembered the first time the Rabbi had introduced me to his family and friends. I'd overheard Golda and the Rabbi speaking afterwards. Her words echoed in my ears as I stood there, dumbstruck. "I have a lot of faith in that boy, Avi. He's got the same grit and determination in his eyes that I saw in you Avi. You must look out for him."

Avi had looked out for me. But how could I explain to her that I had no job, no future, no girlfriend, and that I was about as far from having any of those as I could get? I didn't want to disappoint her. The last time I'd seen her I was only one item shy on that laundry list of deficits. At the time, it wasn't a priority. Women came and went and in those years. I never had to wait long between one girl and the next. I'd learned that it was a lot easier to get laid than to get loved. Eventually though, the novelty wore off and I started searching for something deeper.

"I've been busy," I replied with a sheepish smile.

I rubbed my neck in that awkward way you do when you've accidentally shot your neighbours goldfish bowl with an illegally obtained BB gun. But even that was easier to deal with than the interrogating laser-beam gaze of a Jewish mother.

Just then, I heard a car pull up on the gravel-spread driveway and there were voices murmuring, getting closer to the door to the den. I recognised one. The other seemed familiar too, but I couldn't place it.

"Oi Vey! Are you going to make me carry all of this inside? Give me a hand dammit!"

I was about to run and help when I realised that the request wasn't directed at me. The Rabbi kicked the swing door open and walked in with boxes in each hand. Behind him was the endlessly complaining female voice I'd heard outside. The Rabbi's six-foot frame moved over to the desk adjacent to the filing cabinet and I could now make out the face of the woman carrying the rest of the shopping bags. My heart got stuck in my throat. It was Bella.

"Hi," she said, not moving.

The Rabbi took the bags from her hands. I stared at

her for a while before replying. My mouth was dry and I barely mustered a response.

"Hi," I paused for a few seconds, unsure of what to say next. "You look great."

"Thanks. You too. How was your flight?"

"Long," I said.

The Rabbi emptied the boxes he'd brought in. Everything from Bell's whiskey to fine South African wine lined the length and breadth of the table. I helped him fold down the boxes and Bella did the same. It was safe to say Bella was the only woman who I knew for certain had once actually loved me, but being immature and irresponsible, I had no clue as to the real value of love in those days. I'd been careless and inconsiderate with her feelings, playing fast and loose with that cavalier attitude that most jaded people carry with them. Whatever may have been between us was dead in the water quicker than a harpooned sperm whale off the coast of Japan.

The four of us shared a quiet drink on the patio, enjoying the great outdoors. The Rabbi suggested bringing out the gas barbecue stowed in the garage. Bella and I agreed that it was a stellar idea and helped him drag it out from under a mountain of collected junk. Golda laid back in the deck chair with a margarita in one hand and a copy of Vogue magazine in the other, perusing the pages as if she were on holiday in Barbados.

Hooking up the gas tank was easy and didn't take much effort. We raided the larder for meat to splay across the heavy duty industrial grill. It was fire-apple red and looked like something Satan had constructed on his day off, for the specific purpose of roasting Stalin's iron testicles.

I ducked out with my arms full of packaged meat, cradling a heap of lamb chops, steaks and marinated chicken breasts. It occurred to me that the Rabbi had likely pre-planned for such an occasion but hadn't quite gotten around to hoisting out the flame-spewing grilling machine; or perhaps he'd cunningly calculated the easier option of leaving the real hard work to Bella and me.

3. Counting Kcals In California

Guests began to arrive just as we were organizing the evening's entertainment. The Rabbi brought out his boom box from the den and we piled his CD collection into an old wheelbarrow and carted it out, placing it beside the pool. This, we figured, would leave the choice of music in the hands of the attendees and not down to the three of us. All of us had eclectic tastes which were not appreciated by the general public. Bella had flirted with industrial music for a while and she'd learned to appreciate the incessant bashing of used oil drums against steel toe capped boots. My own ears were terminally tuned into the sounds of the seventies and rarely ventured into the realms of new age pop. The Rabbi himself could listen to just about anything; but his own preferences were a matter of Californian folklore. Johnny Cash, Perry Como and Roy Orbison. These were the three lightening rods that kept him grounded.

The Rabbi announced that the pool cleaner had been round that afternoon and that those who wanted to go for a swim were welcome to, if and when they felt the urge. Skinny dipping was encouraged, imbibing was promoted and mischief was compulsory. Contrary to outward appearances, Rabbi Glassman was not the straight-laced religious scholar he liked to portray himself as. The moment no-one was looking, he clawed out of his buttoned down professional garments and dived into a pair of Bermuda shorts that hung down to his knees. He was like Superman in this regard, a man with dual identities, with his own flash superhero costume to boot.

I asked him about his son. I hadn't seen the little devil since my arrival and I was concerned, especially with all the alcohol that was flowing more freely than a retired pensioner's bladder.

"He's staying over at his mom's tonight," he said. "I'm footloose and free! Free for a day!"

He and his wife had parted ways almost a year after

the kid was born. It was a sad state of affairs. He'd gotten custody of their son when she was deemed an unfit parent by the state of California. The primary basis for the judge's decision was the initially undisclosed fact that she had overdosed on a speed-ball in a downtown drug den in the middle of a school day. She checked into rehab subsequently and went through court ordered detox; but it took Avi many years to build up a workable relationship with her to share parental responsibility. Neither he nor Golda completely trusted her. I noted that the Rabbi checked his phone with regularity throughout the evening.

Avi's religious enlightenment came on the eve of his son's second birthday. Up until then, his main focus and port through every storm had been the health and fitness kick he'd been on since his twenties. He was a fully fledged exercise nut and worked out every day of the week, except on Shabbat. He even hired out his services as a personal trainer. Given his physique, it wasn't surprising that the majority of his clients were women and he relished offering them his 'extra special work out sessions'. It was during one of these that his son had been conceived. Before his spawn turned two, he experienced what addicts refer to as 'an instant of clarity'. He began to recognize that there was something missing within him, and he became driven by a need to search for that something. Two trips to Egypt, a short stay in the holy land and a slew of eastern mystics later, he claimed to know the secrets of the hidden universe, becoming a teacher to countless lost souls   all desperate for answers.

A total of about fifty or sixty people had gathered around his not-so-humble home. I only knew a handful, and most of them only in passing. But the Rabbi certainly knew how to throw a party with pizzazz. The meat on the grill went down well and we had a ball charring the hell out of orders from people we didn't like. Even a live rock band put in an appearance and belted out a tune or two.

Golda had a blast talking up her son to every young lady within five yards of earshot. "I want to see you settle down with a *nice* girl Avi," she'd say to him. "You deserve a *good* Jewish girl who'll look after you. Stop wasting your time on these *shiksas!*"

More people came, and with them more bottles; some with homemade kick-ass concoctions. I sampled some moonshine that was doing the rounds, which nearly killed me.

"It's a hundred and sixty proof! Try it, it'll put hairs on your chest!" said the man with the jug.

"You can't get a hundred and sixty proof," I said. "Besides; I already have a ferret's pelt on my chest."

"Doesn't matter. Take a swig. Trust me, this will make you into a sexual Tyrannosaurus!" he exclaimed.

I spent the next hour bowlegged and babbling like a baboon, extolling the virtues of Salman Rushdie's Satanic Verses to a conservative Iranian. He'd only come over to complain about the noise.

He declared me an infidel and I chased him to his car, armed with a large kebab skewer. Technically, he was correct. I had no time for orthodox religion. But I was far from an infidel and I was offended by his pronouncement. I believed in the unified beginnings of all creation, a sort of collective consciousness of all living things. This was my God, heavy duty tree of life stuff. The Rabbi's teachings had re-affirmed those beliefs.

Bella was standing next to me, shaking her head vigorously. I hid the skewer behind my back and smiled at her.

"You haven't changed one bit!" she laughed.

"Should I have?" I asked her.

"No. I like you just the way you are. You're like Rasputin, except way crazier!"

"Yeah. But sadly I'm not banging the Queen. Then again, I don't think I'd want to. Queen Elizabeth is getting on a bit these days!"

We rejoined the Rabbi, though he was busy sampling a Bundt cake brought over by a German couple. In the distance, close to the rose bushes, I could see Divine and Mario, old friends from the valley. Divine certainly was a beautiful creature and a free spirit; a goddess among mere mortal women, with huge natural tits and a big ass begging to be coveted. Any man on earth would have robbed every bank in the United States and laid it at her feet, just to taste her sweetness. Many already had. But she now only had eyes for Mario. Mario, the polished Italian stallion with 1200cc's of horsepower between his legs. His Ducati was a work of art; a real crowd pleaser. He strode up and gave me one of his custom macho man hugs.

"Max! When I heard you were in town, I thought to myself, 'I must go and see him!' Divine and I were talking about you the other day. I still owe you for that favour," he said.

"No, you don't Mario. It was my pleasure. Honestly, let's not mention it," I said, looking over his shoulder. "Divine! So good to see you!"

"And you sweetie! We were so excited. It's been forever!" she said, hitting me lightly with her handbag. "Next time, don't leave it so long!"

"I won't."

We shared some champagne and chatted for a while. By the end of the night, everyone was utterly plastered. We lit some fireworks, leftovers from the fourth of July, and stared at the moon yodelling at three am. Golda had already retired for the night and the Rabbi urged us to avoid doing anything that would wake her. At first, I thought this was because he was simply doing his duty as a dotting son. But I soon found out this was not the case. Mario took out a small pipe, some tin foil and a seven gram rock. Crack cocaine was a vice I generally didn't indulge in, and certainly never in Glasgow. I'd read stories about how dealers often cut it with drain cleaner or various household chemicals that would send a man to his grave. But being in trusted company, and knowing that Mario only bought from a reputable source, I decided to partake.

High and horny, things quickly descended into a chaotic frenzy. Clothes were stripped and ripped off and unfettered tongues explored pink flesh and lusciously erect nipples. Men were fucking men, women were topping women, and dogs were mating cats. Fluids gushed forth like Niagara Falls and nothing was left that hadn't been ravished. It was as if the Romans were ransacking the West Coast in a revival of Pompeii's finest moments.

By sun-up I was in the guest room with no memory of how I'd gotten there. Only remnants of decaying flashbacks were left in my Swiss-cheesed head. I couldn't bring myself to leave my surroundings for the better part of an hour, afraid of what and who I'd encounter if I was to venture outside of those walls. When I eventually I did, I found that not a single soul remained save the Rabbi and me. The pool was a complete mess, the floors inside were covered in mud and a giant moose head had been placed on top of the toilet seat in the bathroom. I wasn't exactly thrilled at prospect of having a dead animal stare at me while I took a leak, so I carried it out into the yard, where Avi was sunning himself on a lawn chair. I crept up behind him, dropped the moose head on his six-pack abs and ran back into the bathroom.

"You bastard! You fucking evil bastard! I'll get you for that!"

I worried for a while that he might do something in retaliation, but not hearing anything more, I relaxed, coming to the conclusion that it was safe to take a crap without worry of being disturbed. This was sibling rivalry taken to hideous extremes, but such was our relationship. Avi had pulled me out of more lows than anyone. He'd saved my neck more than once. After my depressive episode in New York City, he was the one who'd fronted me the money for a plane ticket back to Scotland. He knew my salvation lay in going back to my roots of thirteen years and not in hospitalization. "A cactus can only grow in the desert, not in a paddy field. America is a paddy field.' he said. I had no idea what the hell he meant at the time.

At 1.30pm, well settled and more awake, the Rabbi suggested we meet Bella for lunch at the most happening restaurant in town. Mr Chow's was known for its showcased menu, high-end prices and celebrity diners. I wasn't sure that we'd get in given our propensity for making trouble and my slightly tight budget, but the Rabbi said this would not be a problem.

"Relax," he said. "The Lord and I have an understanding. We'll get in. I'd better call Bella and tell her our plans."

We cruised in comfort thanks to the Rabbi's air-conditioned car. Tourists were huddled like ants around the Hollywood walk of fame. I was tempted to get out and circle the block. It would have been easy to draw a crowd. They all *expected* to encounter famous people and I knew could fool them all with my Don Johnson style of attire and wrap-around designer Siamese sunglasses. They didn't know that most persons in the public eye were safely tucked away in their secure fortresses, enclosed within the confines of tall walls, watching reruns of Jeopardy. That was, of course, until some freelancing, chancing paparazzi got through the net of necessitated precautions. It was a vicious cycle. I'd been unlucky enough to meet some of these self obsessed 'stars' on my previous visit. I was not impressed.

"Hey, you wanna go to the Universal theme park?" asked my friend.

"What for? It was fun the last time, but I doubt I'd get the same kick out of it again," I replied.

It was obvious he was in the process of planning activities for the rest of my vacation. He knew I needed to take my mind off the stresses I'd escaped from. The valet was on standby outside Mr Chows. We got out of the vehicle and the Rabbi threw him the keys. "You scratch it, you go six feet under!" The doorman peered over his list of pre-booked patrons.

"I don't see you on the list, sir."

Avi stared at him, burning a hole into the other man's retinas.

"Perhaps it's under the name of the other gentleman

in your party. What did you say your name was?" he asked nervously, looking to me for help.

"They call me Mister Tibbs!" I answered, doing my best Sidney Poitier impression.

"Look," said the Rabbi. "We're friends of the management! Now, unless you want to get fired, you'd better let us in. Do we not look like upstanding respectable gentleman to you? You don't want to be branded an anti-Semite do you? Are you bigoted?"

"Let me check again," he gulped. "Yes, I believe we have an opening. Table six. The maitre d' will take you to it."

A sleek Chinese man showed us the way, seated us at the table and handed us a wine list and a menu. The first was not a wise move. I was still in the process of recovering from my hangover. But the Rabbi insisted that it would do me good to add ballast to my light-headed brain. I stared out the window to check for pink elephants and saw Bella talking to the doorman. She pointed at us and I waved her over. The doorman nodded and let her in. She strutted up to the table and ran her fingers through her short jet-black hair.

"I can't believe you got in here!" she squealed.

"Neither can we," I said, looking at the Rabbi who was about ready to order.

A waiter brought another menu over. Bella glanced at it and put it down quickly. She asked Avi to order for her. He chose an expensive Claret, three appetizers, four main courses and four desserts, including Crème Brule. I was a little perplexed by his selection. The waiter opened the wine bottle and handed Avi the cork to admire its bouquet. The Rabbi sniffed it while the man in the red waistcoat poured a sample into a wineglass. Avi swirled the vino around in the glass and then tasted it. I could hear it swishing as it circled his palate. He gave it a resounding thumbs-up and the waiter poured the blood-red liquid for each of us before placing the bottle in the centre of our table.

The spring rolls, quail eggs and carrot soup didn't take long to arrive, but the venison, sliced seaweed and calamari was not dished out in good time so I excused myself to use the restroom. I wandered by the kitchen and couldn't resist the temptation to take a peek. I peered through the small window panel on the swing door and saw one of the trainee chefs preparing some roast beef and Yukon Gold mashed potatoes, which looked extremely appetizing. His colleague was hunched over another plate and at first it was difficult to tell what he was doing. But then I saw. There he was, in broad daylight, fornicating with a plate of jellied eels. His eyes rolled back and a smattering of thick fluid covered the contents. I was not put off eating however, as he was not the cook assigned to our orders; though I did feel a sense of revulsion on behalf of those who'd have to enjoy his handy work.

The restrooms were just past the kitchen. They were amongst the cleanest I'd ever seen; with the most polite toilet attendant I'd had the pleasure of encountering. He dried my hands with a fresh towel and spritzed me with some aftershave or other. I gave him ten dollars, thanked him for his efforts and told him that he was doing a great job and to carry on flying the flag for the spirit of capitalism.

The wank-happy chef walked by me as I made my way back to the table and I saw him ask an old Frenchman if he'd enjoyed his meal. Bella was telling the Rabbi about her new diet. She could eat anything she wanted and not put an inch on her waistline. I gazed down at my bulging gut then at the two picture-perfect bodies next to me. On and on she droned, lecturing me on the benefits of juniper berries, guava juice and fruitarian apple farms. I was not remotely interested, but the Rabbi was entranced.

"Well. There's always the tapeworm diet," I said.

"No way! I'd never do that. Why swallow a tapeworm when all you have to do is count your calories?" said Bella.

"Anyone want to take a guess how many Kcals are in what we've just ordered?" asked the Rabbi, as the rest of our food arrived.

"So, Bella, how's your day been?"

"It was good," she replied. "I went jogging down

Sunset Strip earlier before picking the brain of an old school Hollywood diva. What a trip; she'd forgotten even more than she remembered!"

"That'll happen if you keep Barbara Walters whacked on roofies and chained in the basement," I said. "There's bound to be some permanent damage over time."

"She's not chained in the basement," she chuckled. "I keep her in the attic stoned on psilocybin."

"Dear God! Have you no shame?!" I said. "These Hollywood types just aren't prepared for the sort of madness that can cause. We real people might cope with images of Japanese sumo wrestlers humping our eye sockets; but can you imagine what that kind of hallucination would do to one of *them*? They'd run amok, stealing sausages from other old ladies in grocery stores!"

The Rabbi nearly choked on his sorbet, but I was ready and prepared to perform the Heimlich manoeuvre if it came to it. Bella doubled over with a fit of the giggles. Tears were streaming down her face and she went beet red. But she wasn't one to be beaten, not even in a surreal session of verbal jousting.

"It's not like I don't look after her. I had the doctor over. He said there was a chance it could lead to early onset of Alzheimer's. Actually, she's a very sweet lady, normally or running amok," she parried.

"Alzheimer's eh? I wonder if that would explain her satanic sex orgies with John Warner and Alan Greenspan. Personally I think she's the greatest patriot in history; I mean Greenspan! Only someone who really loved their country could go there," I said.

I wondered if Bill Clinton, America's greatest love machine, had ever hired Walters to polish the Whitehouse flagpole. The Rabbi was in hysterics and Bella was gasping for air. Even I struggled to keep a straight face and it wasn't long before I too was laughing uncontrollably. The Maitre d' shot us a look of utter contempt and told us that we were making the other diners feel uneasy. The self-conscious bastards mistakenly believed that we were ridiculing them.

"So I was thinking," continued the Rabbi, "…maybe we could go sightseeing."

"Sure," I said. "Where did you have in mind?"

"Well I was thinking it might be nice to get out of LA for a while. Maybe go to Miami for a few days. Get some sun, sand and Sangria. All on me of course. Maybe we could make a couple of other stops too."

"Like a road trip?" I asked.

"Yeah. But by plane. First class. Whad'ya say? Come on, say yes. It'll be just like the old days!"

"Sounds like an idea," I said, thinking about it for a moment. "Sure, why not!"

"I would love to come with you boys," Bella chimed in. "But my cousin's coming in from Norco tomorrow."

"Damn, that sucks. Two's company, but three's always better!" said the Rabbi.

"Yeah," I added. "What he said."

"Mom's always complaining about how she doesn't get to spend enough time with the sprog. I'm sure she wouldn't mind watching him for a couple of days."

"Speaking of your son, don't you have to pick him up soon?" said Bella.

"Damn, you're right. We should get a move on. We'll pick up the little man then I'll call my travel agent and make the arrangements for our trip," he said.

We went Dutch and split the bill three ways and left separate tips based on our individual dining experiences. I'd blown a third of my life-savings, which didn't amount to all that much, on an agreeable meal at an average eatery. But I was beginning to enjoy myself and I felt better just being in the company of old friends and I began to reminisce about other friends in other states, scattered across the vastness of America's heartlands.

4. Where The Mammoths Live -
A Safari Through An American Jungle

Rabbi Glassman and I arrived in Miami as dawn broke across the state of Florida. I could take the risk of travelling by plane when I had my spiritual advisor with me. No-one would risk fucking with God in this bible-bashing, Mormon-hating country. Even the average coke fiend has to have some faith in the big guy in the sky while rolling up his dollar bill to inhale the white stuff. "In God We Trust".

There was never any real separation between church and state. America's secularism was simply a convenient cover for military campaigns into foreign territories; sometimes for black gold, mostly for money. Countless wars had been declared against invisible enemies whose very existence was, at best, debatable. First they waged the cold war and 'fought' the 'evil' communists; many of whom were just taking a stand against the rapid cancer-like growth of capitalism. Then came the 'War on Drugs', targeting the young who were calling for the collapse of old establishments in favour of individual awareness. That battlefront had easily been taken when the tools for perceived enlightenment eventually became the very means of mental and physical imprisonment. But this new millennium brought with it a new threat: terrorism. In this century, it was the turn of the Islamic world to brace itself for vilification, along with anyone else who was a voice of descent, and airports were the front lines of defence in this crusade.

We thanked the Transport and Security Authority for their hospitality, left Miami International and checked into Wyndham Gardens, a modernised and trendy hotel in South Beach that catered to happy holiday makers. But it also appealed to high class hookers and their johns; booked in for a few fun moments of unabashed pleasure. Women in these parts were generally looser than old screen porch doors and got banged with similar frequency.

This was a place where a drink bought for the right woman could get you blown. Two might get her friend in on the action, and a twenty stuffed down her bra would buy you a quick fuck in the powder room. My associate and I had already been offered a sample eight-ball by the man in the next room. We didn't decline. There was more cocaine on these streets than in the entire film reel of Scarface. That stain on global cinema screens sparked a slew of copycat dealers. Every one of those insignificant worms saw themselves as the next Tony Montana, clad in silk shirts and cheesy suits, while their girlfriends were kitted out from head to toe in DeBeers diamonds. But the reality was considerably different. Virtually all of them ended up behind bars, trying desperately to avoid being anally raped in the communal showers.

There was a resolute and dire need for a proper mode of transportation. We wanted to *explore*, see things the typical tourist doesn't get to; or perhaps doesn't want to. Most visitors get sold on the idea of the cellophane packaged vacation plan, sucking them into 'fun for all the family!' This was no way to get the true feel of a holiday hotspot. I was on my fourth visit to this cesspool of decadence and I was loving every minute of it. Most of the people who lived in Miami would up sticks in a heartbeat if given the chance, and I could understand why. Being surrounded by wickedness day in, day out was enough to give anyone a huge fuck-off ulcer. But my own character was so horrendously flawed that I thrived on monumental acts of misbehaviour. If the doctors had gotten their way, I would probably have been castrated during early childhood and put on a diet of Ritalin and a daily dose of Spongebob Squarepants to numb my overactive mind.

We rented a Ford Mustang from the Avis people at the desk in the lobby; but we had to promise not to crash into pedestrians at high speeds. Initially, they asked us for our credit card information. But I couldn't oblige as I was classed as 'persona non grata' with most rental, credit and insurance agencies. Over the years, I had been responsible for the destruction of one Dodge Durango, a Ford Probe and a Fiat Coupe; the last of which met its end thanks to several spare canisters of kerosene, stored (for no particular purpose) in the boot of the bugger. The police in Glasgow were not amused by that incident. When asked why I'd done it, I told them candidly "The fuckin' thing wouldn't start and I couldn't be arsed to sell it for scrap." They'd reported me to every authority in the region. I was sure that even Interpol were now keeping an eye on my every move. But the Rabbi, being a man of God, was able to assure the young lady attending to us that we were honourable and upstanding gentlemen; with honourable intentions. I suppressed the urge to regurgitate as I watched them flirt. It was a sickening display of ass-kissing niceness.

"Since you have impeccable credentials Mr Glassman, I don't think there will be a problem," she cooed.

"Thank you sweet child! God Bless your darling soul!" he said.

I watched her give him the keys. The old adage was true; the Lord certainly did work in mysterious ways.

By three o'clock that afternoon, we were driving around Coral Gables searching for a bar I'd discovered on my last trip. There was no sign of it anywhere. And then came the terrible realisation that it had been replaced with a Denny's diner. There was nothing to be done, except to go in and sample the menu. To have quit and driven away would have been a waste of good gasoline. There was also the food factor to consider. My associate and I were hungry. The complimentary breakfast at the hotel had not been enough to satisfy our voracious appetites. But thankfully, extra large helpings of everything were the norm here. No plate on any table was left with a morsel on it. This helped explain the muffin tops we'd encountered on entering; a sight that should never be witnessed by a small child - or an adult lacking a strong stomach. Large women, who were otherwise attractive, chose to wear tight jeans and hot-pants, and the fat just poured out of their bulging waste lines, surrounding their upper thighs and sagging down, down toward the Earth's gravitational centre. Three years ago seeing a thing like that may have done something for me; in those years of mental disturbance I was experimenting with unconventional tastes. Now all it did was make me gag.

Having been fed and watered by the excellent waitresses, we resumed our tour and got a little lost. We'd ended up in Hialeah; this was not a part of town that Florida wanted to accept as being within its state borders. Although the entire city was crawling with Castro's prison rejects, this suburb was a snake-pit of degeneration. There was something about the street politic that created an excess of mayhem. Nowhere was it as evident as in the Walgreens car-park, where we stopped for aspirin and other assorted pharmaceutical compounds. A large four by four with spinning rims was parked two spaces to our right. The reverberating bass beats echoed in its stereo speakers. The tinted windows rolled down and I was sure we were about to witness a daytime drive-by. The Rabbi and I hunkered down in case we got caught in the crossfire. But then, a voice growled and spoke in Spanglish.

"Hey mamacita, why don't you bring that hot little ass over to your papi! Come sit on my lap!" heckled the hyena behind the wheel.

The girl, who couldn't have been older than fifteen, looked visibly uncomfortable. We indulged in a spot of voyeurism and watched her as she adjusted her clothes and walked quickly across the street. Base animal behaviour. It never fails to shock; the amorphous face of evil. In this instance, no actual crime had taken place, yet the look of humiliation and degradation in the young girls eyes was unmistakable. The same was true of most rapes and murders. The perpetrators were innocent until proven guilty; but they were only guilty if there was no reasonable doubt; but no reasonable human being could be free of doubt; so they were innocent by default. Meanwhile, entire generations were being criminalised, shunned and rejected for wanting to explore bizarre ideals such as freedom, hope and love. People hooked on heroin, marijuana smokers and the mentally irregular were all harmful to the greater good. It was this twisted vision of social Darwinism that led many brilliant minds to live on the fringes, creating their own cliques and secret societies.

Suddenly, I heard the opening bars of 2Pac's California Love. The Rabbi took out his newfangled smart phone and answered the call.

"Rachel! Yeah, we just got into town... Actually we were on our way to the mall to watch the cattle in the bull-pen. We could stop by yours afterwards?"

He looked to me and I nodded.

"When are you free? Yeah, I know the address. Cool."

"Ask her if she's got any weed dude!"

"Oh, Max wants to know if... Yeah? Cool. Canadian eh? Cool. Ciao."

He turned to me as put the phone back in his trouser pocket.

"I wasn't sure if you wanted to talk to her."

"I probably shouldn't. Not on the phone anyway," I replied.

Rachel was great. The kind of woman with whom you could talk baseball and shoot the breeze, without that male fear of the conversation turning to pink lipstick and hair extensions. Unfortunately, she was also a sex addict. This posed a problem one particular evening in the spring of 2005 when the electricity went out in her apartment and we were left alone on an idle Friday night. I wondered if there would be that awkwardness in the air when I saw her again. There was also the strangeness of my present predicament to consider. Like Oscar Wilde, I too had a love that dared not speak its name. A felonious feline had clawed her way into my affections. Her cat nature entranced me. But she was wild and dangerous. What would be the consequences of caring for such a hormone-driven, power-mad hybrid? I was certain that the RSPCA wouldn't take too kindly to my manhandling that kind of creature. There would be an outcry. Such things were meant to run free in the forests of exploration.

We pulled into the Dolphin Mall car-park and I searched the glove compartment for a pair of military high-grade binoculars, which we'd brought with us in case we had to watch the action from behind enemy lines. This was not a place your ordinary shopping junkie could handle. The bargain basement sale signs and free snack testing booths were strategically positioned to catch the eye of hungry customers on the go; on the war-path to the next sale. Like F-18s, they could refuel in middle of all the action. They would not otherwise make it through their commerce crazed spending sprees. This was the DMZ, where they fought, tackled and bruised to show the might of their purchasing power. The sight brought us a twisted sense of joy. They were like caged zoo animals being let loose to tear apart their jungle opponents. Little did the fools realise that despite being given the designation of 'valued consumers', it was they themselves that were being consumed.

The sun got lower in the sky and the hour came to see Rachel. Better to bite the bullet and not prolong the impending doom, I thought. My chronic insomnia and jet lag weren't helping my nervous disposition. I fiddled with the radio in the car, trying desperately to pick up some station that didn't have a play list full of bitches, pimps and ho's. I'd once heard it said that rap music was a form of poetry. John Keats probably turned in his grave on hearing that. In the days of Gill Scott Heron, that might have been true. Rap and poetry were indivisible and real to their roots in the good old days. But now it was driven by lesser imitations of Biggie Smalls and Jay-Z. Testosterone induced lyrics glamorised the thug life and young gun-totting troubadours were its victims.

We pulled up at seven eighty six, 16th North West Avenue and made our way to the front door. I was as nervous as an Alabama tick-hound at a bluegrass jamboree. Rachel answered the door. Her long blonde hair swished over her low cut top, contrasting the green material covering her buxom breasts.

"Hey guys, come on in. I was just making margaritas."

I gave a quick wave and smiled slightly before she grabbed me and squeezed herself against my short body. I was feeling light-headed and dizzy from the heat. Her perfume seeped into my senses and I recognised it instantly. Chanel twenty two; the last birthday gift I'd bought her.

The Rabbi brought in a crate of beer from the car and I helped him carry the rest inside. We'd stopped by a liquor store run by Peruvian immigrants and picked up two cases of Budweiser and three quarts of Sangria. Rachel poured out the contents from her blender and the three of us sat silently on the couch and sampled the bowl of nacho chips next to the super-sized jar of dip.

It was only once we'd gone through two bags of Canadian grass, six beers, three margaritas and six capsules of diphenhydramine that we felt truly comfortable. Just like old times. It was then that we were struck with the notion of going for a swim in the neighbour's pool; but before I stripped down, my associate pulled me aside. He was uncharacteristically drunk and it was obvious from his slurred speech that he was not himself.

"She's fuckin' beautiful! I must have her! Bathe her and bring her to my temple. The spirit of God demands it! No, better yet, I'll lick her clean!"

There was certainly some kind of spirit going through him; though it wasn't coming from any divine source. I tried to explain to him that it was an unwise idea to let himself be tempted by a creature of lust, but he was having none of it. In the end, I agreed to give them privacy for their pending 'religious' experience. It did make sense in the long run. If the Rabbi was the victim of her sultry charms, I'd be off the hook, Rachel would get laid, and the Rabbi would have an opportunity to spread his seed as well as his word. I went back into the house and rummaged through the Rabbi's jacket. Jackpot. Car keys in hand, I rushed out to the Mustang parked on the sidewalk. Darkness had finally descended, but a sticky warmth still clung to the night air. I turned the key in the ignition and the engine grumbled before settling into a slow hum. I drove through the Cuban district and coasted around the Miami Orange Bowl stadium, home to the Miami Dolphins for their first twenty-one seasons. Their greatest quarterback, Dan Marino, was a living legend and all-round American hero. But he'd retired in 1999. The Orange Bowl became pretty much defunct in that same fateful year when the Sun Life stadium became the primary host to pro and college football games.

I could see that the all-night bars and clubs were beginning to open their doors to the long suffering masses, all standing in an orderly line; waiting for Lucifer to claim their souls. In a city that gave the lowest circles of hell a run for their money, the savage wasteland of human indecency was all but invisible to the naked eye; hidden in plain sight, paraded out to entertain and shock the squares. The regular Joe, with his Peggy Sue in tow, would never be caught dead in these avenues and alleyways. They would be busying themselves in gift shops with cheap souvenirs promoting Disneyland and the many fine Mom and Pop stores that were springing up on hill tops and highways stretching from coast to coast. Hussies were flashing their tits at every passing motorist and half-cocked potential client. The American prostitute is in a class of her own. She doesn't take shit from anyone and will not tolerate being called a slut until *after* she's seen the green. If you're short of the necessary legal tender, she'll hiss her tag-line at you as you roll down your window: "If you ain't got no money, take your broke ass home!"

I wasn't prepared to risk my disease free status; not even for the finest blowjob this side of Kansas. I cruised on, past the redhead with the big round butt, and onwards, toward the beach. I could see the sand, lit up with lanterns and decorated with fire-eating circus freaks. Volleyball players dressed in skimpy bikinis and jogging shorts littered the seafront, grunting away in the midnight hours while the moonlight reflected off their tanned silhouettes. I stopped the car in an empty parking bay and set off to join in the fun. The bronzed beauty sitting on the Teak patio of the Seaside Bar motioned me to come over and I found myself enjoying a cool Mojito with her while she talked to me about humpback whales and their mating rituals. She was a marine biologist. We swam in the ocean for a while and looked up at the moon and the stars.

"Have you ever made love under the stars?" she asked.

"Can't say I have. There's too much smog in Scotland's cities to see them."

"Would you like to?"

"Sure."

She went down on me and we screwed for what seemed like an unending eternity while the waves washed over us on the shoreline. I was a horny toad in heat. The exhilaration didn't last long. In all the furore of impassioned fucking, specks of sand had crawled into my ass-crack and it was beginning to itch. We washed ourselves off in the warm water and went back to the bar for another round of cocktails and tacos. Spanish songs of love and loss pulsated from two damaged and badly wired speakers on the promenade. Mixed up feelings and confused memories surfaced in my intoxicated mind. I'd left Rachel's to avoid adding to my burgeoning bag of complex emotional problems, yet here I was, embroiled in another kettle of strange fish; out of the frying pan and straight into the napalm.

I paid for the food and drinks and bid the dusky devil-woman farewell. She rubbed her cheek with her forefinger and smiled as I got up to leave. I felt guilty for leaving her there like that, but it would have been foolish to take the situation any further. I didn't know her from Eve. She could have been an axe-murdering escapee from the local lunatic asylum. I quickened my pace as this thought lingered in my mind.

By 4am I was safely back in room 314 at the hotel. The maid had left fresh bars of soap and toiletries in the bathroom. I placed a call to room-service and ordered a Philly cheese-steak and another bottle of Bourbon. Twenty minutes later there was a knock at the door and a tall Cuban in a bow-tie entered, carrying a plastic tray. I tipped him modestly and got down to the business of eating. There was also some freshly squeezed orange juice in a plastic cup, next to the sandwich, which I hadn't ordered.

At 6am I heard someone fiddling with the electronic key-card mechanism. The door burst open and there stood the Rabbi, seething with anger, his teeth dripping with saliva, almost frothing at the mouth.

"Where the fuck did you get to?" he shouted. "Do you have any idea what that... woman did to me?"

"I thought you two were hitting it off. Besides, you told me to scamper, so I did."

"I expected you to come back with the fucking car!" he continued. "She wouldn't let me leave. That... bitch was insatiable! Five times! Five fucking times! I had to call a cab once I was sure she was asleep!"

"I don't know what you're complaining about," I replied. "Sounds like you had a great time."

He wrapped himself in the bed-sheets and rocked himself to sleep, mumbling something about the nature of the beast. I was too tired to give a flying fuck. But I kept one eye open in case he felt the urge to tear my innards apart. We had two more nights to spend in this town and it would have been a shame to have our stay cut short because of the untimely death of one party.

5. An American Werewolf & A Scotsman –
The Naked Truth & The Final Day In Miami

Our three days in Miami culminated in a singular night of hedonistic devastation. We'd used up most of our money in Club Azucare. It was an unusual place, well off the beaten track. This, it seemed, was where the weird and wonderful gathered. Every fetish freak in Florida, along with an array of transsexuals, pansexuals, heterosexuals and asexual amoeba all assembled together in that salad bowl of the South. Black, white, gay or straight; race and gender just didn't matter. The only prerequisite in order to participate in the games was an open mind; open enough to let your brains fall out onto the floor, leaking the grey matter from the back of your skull. I had no problem in this regard. As a Scotsman who'd found his salvation in head-shrinking therapies and mind altering substances, I was prepared for any eventuality. The Boy Scouts were robbed of a real asset when I'd chosen to never join their legions; though they were many.

Thirty-six hours of no sleep and a lot of tequila had left me slightly psychotic. The Rabbi was on the dance floor, making a fool of himself as he practiced his own bastardised version of 'the laying on of hands'. He too had no trouble in adjusting himself to this scene. I suspected that this was due to the influence of his early career, before he became a conduit of God. He was unique in that respect. Not many men would have given up the lifestyle he once had to pursue what he referred to as 'a calling'. In fact, most would have happily checked themselves into a hospital under the care of an excellent physician; if only to sample the free psychotropic drugs.

We'd met before his conversion. I was in Las Vegas at the time with another friend who was facing a serious crisis in his native community, and he'd persuaded me to go along with him on that long drive from New York City. Just north of the Nevada desert was a small Navajo reservation where he'd been summoned by the elders of his tribe, to help resolve a legal land dispute. While there, they invited me to embark on a 'vision quest'. It was to be the first of several. The general idea of it is that after spending a few days buried from the neck down; and not taking any food or water; one achieves harmony with the spirit world. This is mostly assumed to be an urban myth, told to the white man to amuse him. But I found, much to my own astonishment, that it was a real and liberating experience. However, after a week of rough living and being no closer to enlightenment, I decided that enough was enough and I checked into the Rio All-Suite Hotel & Casino in Vegas. I caught the evening's entertainment, the Penn & Teller magic show, and tried my luck at the fruit machines. I'd been told that your best chances always lay in picking one that was closest to an entrance, as they were supposed to be a walking advertisement for risk-loving, first-time gamblers. My grand total from the evening's winnings was zero dollars and no cents.

I drowned my sorrows in a Martini glass and the waitress who brought it over shot me a come hither look. An amorous encounter ensued in a cleaning closet and she and I were soon locked in a deadly game of 'Let's out fuck each other', with no end in sight. I carefully made my way out of that broom cupboard approximately forty minutes later and was met by a well dressed gentleman in a tuxedo, just standing there clapping his hands and congratulating me.

"Dude," he exclaimed. "That was awesome! You clearly have a natural technique with the hotties!"

At first I was concerned that he might have been watching the escapade through some obscure make-shift peephole, indulging some perverse past-time in the city of sin, full of glitz and no glamour. However, I had a personal policy of giving people the benefit of the doubt and thought it best to believe that he was simply acknowledging my magnetic personality. He introduced himself. Avi Glassman; film producer. I recognised his name from my addiction days; those were long and lonely nights. The man was a legend in certain circles and we found that we got along like red-necks at a bluegrass barn dance. Unbeknownst to me at the time, the AVN award ceremony (considered the Oscars of Adult Entertainment) was also being held in Vegas on that day. This was the main reason my future associate was there; he was a keen student of all genres of cinematic endeavour and had a fine eye for talent. He introduced me to three other ladies of his acquaintance and we spent the rest of the evening popping capsules of amyl nitrate and enjoying the pleasures of their company. By the end of the evening, I was satisfyingly assured that these women were extremely well versed in the art of biblical knowing.

Now here we were in Miami six years later. Much had changed. We had grown older and wiser. We had a better handle on things; at least that's what we told ourselves through secret moments of self-doubt. It was the only way to keep the inner dragon at bay. Ours were fire breathing souls, chained in their desire to fly forever high.

My associate excused himself and went to the men's room. By my reckoning, he was gone a good thirty minutes and, for a short while, I was concerned that he might have been accosted by a Bolivian drug cartel. He returned however, but my initial relief turned to dismay when I discovered that at some point between leaving the dance floor and coming back, he had purchased an item that was so peculiar I was left literally lost for words. I stared at him for a good twenty-five seconds while he flapped his arms around a metal cage of a modest size.

"A man outside the rest rooms sold it to me for five bucks!"

"Five bucks?" I enquired. "Did you even stop to think if we needed a parrot?"

"Sure," he replied solemnly. "We need it!"

"You're going to have to explain that one. I'm afraid I can't see the intrinsic value of your newly acquired winged warrior."

"Well," he began. "It's like this. See, we're two free,

foolish and drunk individuals right?"

"Yeah."

"And this is not just a parrot. It's a talking parrot."

"I see."

"So we're like pirates on the open Somalian Seas! We need a mascot to hoist our colours!"

I was not convinced.

"Didn't it strike you as a little bit odd that a complete stranger randomly offered to sell you a creature of the Avian persuasion?" I asked.

"Not particularly," he said. "You remember when that contortionist chick you were dating sold you her hamster?"

"That was different," I explained.

It was closing time and we were asked to leave. The Rabbi carried the bird for a while before handing it off to me. I was in no condition drive the Mustang; and certainly not on the wrong side of the road. I climbed into the right side of the car, threw the Rabbi our car keys and clutched our feathered friend as we sped through the dead end streets. The journey back to South Beach was bitter-sweet. Not only was it our last morning, but it was also likely to be my last trip in Miami. The economic mess was driving out the mad ones, the bad ones and the beautiful ones, and bringing in unoriginal big suits with their big banking bonuses. They were the only ones left who could afford to keep throwing away good money after bad. It was their final desperate attempt at holding onto some measure of control. Those of us aspiring to be original always knew in the back of our minds that 'control' was nothing more than a fool's illusion. They got their freaky kicks from having it; we got off on bringing down that man-made wall brick-by-brick. But this city was now lost.

Back in the suite at the Wyndham, the shadow of impending doom merged with our toasted heads, creating a terrifying mix of rage and dread. The talking parrot hadn't spoken at all in the time I'd been carrying its cage, which seemed to further agitate the Rabbi. I set it down next to the mini bar. The Rabbi, irritated at having purchased the defective squawker, started banging on the sides of the cage.

"Talk to me you hideous bastard!"

There was nothing but silence and an incredibly unnerving calm came over the creature. It was studying *us*. I threw a towel over the cage to prevent it from learning too much.

I was soon hit by an urge to create a new type of table tennis. I was still harbouring a deep-seated anger toward Raphael Nadal for losing in the Wimbledon final. It was an abysmal performance, unworthy of any talented sportsman. It was this, I think, that led to us using the fire axes in the hallway to create a fair and fun competition, where two sporting gentlemen like ourselves would be pitted against each other in a deadly game, full of real mortal danger. The rules were simple. There was no need for any cricket, basket or ping-pong balls. Whoever chopped both legs off the coffee table first would be crowned king-champion, and this certainly was the sport of kings. But I was easily defeated by a man who had God on his side. It seemed only a logical progression for this fine game to find another arena. Sadly, the sheet-rock walls did not survive intact, and we knew then that the credit card the hotel had on file was destined to be charged incalculable and serious sums for heavy damage inflicted on hotel property. At eight o'clock that morning, we were fully packed and ready to leave for New Orleans; our next stop on my tour of old stomping grounds.

The only thing left on the to-do list was handing the car back to the rental agency. My associate approached their desk and spoke to the same girl that saw us when we arrived. I was left holding the parrot. The Rabbi had no problem taking care of the situation, despite the strange scratches on the driver's side. They looked like claw marks. How did they get there? Had some hell-hound attacked us last night? Was one of us a werewolf in sheep's-wool clothing? At any rate it didn't matter. She signed off on the paperwork.

"I want you to have my prized parrot as a token of my appreciation," said Avi, as he took the animal and gave it to the stunned but overjoyed girl. It glared at us with a look of evil intensity, *knowing* that we'd pawned it off on yet another unsuspecting soul.

We were soon in a taxi with our luggage, on the way to Miami International Airport. They were hardly likely to start a nation-wide manhunt for two Jewish gentlemen with violent tendencies, just because of a few small marks on an automobile. And if they did? I had a British passport. Surely the British consulate would intervene or send in the SAS to facilitate my release from prison. Unless I ended up in Guantanamo Bay or in the hands of the CIA, like that poor young computer hacker.

But we couldn't afford to think like that. We had to remain positive, stay focused on the road ahead. The prospect of going back to New Orleans was a little bit like returning to the scene of a perfect crime; there's a little voice tells you it's a bad idea - but you can't help swelling with joy every time you remember that brief moment you almost got away with it.

Mason, my old drinking buddy would be there to welcome us with open arms and sharpened fangs. Mason Lorn was, and still is, renowned for his skills in creating permanent vampire teeth for goth kids, lost to the extreme edge of alternative culture. His own fangs, he told me, were present since birth. I often wondered if in fact he really was the spawn of Dracula. During the day, he sun-lighted as a graphic designer of the highest calibre. 'Vampyrism', I learned, was a proper religion in its own right.

It was Mason who'd acquainted me with the underground subculture of vampyrism and blood-letting that was rampant in New York City. New York was a strange place to be in 2002. The aftermath of 9/11 left a big hole in the spirit of the entire city. We all found ourselves searching for some sense of meaning, scared shitless by the possibility of chemical or biological attack by some suicidal terrorist fuckwit looking for the door to paradise; all so he could surround himself with virgins in a mythical promised land that rivalled the heathenish fevers of ancient Babylon. This was not an easy thing to get our heads around and we were all left confused by these kinds of unprovoked abominations. Of course, no-one could predict we would set loose our righteous ire through an unstoppable war machine. But for a brief moment, those of us who'd witnessed the tumbling towers were one, irrespective of religion, colour or creed.

Internally for many, it was a time of deep grief and I personally looked to the world of the weird to find the answers. And so started the search, the voyage of discovery, which led me to New Orleans and, in the course of the events that unfolded, to Mason. But it was during his time in Manhattan that he showed me portals to places I'd never known existed in the heart of the city. The 'Vampyre' freak culture was loosely attached to the bondage, domination and sadomasochism (or BDSM) scene, and it blended elements of Gothic culture, spiritualism and folklore. At the top of this heap of weirdness was Father Christian; a long-haired lunatic in Jesus sandals; and he had as many screws loose as a nut factory. But he was worshipped like a God in the cult-like circles of the strange and always travelled with an entourage of submissive slave girls. Admittedly, I was intrigued by his philosophies and we became fast friends. But on one eventful night, in a place called 'The Red Room', our association came to an abrupt end. It wasn't unusual to hear loud screams of pleasure or pain in those situations, but it was the cry of 'Help! Help! Rape!' that made me spill my Johnny Walker all over the stylish burgundy carpet. I rushed head first into Christian's private room, which was a major no-no for any initiate. A young woman was sobbing on the floor. She looked like a bruised up thanksgiving turkey that had been basted and mauled. I felt compelled to hold a pen knife to the evil bastard's balls and for reasons that don't need explaining, I was promptly ejected, beaten and barred from the whole scene. Mason felt responsible and this whole thing put a strain on our friendship for some months. But a bottle of Glenmorangie and introducing him to his present fiancé helped us both bury the hatchet; figuratively speaking.

New Orleans had always been one of my favourite haunts, especially the French Quarter, and particularly during Mardi Gras. Hurricane Katrina had brought with it a destruction that not only led to the deaths of countless innocents, but also decimated the hopes and dreams of thousands. I was told that the chaos and panic that swept the streets was unparalleled in its viciousness and ruthless cut-throat nature. Shops were smashed in, cars were vandalised and women were raped and sodomised by passing thugs without a scrap of decency. Yet the spirit of those people was unbreakable. It was not unlike the spirit of most Glaswegians. Perhaps that was why I felt a kinship with the people there. They were as tough as they came. Hard nuts to crack; but some did, and they were still picking up the pieces.

The Rabbi and I checked our luggage at the appropriate desk, passed through the pornographic body scanners and waited to board our plane. It was a generally joyless experience and I hated every minute of it. There was nothing to do. We occupied ourselves with unabashed ogling, but that became boring very quickly and we indulged in some idle conversation instead.

"Man this has been one whacked out vacation. I owe you."

"Don't be silly," he said. "I think in some ways, I needed this more than you did. It's not easy getting old."

"You're not that old."

"True. But I'm getting there. When you have a kid, it ages you beyond belief!"

"I guess. I wouldn't know. I've never given much thought to having any. I'd need the right woman for that."

"Yeah. So, what's it like being back in old US of A again?" he asked.

"It's a funny thing. I'm not sure if this makes much sense, but it's like going to see a house you used to live in."

"How so?" he asked.

"Well suppose you go back and find someone else living in it. And then find out that they've redecorated the whole thing. It's nice to get the smell and feel of it again, but you know it's changed too much for you to be able to move back in."

"Makes sense."

I got up to get coffee from the Starbucks kiosk in the lounge. Just as I got my hands on two skinny lattes, the bing-bong from the PA system alerted me to the fact that an announcement was about to be made. Our boarding call came. We'd been waiting at the wrong gate. We raced to the other side of the airport, hoping that we would find ourselves in the right line, or at least on a plane that would take us somewhere near the general vicinity of our intended destination.

6. The Final Trumpet Blows On The Bayou:
The Last Refuge Of A Scurrilous Scoundrel

We arrived in New Orleans at around 2pm and waited patiently for our suitcases at the baggage carousel. It occurred to me that I hadn't written more than two lines in the travel journal I'd intended on keeping. Most of my time thus far had been spent ticking off boxes on some subconscious to-do list, birthed in the dark recesses of my warped mind. I needed to buckle down and make a proper start on the thing, and maybe think about finding a proper job on my return to Scotland.

Without a consistent and guaranteed income, no man can support himself. There were things like food and rent to consider, and I was already three months behind on the latter. With the damage I'd inflicted on my flat in Glasgow, I knew the landlord wouldn't be hard-pressed to decide on a swift eviction. There wasn't a wall or a door that hadn't experienced a frenzied attack with a knife, crossbow and the occasional Japanese samurai sword. I had pretty much lost my deposit the very day I moved in. But right now, none of it seemed all that important. I was a million miles away from those troubles.

Mason greeted us at the Louis Armstrong New Orleans International Airport and we sped away from the great Satchmo in the sky in his beat-up cherry-red Chevy Nova convertible, zigzagging through the traffic toward Mason's house. Very little had changed since the last time I'd visited. It was comforting to know that while the rest of the world was tilting on its head, rolling down and falling over itself, there was one corner where things seemed to be going at their own steady pace. The French Quarter was bursting at the seams with an influx of tourists. The energy was amazing. It was like being plugged into a 240 volt mains socket, and the current was surging through my every nerve ending. We arrived at 620 Philip Street and got out. Jewel, Mason's fiancé, met us at the landing and offered to help us carry our luggage. The Rabbi and I politely declined. Despite our personal failings as morally bankrupt and depraved creatures, I was still a Scottish Gentleman, and he a holy man from the city of angels.

Jewel was a remarkably voluptuous and beautiful girl. She was of Vietnamese heritage by birth, but had been adopted by an American family at a young age. To describe her early life as turbulent would have been an understatement. She resented her birth parents for having abandoned her. She had no memory of them, but she couldn't understand *why*. Was there something wrong with her? Had they known that she was... different? Unable to reconcile this within herself, she had a total psychotic break from reality and began to push the limits of consciousness to extremes, testing herself in numerous fucked up ways, racking up an uncounted number of heinous transgressions, just to see where the line was. The family that had adopted her also gave up on her and set her free to roam the road of self-discovery. Yet even though she had every reason to become cold, her heart was open and her soul was warm. A part of me had once been tempted to make a move on her, but that was long before she and Mason became an item. He told me about his feelings for her one night in the middle of a drunken brawl with four Irishmen, which was not the most opportune of times to do such a thing. But after learning of his feelings for her, I did what I could to bring them together and they hit it off like two peas from the same pod. It was the least I could have done for a friend who'd stood by me; through violent incursions into perilous territories and personal tragedies that took me to the top of the Brooklyn Bridge, ready to take a nose dive into the black water below. The six degrees of separation meant that everyone in my social circle eventually met everyone else, usually at some party or shindig thrown by some acquaintance or other. It was at one of these, though I forget exactly which, that the Rabbi came to meet Mason. Finding each other to be of sound character, we became the three amigos, wondering the lonely freeways of manly endeavour. It felt good to have the troupe together again.

Not long after settling in, the four of us headed down to St. Charles Avenue, where the infamous and historic Pontchartrain Hotel stood. I'd stayed in it without major incident during my first vacation. Sadly, its doors were no longer open. Mason told me that they were converting it into a residence for the retired. We looked on, admiring the building; the result of hard labour and artistic inspiration. There were no words to truly describe its elegance. Majestic came close, but we dared not use it for fear of demeaning the value of other equally well-constructed edifices. We hit Magazine Street next; a shopping hub of sorts, where consumerism still had a human form. Several antique shops were elegantly positioned between dispersed clothing and grocery stores. A few sold vintage bric-a-brac, which interested the Rabbi tremendously. There was a quiet dignity to be found here that was not found in most centralised cities. We mulled around for a while, poking our heads into a hat shop and measuring up the local tailor before deciding that there was more to life than harassing local businesses.

The New Orleans Mint demanded a look-in. I'd unintentionally avoided it the last few times; mostly because it represented a sort of metaphorical birthplace of money, which I had always regarded as an evil that had to be tolerated, but which always came to collect. There was either too much of it, which brought people their own unique set of woes; or too little of it, which presented its own set of sorrows for us, the terminally poor.

The mint had once played a prominent part in the beginnings of the country, helping it to rise from the ashes and rebuild the lives of so many after the civil war. In a way, the North was still fighting the South; it was a bit like Scotland and England. There were two distinct and separate cultures occupying the same space and time; growing, negotiating, trying to find an acceptable status-quo. And this building housed the memories of a very important time and place, harkening back to another era of hardship. But it was now a museum, showcasing rare coins and minting machinery from its days of glory. Unknown to me however, was that there was also a jazz exhibit housed within its walls. It was the most interesting thing I'd seen all day. This was where distinct and fresh new sounds took root; where men like Bunk Johnson, Jim Robinson and George Lewis had learnt and plied their trade. And of course there was my personal jazz hero - Mr James Booker esquire; The Bayou Maharajah; The Piano Prince of New Orleans. For me personally, going to New Orleans was like going on a holy pilgrimage to Vatican City. This was the Mecca of musical genius. I could have stayed for weeks just soaking up the information on each plaque and under each instrument; but I knew my companions did not share my enthusiasm for jazz so I thought it best to leave before I bored them with my trivial knowledge of music that was not to their own tastes.

We refuelled on soul-food and soda-pop at a nearby restaurant and thought it a good idea to tour the port afterwards. As anyone from these parts will tell you, there is only one proper way to look into the murky depths of the Mississippi River, and that's by sailing on the last authentic steamboat still fit for sailing; the Natchez. We got four tickets and trundled onto the vessel.

On the deck of the riverboat Mason was unusually quiet and appeared agitated. I assumed it was because I'd insisted on drinking eight cups of coffee, which put me in a caffeine crazed state. I was horribly hungover, so it seemed the logical thing to do. But the side effect of this cure was that it made me very hyperactive, and I found myself talking at a speed that made Mario Andretti look like a pensioner on a kid's tricycle. I contemplated the potential number of Youtube hits for such a spectacle before asking him why he was troubled.

"It's Jewel," he replied. "She breeched the terms of her parole again and they're talking about putting her back inside."

It's important, I think, to mention that Jewel, like me,

had a nasty habit of getting herself into, and most times out of, all sorts of trouble. There weren't too many left that were deranged or insane enough to live the life of a true outlaw. But Jewel and I were different in this regard. We were the free range crazy, roaming the cruel fast-tracks of existence, constantly searching for new and better kicks. Like the fabled swamp monster that lived in the Honey Island wetlands, we answered to no-one, lived for no-one and would die for no-one. We were the parent-less children of a desperate society that needed us more than we needed it. But this sort of lifestyle could be wearing on loved-ones.

"Don't worry about it," I told Mason. "Unless she molested a state trooper with his flash-light, they won't pay much attention to a multiple felon who's fractured the occasional law."

The prison system was too crowded to put away every oddball and degenerate who broke the rules. My own personal experience had taught me this. But I was worried that a parole officer would perhaps not see things that way. They didn't give a damn about the whys. They were small fry with large chips on their shoulders and had a whole lot of power to boot. But they were more dangerous than any big fish with an atomic arsenal of legal knowledge. Some were notorious for demanding sexual favours in exchange for lenient treatment. I wondered if this was perhaps what was really troubling my friend.

"She loves you," I told him.

"I know," he said, sighing.

"Well, just make sure you hire a good attorney just in case," I added.

"Yeah. We plan on doing that. You're probably right though. This whole fucking thing will blow over," he replied. I wasn't sure if he was trying to reassure me or himself.

Then a voice suddenly yelled.

"I'll pray and beseech the Lord to grant you freedom from these demon troublemakers!"

Folk on the boat snapped their necks round, tutting and muttering at us, and looks of disapproval beamed out from their conventional heads. But they quickly resumed their mundane activities.

The Rabbi's pronouncement made us all feel edgy. We knew that when he spoke, mystic transmissions to a force beyond our comprehension were taking place. None of us dared to question him on the how and why of it all. The man, though I'm not sure if he *was* just a man, had a way of making things happen. This made us all wonder if he, like Moses or Nostradamus, was a prophet, here to herald in a new century. He certainly believed he was.

The Rabbi and Mason took one of the many guided tours around the boat. Jewel and I opted to stay behind and take in the sights. We watched on as the sun set slowly across the bright blue sky. The changing shades of orange and red brought with them a true joy that only comes when you witness pictures being painted on the canvas of reality. Jewel broke the silence.

"Max... There's something I've always wanted to ask you," she said, hesitating a little.

"Sure, ask away," I replied

"Well... It's... I was wondering... How come you never ever asked me out?"

I wasn't sure what to tell her. I'd never really thought about it before. Most of my life had been a never ending sequence of things that happened; what actually was, instead of what might have been. I was, I suppose, afraid of looking any deeper than that. Afraid that I might find something so broken inside that it could never be repaired.

"Well J, when you have one damaged soul that's smashed beyond repair, it's not such a great idea to put it in an ice bucket along with *another* one that's also cracked," I told her.

She clearly didn't like the answer. It was plain to see that I'd inadvertently upset her. It was the honest truth as I saw it. I felt an inclination to apologise, but seeing no fault in what I'd said, I refrained. Perhaps it was that bit about being cracked. She didn't like it when I referred to myself as cracked, fucked or damaged. She'd always been a strong advocate of my positive attributes and I'd long suspected that she harboured an unspoken affection for me. I tried to dispel the rising tension.

"Mason's a great guy," I said. "You really lucked out in that prize draw! Not even the lottery guarantees that kind of jackpot.

"And I really wouldn't worry about the parole thing. It's nothing more than a fly in the soup."

She nodded and smiled as she saw Mason and the Rabbi making their way back to where we were. Mason was well and truly besotted with the design and structure of the glorified skiff. The Rabbi however, was unimpressed by the boat. We all agreed it that it was a fine feat of human engineering and that it served its purpose well.

We disembarked after the cruising along the river and went back to the apartment for a quick change of clothes. Mason suggested the idea of checking out the local night-life and it didn't take much to persuade Avi and I to go along for the ride. By 10pm, we were suited and booted to the hilt and it was time to find the weirdness that was Club 735. Suitable attire was essential if we were to get in without being noticed as outsiders. The more bizarre the better. I donned a dazzling blue Hawaiian shirt over my washed out jeans while the others kept to their tried and tested wardrobes. Mason was still sporting the black on black look, with leather pants that were one size too small and Jewel had slipped into her sultry satin red dress, ready to rock. The Rabbi wore a fairly conservative cool blue suit with a twist. Underneath his bespoke jacket was a frilly lime green shirt that even Liberace wouldn't have experimented with.

Yet, despite our self-congratulating sense of style, we soon realised that we were the most under dressed people out on Bourbon Street. The Steampunk generation had gained momentum and gaps were being bridged between Victorian Gothic, grunge, punk, goth and Emo. New styles were emerging from all over the place and here we were, already antiquated like the discarded bobbles on

Magazine Street. But we soldiered on. We could still show the young generations a thing or two. They still took their cues from us and we would readily oblige.

Deep in the heart of Club 735, DJ AfroDizzyAc's set was pumping out supersonic tunes that were splitting atoms in the atmosphere. The people at CERN didn't need that overblown Hadron Collider. Millions of tax-payers' dollars could have been saved if they'd spent just one hour during their weekends in here.

In the middle of the dance hall, a jaw-dropping rope suspension and strip show had begun. The dexterity and skill required was astounding. The girl herself was a gorgeous blue haired beauty. I felt a stirring in my lions as I watched her take off her bra, twirl it around and throw it into the crowd. I was right at the front, next to the performing area and the loud speakers, and I saw her wink at me as she extended out her forefinger and beckoned me to follow her every move. Near the end of the act, she flexed her calves and did the splits, and I felt an overwhelming desire to lick the small of her back. Luckily, I was able to resist the temptation. The coolers were on the lookout for that sort of deviant behaviour and they didn't look kindly upon the exchange of precious bodily fluids in public. I decided instead to go to the bar and buy my friends a round of drinks.

I pushed my way through the mass of human flesh, until I got to the naked barmaid with heavy make-up and colourful full-body tattoos. She approached me as the music pounded in the background. I admired her artwork for a moment before I heard her speak.

"What is your pleasure, sir?"

I knew what my pleasure of choice was, but I knew that would be difficult to communicate to this devilish delight of a demon princess. I opted to stick to a list of requested beverages.

"Two Jack Daniels, one Bloody Mary and a Grasshopper," I replied.

I watched her trot off to the shelf where the bottled

liquor was kept and admired her sweet posterior while she measured out the alcohol into two glasses and mixed up the tomato juice for the Bloody Mary. She had two puppy dogs inked above each breast and on either side of the perfect cleft of her ass, were two bluebirds. She returned carrying the orders in her arms and I picked them up them carefully from the counter where she'd placed them. My friends were all gathered at the far end of the club, next to the supporting ledge that ran the entire circumference of the place. It was going to be another night of hard drinking and sinking into moral oblivion; and it had just begun.

7. To Sleep, Perhaps to Dream - A Fond Farewell To Outstretched Arms

It was 4am when we made our way back to the safety of our refuge. The streets were packed with revellers making their way back to their own abodes. I was still buzzing from the five bottles of Bud and two Bacardi Breezers I'd drank on top of what I'd already downed. A private jam session was taking place in my head. There's nothing more gratifying than having a great tune jangling in your head at morning o'clock after partying hard. Even endless hours of debauchery can't compare to the high that comes from the musical genius of certain artists. It gives one a solid sense of satisfaction.

My shirt stank of rum and I could detect the smell of sex in the warm air. Mason and Jewel had been bumping body parts at some point earlier in the evening. My only bone of contention was that I'd missed out on all the action. I'd been too busy; engrossed in a conversation with the shaven headed, tattoo sporting barmaid. The subject matter - the pros and cons of scrotal piercings - didn't really require any serious level of thought, which made it easy to follow. But I was rudely interrupted by the Rabbi.

"We've run out of beer money!" he screamed.

At first I was angry with him, but I understood all too well the seriousness of the situation. Without an adequate intake of alcohol, we would find ourselves waking to the chronic terror of reality. Had this happened in our early years, we simply would have killed ourselves and checked out of this godforsaken Earth life. But if it happened now, it would require something considerably more drastic. It was then that I remembered the secret stash of money I always kept pinned to my underwear in case of an emergency, and this definitely qualified as one.

When I turned back round, the barmaid had disappeared and I was left clutching my rum with just the Rabbi for company. If only I'd acted on my earlier impulse to molest the stripper, I wouldn't have found myself alone with that damned song swirling in my head. I couldn't even remember who sang it, which served only served to frustrate me further.

I must have started singing aloud because the residents of Philip Street began hurling insults in our direction almost immediately. We stood there, swaying on the steps, as Mason searched through his pockets for the key to his front door. It was a tense moment. We all experienced the anxiety, feeling sure that we were one step away from having our mail redirected to a temporary space on the pavement. The New Orleans Police Department didn't look too kindly on the homeless. Thankfully, we were saved from being bludgeoned for vagrancy when Jewel reached into her purse and rattled the key-chain in her hands.

Inside, the house was small but homely in a strangely traditional sort of way. There were two uncomfortable single guest beds set up in the living room. I didn't understand why they'd gone to the trouble. They knew I was set to leave for Chicago in four short hours. Still, I thought, better get some rest before being subjected to the trauma of airport security again.

I had no intention of straying anywhere in the windy city. Were it not for the fact that I had to change flights at O'Hare to get back to Glasgow, I'd have avoided that entire wretched urban hell-hole. It was full of dullards and winos, and provided little in the way of excitement. Those kinds of quiet cities, run by mobsters and pimps, perplexed me. It didn't make sense to fill a place up with people, then watch them waste away. Each counted the minutes until they got their next heroin laced hamburger fix and maybe a meagre social security cheque to feed their habit.

The window had been left open and the sound of stray dogs fighting on the side-walk echoed through the alleyways. Images danced around the walls as shadows flickered from the dim street lights. My brain slowly switched off and I dreamt of a girl who sliced up her heart to satisfy my hunger.

With morning came the rush to pack my belongings in some orderly fashion. I hadn't brought all that much to begin with; which should have made it easy. But the difficulty lay in trying to find my lucky cream coloured socks. I was wearing them when I arrived, I was certain of that. After forty-five minutes of searching, I finally discovered them in the garbage can. I immediately knew what had happened. In my tired and drunken stupor, I mistook the large blue cylinder for a laundry hamper. There was no time to put them in the washing machine, so I washed and rung them out in the bathroom sink while I showered. And thanks to Jewel's very expensive hairdryer they were instantly bone dry and ready to wear.

"MQB! Were you using my fucking hairdryer?" she scowled.

I had no idea how to explain why I was using her personal high-grade appliance to dry a pair of $5 socks from Walmart. And there was no way that a bald man could get away with saying that he was borrowing it for personal grooming.

"No!" I shouted back. "Ah... That's just my electric razor... It's got one of those very noisy beard trimmers. I'll be done in here in a minute damn it! Don't you come barging in here woman! I warn you, it's not a pretty sight!"

I heard her walk into the kitchen and turn on the percolator. I quickly put the hair-dryer back where I found it and quietly walked out of the bathroom to finish gathering my things. I was beginning to feel uneasy about going back.

"Om Mani Padme Hum." I recited this Buddhist mantra repeatedly as I put on my snake-skin shoes.

I'd spent several months at a Buddhist retreat in northern Scotland during one particularly horrendous phase of unrequited love. I don't know if it was the calming influence of the monks at the Samye Ling temple, or simply the fresh air that gave me a feeling of oneness; but I soon felt healed and unburdened. This feeling didn't last long however. One idle afternoon, I was discovered with a past issue of Playboy magazine featuring Pamela Anderson as the centrefold. That woman had plagued my early years with her broken promises of sweet suffocation. Her lips never moved; they didn't have to. Her eyes did all the talking that was necessary. After being deemed a bad influence on other lost truth-seekers I was politely asked to leave; which I did, thankful that I had gained a profound understanding of the cosmic order of things.

I fumbled through my multi-coloured Nike baseball jacket for my passport and airline tickets. Passengers, like pilots, have to perform a series of pre-flight checks in order to maintain industry standards for cattle-class. And we paid dearly for the privilege of life in the age of air-travel. There were fuel taxes, airport taxes, landing taxes, carbon taxes, baggage taxes, travel insurance, life insurance, death insurance and of course ensured insurance. It was inevitable that some greedy bastard somewhere would come up with the idea of charging money for using the on-board lavatories. If you couldn't afford to pay, you would suffer the indignity of not making it to the toilet on time while two air stewards wrestled you to the ground. I was sure that this was going to result in high sales figures in the incontinent underwear market. So sure, in fact, that I'd invested in one such company during the previous summer.

With everything packed and ready, I folded up my guest bed. The Rabbi was set to leave for L.A. the following day, so I suggested that the four of us have breakfast at a small coffee house on Bourbon Street. The sunshine beat down on us as we strolled along, taking in the warm hues bouncing off the passing cars.

I ordered blueberry pancakes as we sat in a secluded area, shielding us from the heavy heat outside. Café Beignet was like something out of an Edward Hopper painting. Plates of Belgian waffles and omelettes were brought to the table for my compatriots and we sampled portions from each of our respective orders.

"It's been a blast having you down MQB. Wish you were sticking around for a little longer," said Mason, attacking the fresh fruit on the side of his plate with a dull fork.

"It's been good being down man. But you know how it is with me. I can't sit still in one place too long. You start doing that, you become part of the furniture, and I don't want to shuffle off this Earth like a used paperweight," I replied.

He nodded and smiled. His sharpened teeth sparkled as small beams of sunlight hit them. The Rabbi ate his omelette in silent contemplation. I could see from the pained expression on his face that he was missing his son. But his mother was sure taking good care of the boy whilst we'd embarked on this spiritual expedition.

"You'll be back home tomorrow my friend," I said.

"Yeah. It's been great hanging with you guys," he said, "...but I gotta tell ye, it'll be good to get back home. Hey Mason, how much would it cost to get them kinda teeth?"

Mason stood up and walked over to look at his teeth, hovering above him as if he were an actual dentist giving a proper consultation for a thousand dollars an hour. Jewel stretched out her hand and took mine as it lay flaccid on the table. She pressed it firmly and opened her mouth to speak, but no words came out. I gently put my free hand over hers to tell her she didn't need to say anything.

The two men were finished with their discussion and had come to the conclusion that it would be too expensive and generally pointless for the Rabbi to even consider getting fangs. I agreed and quickly finished off my coffee.

"Well dude, we'd better get you to the airport I guess," said Mason as we walked back.

"Yeah, the clock is ticking I suppose, and they do say that you should ideally check in two hours before take-off," I said.

We loaded the luggage into his car as I said a tearful goodbye to my friends, who decided to remain at the house while Mason dropped me off. Jewel held me and I almost didn't want to let go. I bid farewell to the Rabbi and we shook hands and hugged. The car ride to New Orleans

International Airport was short. Little was said by either of us. One question kept going through my mind, "Why are you leaving again?", "To go home." I told myself. Home. It seemed like such a strange word. Nowhere had really felt like 'home' in a long time; at least no geographical place. The one moment in twenty years that I had felt remotely close to 'being home' was in the arms of an untamed cat-lady. I'd trusted her enough to warrant the thought of give her my plant. But she was a wild card, and ranked high in the stakes of uncertainty.

The car pulled up at the kerb as we approached the designated unloading area for transatlantic air travellers. Mason and I shook hands and thumped our chests as a sign of our enduring friendship. There was no need for any fond farewell. I knew I'd see the solemn bastard again someday. And even if I didn't, there was an unspoken bond between us as friends and as men. He popped the trunk open and I took out my bags before going into the terminal building. He waved and drove off into the distance. I looked at my watch. It was high-noon precisely.

Inside the terminal building, I strained my eyes to read the information screens listing flight numbers and departure times. I moved closer to try and see the assigned check-in desk for my airline. I was at the wrong end of the damned building again. There wasn't a moment to lose. I dragged my suitcase along the marble tiling and raced toward the appropriate desk. There was an extensively long queue of lost souls all waiting to be accepted into the bosom of a sardine can with wings. I was in no immediate rush to board, only to check in and make it through security. Finally, my turn came.

"Hi, do you have your passport and ticket?"

The brunette woman behind the service counter seemed pleasant enough. I reached into my trouser pocket and gave her my travel documents.

"Please place your luggage on the belt," She said.

I did as she asked. The steel weighing machine beeped and the display flashed with '15 Kg' in big red digits.

There was a large whirring sound like a garbage compacter and suddenly my bags were gone, delivered into the hands of some half-witted handler who'd toss them around like it a bottle of cheap aftershave. I was glad I hadn't packed anything remotely fragile.

The security area wasn't too much trouble, although I did have to remove my snakeskin shoes. By this point, I was used to the indignity of being scanned and prodded like a prized bull in a meat market. Outrage had given way to apathy. But I still felt great pity for the dozens who were forced to go through the same thing. It's a curious thing. You only realise certain injustices when you witness them being visited on others instead of yourself.

I bought the latest issue of the New York Times and flicked through the pages while I waited for my boarding number to be called. The biggest news on the front page was the president's plan to raise the debt ceiling; plans that were being stalled by the Republicans in the House of Representatives. What troubled me about the whole affair (which had been talked about endlessly on radio shows) was the complete lack of foresight on the part of our fearless leaders. 'Oh, Obama you misguided fool!' I thought. 'Surely you realise that raising the debt ceiling will only lead to a bigger mess.' There'd been no real financial growth since the recession, and there was still the matter of an outstanding debt that ran into the trillions. 'All you've done, my dear Barrack, is to secure your own term in office till 2012. Like Pontius Pilate, you'll leave America to face the cruel tortures of the tea-bagging right-wing crazies.'

The UK was virtually in the same boat. I suspected that even two generations down the line, there would be little in the way of change. The rich always got richer and the poor got nothing for their troubles except a stamping from the size 10 shoes of some Tory, Liberal or Labour peer with a duck pond; who of course needed our charitable donations to keep it clean enough to wash his dirty laundry in; away from prying public eyes.

The East African famine barely got a mention on

page eight. Those horrific images we'd all seen on our TV screens during the eighties hadn't made a damned bit of difference. Governments were still selling arms to ruthless dictators in exchange for their blood money. Meanwhile, earthquakes were rocking nuclear reactors in Japan, economies across the world were on the verge of collapse and innocent children were starving in places with unpronounceable names. And there wasn't a fucking thing Bob Geldof could do about it.

The loud speaker sounded off and broke my train of thought. "This is Continental Flight sixty-three from Louis Armstrong New Orleans International to Chicago O'Hare which will shortly be ready for departure. At this time we would ask all passengers seated in rows five to sixteen to begin boarding now. Thank you."

I was seated next to a hockey fan wearing an Anaheim Ducks t-shirt and I felt sure that meant trouble. But the time passed quickly. I arrived in Chicago feeling refreshed and ready for the remainder of the journey. On exiting the plane I followed the signs for connecting flights and found myself joining another long line for yet another security screening before being allowed to resume the search for my departure gate. Having no hand luggage made it easier, but I would still have to remove my stylish footwear, which was an inconvenience. The pressure was mounting and I started to feel nervous. I had thirty minutes before the gate would close and I didn't want to miss the flight because of some security guard's annoyance at my excellent fashion sense.

I ran to the gate with ten minutes to spare and arrived to hear my boarding call. Once I was on the plane, I sank into my allocated chair and breathed deeply, relieved that I had made it. The com system pinged and the captain's voice came on to make its usual announcements, telling us about the cabin crew, their star-signs and the projected flight time. Six hours and thirty-five minutes. That somehow seemed reasonable. It would give me time to rest, sleep and work a little on the travel journal.

Once the metal bird was in the air, the stewardess came down the aisle with a trolley choc-full of goodies. I ordered a small Southern Comfort and sipped it slowly from a plastic cup. I listened to the old Texan couple beside me who were talking about seeing their grandchildren again after three years. The baby boomers were still going strong. I took out a pencil from my shirt pocket and began scribbling on the notepad that I usually carried in my back trouser pocket. High above the clouds, I crashed out as we flew over the clear ocean.

8. Glasgow Smiles Better -
The Prozac Fairy Makes A House-call

Thud! The landing gear hit the tarmac with all the grace of a Welsh rugby player doing the tango. I noticed that my ears had popped whilst we'd been in the air. I began making moose calls and blowing air bubbles into my inner canals to rebalance the pressure. It took a while before I could hear properly. The speakers pinged again.

"Ladies and gentleman, welcome to Glasgow. The local time is seven fifteen in the morning. The weather on this Tuesday morning is at a warm twenty degrees Celsius, with Sunny skies and a slight chance of showers. If you're on holiday, we hope you enjoy your stay and look forward to serving you again. Please wait until the plane has come to a complete standstill before removing your seatbelt. Take extra case when leaving the aircraft and when removing items from the overhead lockers. My name is Karen and on behalf of the cabin crew and myself, we'd like to thank you for choosing to fly with us today."

The other flyers all scuttled and screeched, like feral monkeys let loose in Edinburgh Castle. I gathered my thoughts and waited patiently for them to leave before getting up. I thanked the flight attendants standing by the door and walked into the narrow corridor that led into the main building. Immigration wasn't a problem as I was just another Scotsman returning to the dear green place. All I had to do was state my name and flight number.

It was an endless walk to baggage reclaim and we had to wait a good twenty minutes before the conveyor belt showed any signs of movement. It took another ten for bags to start appearing. We watched them snake around the carousel. My fellow travellers were launching themselves at their luggage, to get at it before some dope-dealer with hopes of selling their Bermuda shorts for drug money. My own battered 'Marco Polo' case didn't take long to make its way down. I casually lifted it off the belt and headed through Customs & Excise.

"Yes," I thought. "This is how it's supposed to be. Nice and easy. No muss, no fuss, no hassle."

Just then a customs officer walked towards me.

"Oh shit!" said a voice. "Not again."

"Sir, could you walk this way please?" said the man, in a calm, firm tone.

I did as he asked and paused, like a show dog waiting for his master's next command.

"Could you open your suitcase? We'd like to examine it."

Every portion of the suitcase was thoroughly poked and prodded and searched through. He used a roll of something resembling sticky tape to take samples of dust and other assorted particles. Another shorter man joined in the fun and brought what looked like a miniature vacuum cleaner to the party.

"We've detected trace amounts of cocaine with your belongings," he said.

"Cocaine?" I mumbled. "I don't understand. I don't know what you're talking about!"

"There's no need to get worked up sir, It's too small an amount to be of concern to us. Where are you flying in from?"

"New Orleans," I told him.

"Ah. Someone probably passed you money used in the consumption of a class A drug. Those bloody Americans do love their drugs! Be careful in future. You're clear to leave."

A mixture of shock and joy bubbled up inside me. This was infinitely better than the American method of doing things. I thanked both men and walked toward the exit. The happy feeling soon subsided when I realised there would be no-one to meet me with open arms here. The only person that could be relied on in this foul place was myself. I stood in line at the taxi rank and when my turn came and I got into a white Volvo with a large 'Renfrew Taxis' sign on top.

Within fifteen minutes I was at Howat Street. I paid

the driver his due and hauled the suitcase up the first flight of stairs. I took a deep breath and unlocked the front door. A sea of mail crunched under my feet. I could see from the envelopes that they were mostly junk. Some promised a cash prizes of a hundred thousand pounds, others offered cover for the over fifties. I knew I wouldn't qualify for either.

I opened the letters that seemed worthwhile, praying that one might contain a cheque I was owed for work. I set down my suitcase in the hallway and paced around, scanning through the post for anything of importance. There were a few reminders for unpaid bills, some going as far back as May. I threw them into the abyss of the kitchen trash can. If it they wanted the money bad enough, they'd remind me again next week, same bat time, same bat channel.

I rifled through the contents of the Marco Polo, unpacking and separating the washed articles from the unwashed. With everything done that needed to be done, I took off my snazzy shoes and placed my lucky socks in the hamper. My feet were prone to sweat a great deal and it seemed a sensible idea to wear a fresh pair later in the day.

I sat down at my desk in the living room and glanced over my calendar and opened some more letters. Bingo! There was the cheque I'd been expecting for an odd job I'd taken on before leaving. I'd inked something on the 2011 Swimsuit Calendar prior to my trip. On closer inspection, it was a note I'd left to remind myself that I'd RSVP'd to an event set for today. A local author had the brilliant but bizarre idea of reading aloud his latest novel from start to finish, while standing in the middle of Buchanan Street. Aloysius Drummond was one of those strange people whose creative spark attracted a vast array of interesting characters. Women were especially susceptible to his brand of intelligent madness. It would be interesting to witness, if only for my own sick amusement. And if he took offence? I'd simply say that I was laughing hysterically *with* the man; not at him.

I thought it best to get some shut eye before

catching this public spectacle of self-flagellation. I picked up my mobile phone and connected it to the charger in the bedroom as I lay down on my foam mattress. Kandy, the girl who'd become a source of vexation, had been in my thoughts a lot. I decided to send her a text, in the hope that she'd agree to come over.

"Hi. Back from vacation. Feeling supercharged. Can you come over?"

The phone beeped with a message alert.

"Glad ur back. Did you have a good vacation? Was in London myself for a few days. Yes. I can come over for a bit after work."

I tapped out a reply on the keypad.

"Had a great time. Hope you had a good time in London. Will see you later."

Beep.

"Will come down around 8.30. K."

At one o'clock I was rudely awakened by the noise of a beer barrel delivery to the Old Govan Arms across the road. 'Sweet Jesus', I thought. My head was pounding with extreme pain; akin to a thousand rodents dancing and clawing their way through my frontal lobe. I got up and flicked open the blinds.

"Keep it the fuck down out there! Decent people are trying to sleep!" I shouted.

They shrugged and carried on. That was the Govan way. People often spoke of the poverty and deprivation that existed in these old tenements. While this was superficially true, it lacked real perspective. We looked out for each other. The money-rich city kids and third generation immigrants lived off the fat of their parents income; buying fancy cars, and rubber-lined condominiums; but *we* were busy building bridges to the real future, and that depended on treating your neighbour as you did yourself. A long-haired hipster preached the same thing once. His name was John Lennon.

I took a quick shower and donned my favourite orange short-sleeve shirt over my jeans. If I was lucky,

Drummond would still be reading to jakeys and shoppers; inadvertently educating them and raping their minds subconsciously as they heckled and spat glue-like sputum in his direction.

The bus stop around to the corner made it exceptionally easy to get to the city centre. The number twenty-three was especially excellent due to its reliable ten minute service. The bus arrived promptly as expected and I climbed aboard, surprised by the Polish blonde woman behind the wheel. I paid the fare and glanced at her badge. 'Olga' punched out a ticket faster than I could blink.

"Your change," she said, with a thick East European accent.

I clutched the coins and the ticket stub in my hand, searching for an empty seat. I made myself comfortable and looked out of the large fibreglass window. Clouds were beginning to appear on the horizon. As we passed near Elder Park, I noticed the unending row of scaffolding on both sides of the road. New soulless brick homes were going up where the world famous shipyards once stood. It brought a certain sense of sadness to see so much changing in the place where I'd grown up. The whole area seemed a little darker.

We came to the fork of Paisley Road West and Govan Road. The stone angel above what was now an Italian restaurant looked down at us from up-on-high. I could have sworn I saw it smile as the traffic lights turned green.

Commuters piled on at each stop, many were from different cultural backgrounds. I remembered how I used to be one of the few non-white faces in a then emerging new Glasgow. Now, thanks to government funded programs, a large influx of people were flowing into an already strained and impoverished city. It was beautiful to see and learn from the variations in lifestyle, but what had been completely ignored was that these people also had needs. Food, clothing and shelter were a human right according to the United Nations. But the greed of those with political motivations had caused tensions to flair between settled Scots and settling outsiders, both of whom were entitled to (and required) those basic essentials. The tension escalated one year, when a series of stabbings and riots took place across the Sighthill area of Glasgow.

There was a mass exodus at the stop on Oswald Street and we all thanked Olga for getting us there. It was a short walk to Argyle Street, and from there onto Buchanan Street. The revamped House of Frazer, complete with restaurant, seemed emptier than usual. So did most of the other stores. The usually busy Argyle Arcade was faring no better, despite being home to every jewellery store imaginable. The last time I was in there, I saw a diamond ring, selling for the princely sum of fifty thousand pounds.

"That's nothing," said the Jeweller. "Last week we sold a bracelet for a hundred and twenty thousand pounds."

'Who are their customers?' I wondered. It didn't seem likely that any Glaswegian of my acquaintance would have that sort of cash lying around.

There was a cheque cashing place a few yards down. I stopped in there and handed them my cheque. They took a percentage, which irked me, but there was nothing to be down. I needed immediate access to my money. The man behind the plastic window counted out the money and handed it to me through the metal drawer. It made him look like Hannibal Lecter.

I carried on walking up Buchanan Street and I saw Drummond a few feet away from the old Tardis-like blue police box that was now used as an ice-cream vending station. Crouching on the ground, hanging on his every word, was a bevy of beauties, staring longingly at his six-foot three-inch slender frame. I remembered that I'd seen something similar in New York.

'Bugger!' I thought. The man seemed to have the luck of the gods. No questionable junkie types were in sight. There was no humour to be enjoyed at his expense. I deduced that this harmonious scene must have come about because of his choice of clothing. The man was smart. His dark Mafia suit screamed 'Fuck with me at your peril! I'll slice you into tiny pieces and stuff you in a deep freezer!' A scarlet rose in his lapel added to the menacing tone. Women always went for the bad boys. He greeted me while he read and I nodded in acknowledgement. I assumed the lotus position on the ground and rolled up a cigarette, listening carefully to his punchy prose style.

J. Daniel Solomon, a gifted writer who'd spent his thirties years living in an Israeli kibbutz, was also in attendance. In an earlier life he'd been a practising lawyer. I'd never bothered to ask why he'd left the profession, but I assumed it had something to do with the gritty realities of crime, or seedy divorce cases revolving around midget sex maniacs and animal prostitution rings. He moved over to where I was and we exchanged pleasantries, careful to avoid breaking the Drummond's concentration. The two of us agreed that it took a certain level of psychosis to attempt something like this, and a sense of pride overtook us. Who else but a Glaswegian would think of doing something this disturbed; inviting public ridicule instead of avoiding it?

"... I thought you were in America?" said Daniel.

"I was. I got back this morning. It was good. How've you been? How was your trip to France?" I asked.

"It was very nice. I managed to get a start on my third book," he said.

"Is it a follow-up to the last one? You might end up like George Lucas and his Star Wars saga if you're not careful!" I said

"Yeah. It's a follow up. But it's more along the lines of another book I read, which focused in the inter-personal relationships between middle-aged men. I caught up with some old friends from university and I found it interesting how our lives had taken different turns," he said.

"Sounds heavy... but good," I said.

Drummond's publisher, Matt Bergland, was filming the event for his company's promotional material. An edited video of the whole escapade was later uploaded to Youtube.

Boredom eventually overtook me and I bid them all a good day. I strutted down Argyle Street, toward Glasgow Cross. There was a small photography shop in Merchant City, which I often wandered into on days when I could afford to. My interest in cameras began at the age of ten when my grandfather bought his very first Minolta. He was quick off the mark and learned all he could about lighting and film developing, going as far as converting his bathroom into a make-shift darkroom, much to the annoyance of my grandmother. The family appointed him 'chief photographer' at every family occasion.

My father followed this up one year by urging everyone to pitch in so he could rent a video camera. We all got a kick out of that. We'd gone for months living on boiled rice and bread, but when the bastard sized behemoth arrived one afternoon, that didn't seem to matter. We all took turns being BBC cameramen reporting on the Beirut conflict. My grandfather also had a fondness for practical jokes, and the fact that he could get one on tape pushed his inventiveness to new levels. There were banana skins, empty tea cups, and buckets of water placed above doorways. My father did not appreciate us being in cahoots and blew up like a mushroom cloud of radioactive anger. I inherited my grandfather's twisted sense of humour as well as his flair for photography, but also embedded somewhere in my genetic code was my father's violent temperament.

It was 4.30pm, but there was still an hour left before closing time. On the second shelf in the window, priced at £300, was a 17-85mm EF zoom lens that would fit perfectly onto my 18 mega-pixel Canon 500D. I stepped inside and saw Jeff the manager standing behind the counter.

"Max! Good to see you young man! What can I do for you today?"

"The Canon 17-85mm in the window there. Can you put it aside for me? I'll be back for it next week."

"I can do better than that my friend. Since you've been a loyal customer, I could give it to you on credit."

On credit? What was he thinking? Obviously he

didn't know about my general habits regarding previous possessions that were also bought on credit. Of course, when I say bought, I mean never paid for.

"Sure, that would be great!" I said.

Jeff removed the lens from display and wrapped it in cloth and bubble-wrap.

"Do you need a carrier bag?" he asked

"Yes, I think so. It might rain later on."

I smiled with a sense of accomplishment and headed to the St. Enoch Square Underground. Glasgow's subway system was second to none. It was one of the most effective means of public transportation. I alighted at the Kelvinhall station and went by foot to the Kelvingrove Art Gallery and Museum.

It boasted one of the largest art collections in the world, with numerous paintings by well known artists. They had rules about food and drink that were punishable by testicular electrocution, but I smuggled in a can of Miller I'd bought at a nearby snack store. Although it bulged out a wee bit in the front pocket of my jeans, the orange shirt hid it well. And if a security guard asked? Well, I was just very pleased to see them.

By seven pm I had seen everything and I felt it was best to head home in good time to meet Kandy. The subway journey on the way back was shorter and before long I was at the stop for Govan. On exit, I noticed droplets of water hitting the pavement, shimmering in the light as they trickled down into the gutter. I bought a newspaper from a street vendor and tucked it under my arm, aiming to catch-up on the latest goings on in the dry safety of my house.

The walk home gave me all the exercise I needed and I felt tired and lethargic from the day's activities. I spent a few moments composing myself and read over the paper. Rupert Murdoch, the Australian/American tycoon, had been implicated in the phone hacking scandal.

I'd heard brief whispers about this during my trip. I knew that he'd taken a beating like a red-headed step-child on the Wall Street stock-markets, but I hadn't really understood the root cause behind the whole thing. After reading about the obscene practices of our so-called free press, I was incensed and outraged that some members of the Metropolitan Police had been in league with crime-happy journalists, illegally hacking into the phones of private citizens, all for the sake of selling more newspapers and, perhaps, for their own sick pleasure.

But that wasn't the worst of it. This abhorrent behaviour was visited on the families of murder victims, causing them deep distress and raising false hopes. Their voice-mail messages were accessed by unknown parties and then subsequently deleted. A parliamentary committee had been set up to investigate the whole issue and they summoned the mighty Rupert and his bastard progeny to answer for these heinous actions on their watch. The slippery fucker had effectively refused to respond to any of the questions put to him, feigning memory loss and towing the old party line - "I know nothing."

Yet the leading news story on the front page of every newspaper that day was about an angered member of the public who'd rightly thrown a custard pie at Murdoch Sr. I felt a gnawing animal digging its way out from within the pit of my stomach. How much more of this cheap bullshit could we be expected to take from that stupid skin stealing freak? He already controlled what we watched on TV, told us who we should vote into Downing Street, and it was his corporation under Fox News that had declared the 2001 presidential election in favour of George W. Bush.

Who gave a fuck if he had a paper plate of shaving foam thrown at him? If there were such a thing as real justice, he would be decomposing in the innards of a giant squid. No ordinary human being normally had that much excess skin hanging from their face. The only possible explanation was that he had been stealing the skin of unknown victims, during some kind of weird demonic sex ritual involving a headless kangaroo, a succubus and the Red Chinese.

The buzzer rang and shook me from my vitriol. I clicked the entry button and peeped through the keyhole. It was Kandy. She was early. The Yale lock clicked and I invited her in.

If there was a word that described her, it was 'petite'. She stood at five-five and had curly brown hair. I presumed it was dyed because I'd seen a hint of blonde in her roots once. Her green eyes reflected innocence but behind them was a razor-sharp brain of lethal cunning and intensity.

The warmth I'd seen in her before my trip was gone. In its place was an edgy energy and the gaze of a predator with a mind to kill. She strode into the kitchen and asked for one of my cigarettes. She was the epitome of a femme-fatal right out of some dime-store noir novel.

The atmosphere was tense. We chatted for a while about my vacation. I asked her about London. That was when the vibe turned nasty.

"It wasn't a great time. Last time I flew down with my friend Linda. This time I went by coach, which was a bad idea. I stayed with my ex. We fucked like rabbits, breaking up, making up and making out."

I felt my blood begin to boil and it rose, unstoppably upwards, searing my temples.

'Calm down,' I told myself. 'Maintain control. There's no need to let the situation get unpleasant. Om Mani Padme Hum.'

She asked me to read her some of my work on the travel journal I'd told her about. I obliged, trying to maintain a Zen state.

"You're an amazingly talented writer," she said.

She began to sensuously stroke the plant sitting on my window sill.

"Don't you touch my plant!" I yelled

She seemed stunned by my reaction.

"I should go," she said.

"That's probably a good idea," I replied.

She struggled with the sticky lock, trying desperately to escape the ugliness of the situation. I held her quickly, hoping that the pure emotion of love might quell the torrential downpour of negativity. It did some good, but the damage had been done. I spent the rest of that evening slashing through the newspaper with my flick-knife, in the vain hope that the deepening jealousy and anger would expel themselves from my core.

The following day seemed no better. Despair crept in and militantly joined forces with malicious feelings of hate. There was but one course of action left open to me. I picked up the phone and dialled the pre-programmed number.

"Good morning, Dr Mullin's surgery. How can I help?"

"I'd like the first appointment you've got please," I croaked.

"I've got one space at 9. 30 Am," said the pleasant feminine voice.

"Yes. That will do very nicely," I replied.

I dragged myself out of bed and made myself presentable. The clinic was relatively empty bar two other patients who had their eyes fixed on the screen overhead, spouting good health and well-being sermons, all sponsored by one drug company or another.

"I'm here for my 9.30," I told the receptionist.

"Take a seat. The doctor will be with you shortly," she said without looking up.

After a few minutes a droopy eyed old fat man came out of one of the treatment rooms and called my name.

There were three chairs opposite his and I couldn't decide which to take. I paced around the room nervously.

"Well, I'm heart-broken, depressed and spent yesterday evening having fantasies about disembowelling Rupert Murdoch."

"Interesting," he said as he clicked on his computerised prescription pad.

The printer on the other side of the room whizzed. He leapt to his feet and thrust a piece of paper into my hands.

"Get this filled in our pharmacy at once! As your

doctor, I'm recommending sixty milligrams of Fluoxetine - Prozac - twice daily. More if you need it!"

9. The Scales Of Two Cities -
Lust & Lamentation Make The World Go Round

I tried to maintain balance as I made my way to the bathroom. My legs felt like jelly. I could hear music playing in the background. I'd left the CD player on repeat through the night. 'Unchanged melody' rang out in all its glorious agony while I evacuated my bowels. I flushed the toilet and washed my hands with coconut fresh anti-bacterial soap. My bloodshot eyes glared in the bathroom mirror; the redness burning into the wall behind. I was endlessly drifting through an ethereal mist, sedated on prescription pills, bottles of bourbon and piss poor 80's pop music. My fragile mind had been fractured by pervading morbidity. There I was, ripped up, hyped up and doped up; forced to conform in the opium den of emotional angst.

I slid the panel on the medicine cabinet and picked up a small carton. 'Warning, May cause drowsiness. Take only as directed', read the label. I popped three pellets from the packet inside and swallowed them as I pulled on the cord to switch off the light bulb.

I walked into the living room, hit mute on the CD player and pressed the 'on' button on the television remote control beside it. The sight of a fifty-inch news anchor greeted me. He was interviewing a spokesman for the British National Party. The man had a great deal to say on the ever present issue of immigration and 'the great Muslim debate'.

"Radical Islam and Muslims in general are taking over this country! They want to implement Sharia law in all of England. We can't let other people dictate our way of life. We are British and we must be proud to be British!" he said.

His concept of nationalism brought images of a howling Adolf Hitler to my mind. It struck me as odd that any rational human being, who was part of an overwhelming ninety-five percent majority, would feel threatened by a mere one percent of the population. But I did understand the fear. When people didn't feel their voices were being heard by all mighty institutions that were designed to represent them, then it was only natural that they would descent to the level of stupid apes, seeking someone to blame in a perverse undercurrent of mass hysteria: the enemy within. The media relished every opportunity to propagate just that.

The BBC budget was paid for through mandatory TV license fees. Government imposed legislation made it a crime to be without one, and I didn't have one. If only Stalin had thought of it. He'd have revelled in rounding up many more 'criminals' in his Gulags. There were 'independent' media outlets, of course; but they too had vested interests that usually aligned with government policies and their spin-doctors. The hacking scandal had brought much of this hideous corruption and collusion to the attention of John Q. Public and there was no getting away from the murky depths that the rich and powerful had sunk to.

I was in the middle of trying to follow the BNP man's explanation on why his party wasn't racist when the phone rang. I was in no mood to speak to anyone, but the damned thing kept ringing. It stopped before ringing again a few seconds later.

"What!" I yelled, ready to smash the handset against the mahogany desk.

"Jesus, Max! It's James. I was just calling to tell you that there's a Syrian poets gathering tonight at the Centre for Contemporary Arts in Sauchiehall Street. Thought you might be interested in coming along."

"Jimmy, I'm not really feeling too great right now. Doubt I'll be there. When's it starting?"

"Tonight at eight. If you can make it along, it'd be great to see you there. There's some people I'd really like you to meet. These guys have gone to a lot of trouble to get here. Take care."

I looked up at the pendulum wall clock as I hung up the phone. It was already two-thirty in the afternoon. The overcast dull weather made the idea even less appealing. But the condition in Syria was worsening. President Al-

Assad's crackdown on his own people had resulted in the death of hundreds of innocent protesters. These poets had taken a big risk in travelling thousands of miles to come to Scotland; all so they could share their art and plight. It seemed only to be good manners to go four miles to see them.

The situation with Kandy was still troubling me. I didn't like the way things had been left. I called my friend Elayna who was now living in Liverpool, hoping that as usual, she would have some wise words on how to restore karmic order and universal harmony.

"Eli? Hey! It's Max!"

"Max! Great to hear your dulcet tones! Are you back from your trip state side?"

"Aye, I got back yesterday. Eli, you know it's always great gabbing with you, but I was hoping you could offer your usual sound advice on something that's got me running circles round my brain."

She listened carefully as I told her about the whole truck-load of problems I was having. She muttered something about scones and the lack of them south of the border between taking sips of tea. I rolled up a cigarette as I talked and flipped open my Zippo lighter, waiting for her sage response before striking the flint.

"You're a fuckin' idiot," she said. "Why did you handle it so badly?"

"I got jealous and angry," I said.

"You need to fuckin' apologise quick-style if you want to make things right." she said.

"Me!? Why? Hey, I wasn't in the wrong here!"

"Yes you were!" she insisted. "You should call her right after you put the phone down and grovel. This isn't the fucking fifties Maxwell. Things have changed."

"What the fuck are you talking about woman?" I said. "Don't you think I know that? But let's be honest here a second. I'm an alpha male. I hate the subjugation of woman, but I'm not inclined, or built, to grovel. Besides I can't call her. It'd be too bloody awkward."

She thought for a moment and I could almost hear the gears ticking in her mind.

"...Fine. Don't grovel. You're such a moron sometimes! I'll tell you what to do. Write her one of those wonderfully honest letters that you're so good at writing. After all, that's why we're still friends isn't it? Well that and your tyrannosaurus like stamina. You were always the one that got away," she said, with a flicker of regret.

I was a left a little red and embarrassed by her comment. Back in the day, we weren't exactly friends and we weren't exactly lovers. We'd been something in between that never quite gelled. It was always a case of wrong time, right location; or right time, wrong place.

"Cheers ears. I knew I could count on you. I'll send you some scones and a case of single malt as a gesture of my thanks. Ciao baby-doll"

I placed the handset back in the cradle as I mulled over what she'd said. Perhaps she was right. There was no real harm in sending Kandy a letter, if only to set things right. I swung open a desk drawer and took out a piece of expensive writing paper and rummaged around in search of a decent pen.

"Dear K,

I've chosen to write this letter to try and explain my recent actions and behaviour. A conversation with a friend today made me realise that I'd acted like a child throwing a rattle out of the pram.

I don't think it was wrong of me to be a little miffed. Clearly, there were things that had been building up in what Jung what have called my shadow side. But it was wrong of me to let this darkness permeate into our sphere of communication.

There are some ailments for which God grants us no cures. Things that vex us in our troubled moments. Sores that tear through soft flesh, and memories that haunt us through our years; fierce terrors that burn into blackness.

I'll clarify that last part for you. Contrary to popular belief, I'm not Superman. I am, in fact, a man. And as a man, I'm imperfect. I carry scars from the past and you already know about the heart-stabbing pain I suffered at the hands of Selena.

I do care for you very much. But I'm sure you'll agree that with you not knowing what you want in life and love, and with me not knowing where I belong in your life, it doesn't make for a stable friendship or relationship of any kind.

I'm also sending you a piece of sheet music, which I came across on my travels some years ago as a peace-making gift.

You're the harmony in my soul. I've never met anyone quite as captivating.

Love on ya, M."

I stuffed the sheet music in with the letter and licked the envelope, sealing its contents. I considered whether I should actually mail the thing. No, best to do it. One less thing to worry about.

I poured myself a small glass of bourbon and took a swig to clear my scattered mind. With my frustrations finally down on paper, I felt a slight sense of relief. But perhaps that was just the medication, or maybe the bourbon; or it could have been the combination of the two. Either way, it didn't matter.

I thought about all the times I'd spent in Kandy's company. It was then that I realised I was prepared to take her good, her bad and her worst, which was a first for me. I wondered how many other men were sitting in their comfortable chairs thinking the same thought, feeling the same feelings, for her.

10. The Ballad Of A Kandy Coated Toffee Apple

She lay on the bed next to me wearing a pair of my baggy pyjamas and my black talent scout t-shirt, exhausted from the emotionally draining few weeks she'd been through. Nothing sexual had happened. We just lay there, peacefully, staring at the ceiling, talking about our respective dreams for the future. Hers revolved around fame and fortune. Mine were simpler; to keep breaking rules and regulations and red-tape until I grew old or killed myself in some spectacular fashion.

We'd spent the evening in my flat, watching DVD's and drinking hallucinogenic teas imported from the Himalayas. I'd kissed her during the directors commentary, but she stood there, quiet and stiff as a board. I figured maybe I'd gotten my wires crossed and decided to call it a night. She was too tired and too high to make her way home safely at three o'clock in the morning. I offered her the option of taking the bed while I would sleep on the couch.

"No," she said. "You don't have to do that. I don't mind sleeping next to someone."

"OK," I said. "But I warn you. I sleep like an eleven stone baby. Don't be surprised if you hear me burping, farting and snoring through the night."

She laughed.

"That's disgusting!" she said.

I smiled at her and gave her a quick peck on the cheek before closing my eyes and lowering my head onto the duck-feathered pillow. I was beginning to nod off when an angelic and gentle voice suddenly said

"...Do you want to see my breasts?"

This doe-eyed twenty-something old had caught me completely by surprise. What was the appropriate response? Yes? No? Phone a friend?

"Of course I do," I said as I reached over to kiss her again.

Her lips were soft and sweet. She took off the t-shirt

and covered her nipples with her hands, nervously smiling in a sleepy haze. Her hands dropped to her side and her milky white skin glowed in the mild light of the scented candle by the window.

Things were heating up. She gazed blankly at the floor.

"I can't do this," she said.

"You don't have to do anything you don't want to," I told her.

I held her close for a few moments and we both drifted off. A few hours later, I was woken from a deep sleep, realising that she was grinding against me uncontrollably. Naturally, I responded in kind.

"I want you inside me! I want you to fuck me hard!" she whispered, breathless from the dry humping.

Night passed into day and I got up to replenish precious bodily fluids while she slept. I prepared a smorgasbord of various treats for breakfast, including fresh blueberries. She'd told me once they were her favourite kind of berry. I quickly popped down to the shop around the corner to buy her fresh flowers as a parting gift, in case I never saw her again. Kandy was about as unpredictable as they came. No-one had ever figured her out; which made her interesting.

When she came out of the shower, I sensed that things were already different. The weather was warm but her aura was cold. She sat quietly at the small table in my kitchen, munching on the crunchy marmalade toast and scooping up blueberries by the handful. I lit a cigarette and inhaled the smoke deep into my lungs, hoping that the toxic fumes would kill me before the conversation became awkward.

"I have to go soon," she said. "I have to meet someone who might put my band on the map."

Kandy was an indie generation rock chick who'd grown up with the cheap factory produced music of the 80's. It eventually bored her and she found herself drawn to the underground club beat scene, with hardcore rhythms and hardened disc-spinners. Her life revolved around fast base lines and faster living; a succession of quick fucks and fumbles in a search for some unknown.

I'd met her purely by accident. They say bad things happen in threes: maybe it's true. That same day, I'd gotten into a fight with a freakishly strong homeless woman, who proceeded to steal my pimped up manly chrome toaster. That should have told me something, but I didn't realise that in the same evening, I would find myself attracted to a flower loving, hot-stepping crazy girl. She was performing at the Victoria Bar, with all the passion of a wildebeest in heat. I couldn't contain my enthusiasm and immediately after the show I introduced myself. We found ourselves sizing each other up in the equivalent of a scorpion mating dance.

As I got to know her better, she told me things about her past and her childhood. Things that filled me with rage and anger. A history of sexual abuse had turned an already troubled child into a hell-raiser of epic proportions. She kept running into the arms of every gruesome son-of-a-bitch she had the misfortune to meet. For a lot of them, Kandy was simply their fuck toy, a dirty little secret, a fetish they indulged in to satisfy their needs. I became the latest in a long line of no good bums. I had no pity for her. She wasn't a victim; not as an adult. But I did have all the love in the world for a girl who wrestled with her demons daily. It took its toll.

To see an otherwise intelligent woman go through moments of extreme suffering and frustration pained me greatly. In Islam the notion of Jihad is often spoken about – the struggle. Many thought it meant a literal battle. From my own experience, the toughest wars to fight were the ones we fought when no-one else was looking; when hopelessness set in and the devil you knew came calling to collect his dues. It seemed a strange thing that we lived in an age when we could wipe each other out with Uranium smart bombs, but we'd yet to invent anything that could heal the wounds inflicted on the spirit of another human being.

Kandy's spirit had been broken and remoulded in two parts. Psychiatrists called it bi-polar disorder. They say it has to do with genetic predispositions, or overwhelming circumstances. Whatever name they gave it, whatever reason they gave for it manifesting itself, there was no actual cure. There were however, plenty of drugs produced by pharmaceutical companies to reduce or manage the symptoms. Kandy didn't believe in using drugs; legal or illegal; it didn't matter to her. She once railed at me for what she called my excess use of medication.

"You're no good for me," she'd said. "You're too much of a chemical freak!"

Perhaps she was right. She was heavily into alternative therapies, and I had nothing but disdain for them. All I'd seen in the new-age miracle market were charlatans looking to make a quick buck; or fake messiahs showing the way to the kool-aid machine. I was all for philosophical ideologies that challenged the system; religious or economic; but few, if any, had altruistic reasons for propagating their newfangled quackery. Usually some insider blew the whistle on whatever angle they were playing and the whole house of cards came tumbling down.

I sometimes wondered if Kandy and I were little more than fuck buddies. We didn't even qualify as friends to fall into the 'friends with benefits' category. What added to the confusion was that I was not the only rooster in the hen house. Most women realised that their power lay in being able to limit who got access to their souls and beds. Kandy was not so discerning. It occurred to me on more than one occasion that maybe she got her rocks off watching men fight over her in a jealous heat of primal passion.

Did that make her sick? Not in my eyes. She was a product of her environment. If she was seen as sick, then it was a reflection on those that saw her that way, instead of her. She had the kindness and compassion of the Dalai Llama in the best of times, and it was this that I found to be her most attractive quality. These traits were rare to find in anyone, and I certainly didn't have them, or need them. I envied those who did.

Kandy's main release wasn't sex or even booze, but rock 'n' roll. Writing songs and singing till her heart bled brought her a sense of peace. It was her confessional, where she communed with her spirit guides. A way for her to reconcile the truths that conflicted within, bringing together that half of herself that she could barely face with the one that gave her the strength and resilience to carry on day to day.

I didn't see or hear from her again for over a month. I assumed that she'd keep herself amused with her other 'interests'. When she finally did call again, I found that my suspicions were correct. But the green-eyed monster showed no signs of appearing. I figured since we didn't have any kind of defined relationship, there was no justification for allowing those kinds of feelings to surface. I had no idea how quickly that would change.

"Hey Kandy, How you been kid?"

"Hi Max. I'm good. New job's going well. I got that position as a support worker! I told you about it remember?"

I couldn't remember.

"Got a glowing report from my boss too! Want to read it? I'll email it to you."

"Sure, send it over. Kandy, I got to see you again babe. I'm missing you like crazy," I said.

I'd been pushing myself to the limits with odd jobs and an equally intense nightlife, leaving almost no time for social activities. I had a fire in my nuts and I had to do something to relieve the stress. I wanted her. I needed her.

"Well, I would love to see you, but I'm pretty busy. We could meet tonight... let's say around 9.30. There's something else you should know. Robbie came down and spent the weekend."

Her voice sounded strained. Was it worry? Fear of my reaction? Perverse excitement?

"I see," I replied.

"Are you mad?" she asked.

"No, I'm not mad."

"Oh," she sighed, sounding almost disappointed.

"I'll see you tonight at 9.30."

I showed up at half past nine on the dot as we'd agreed and knocked with my usual four knocks. She seemed surprised as she answered the door. I'd never been late, so I wasn't sure why. She invited me in and we embraced quickly before I made my way to the Ikea couch in the middle of her living room. I'd walked there from a small tea-house nearby on Pollockshaws Road. There was no question that I was out of shape. I hadn't renewed my gym membership in months and that may have been part of the problem. I wiped the sweat off my brow as she walked into the kitchen.

"Do you want a cuppa?" she shouted.

"Yes, thanks, that would be great," I said

She set down two mugs on bourgeois coasters, filled with very weak tea. It was how she liked it. I didn't understand the point of going to all that trouble of making tea, only to sip on what amounted to water and milk. I put it down to personal preference and gave it no further thought. She made herself comfortable beside me and we talked about her work and issues that were plaguing her life. I didn't have much to share because of the daily sense of sameness that was ever present.

"My feet are killing me!" she said.

"Would you like a foot rub? Some say I have magic fingers, as you might know."

I gave her a cheeky smile and she moved her feet up to my lap. I massaged her left foot gently as she lay back quietly, closing her eyes. My pulse began racing when I moved onto her right foot. She pulled up her skirt past her knees and rubbed her thighs. My hands made their way upwards, cupping her calves. She had sensuously long and sexy legs and she knew I was getting more turned on by the second.

"Are you hard?" she said.

"Hard as a rock," I replied.

Her lips met mine and we kissed gently before I felt

her supple breasts against my chest. We made out in what seemed like a perfect moment, frozen forever in eternity. Her hand reached down to my belt buckle and she bucked as I my crotch rubbed against hers. It wasn't long before my jeans hit the floor and the sound of buttons popping echoed through the room. Then, out of nowhere came the words.

"I love you Kandy."

I kissed her neckline, while in the back of my mind, my subconscious was mulling over the implications of the last moment. 'What the fuck did you just say?' it asked, 'Are you fucking crazy? ...Don't tell this girl you love her! ... She's dangerous!... You're insane!'

It was two am. Kandy looked up at me as I cradled her in my arms, her hand in mine. She broke away and had the same distance in her eyes that I'd seen the last time. She got up and paced nervously through the apartment, clearing up bits of clutter, packing away boxes of make-up and accessories. I'd once read in a medical journal that obsessive compulsive disorder sometimes also affected people who were bi-polar, especially when the sufferer became overwhelmed with conflicting emotions.

"You should go soon," she said. "I have to be up early tomorrow and..."

"You don't have to explain," I told her.

I held her close again and placed a kiss on her forehead.

"I meant what I said earlier. I love you."

"I... love you too," she said, as her lip quivered slightly.

I left and made my way toward the main road, hoping that I'd be lucky enough to catch a taxi. It was a warm night, and I was prepared to walk all the way back to Govan. Luckily, my hunch paid off and I saw the glimmer of an amber taxi sign rushing down in my direction. I flagged it and got in.

By the time I got back to my flat, I was feeling uncertain and on edge. I'd left the lights to prevent intruders from breaking in and stealing my plant along with my beloved Barry Manilow LP collection. I picked up the phone and placed a call to my old friend and spiritual advisor in Los Angeles. It was still early there because of the time difference.

"Rabbi? It's Max. I'm feeling fucked up and a little lost. I wasn't sure where else to turn."

"Hey buddy. Long time no speak. What's got you all dizzy up in the head there? You want to talk about it?"

"It's this girl I met. I don't know what the fuck to do. I really like her, but my head is all over the place," I replied

"Listen dude, why don't you come over state side for a few days. I could use the company. My dime. I'll get your tickets sorted out for next week. We'll go to the old haunts, see if that helps take your mind off things," he said.

"I don't know man. I mean I've got a lot going on over here and..."

"Clear your schedule! You're flying over. No arguments," he said, hanging up the phone before I got another word in edgewise.

The more I thought about it, the more it seemed like a good idea.

11. A Cultural Cataclysm in a Dear Green Place

It was another wet Wednesday night. It hadn't stopped raining since the day before. The weather forecast had predicted exotic temperatures and more sunshine than Aruba. They may as well have hired voodoo shaman priests to do bone readings instead. Perhaps if they did, they'd have had a better accuracy rate. It seemed silly to expect a tropical climate in a country that experienced long winters colder than Siberia. Last year, the whole of London had ground to a complete standstill following an inch of snowfall. I recalled how we in Scotland, had laughed at the time, proud of the fact that we were tougher, made of sterner stuff. It was only when we got record amounts of the tiny white flakes, blanketing our every town and glen, that we took the problem seriously. That was when we stood shoulder to shoulder with our English counterparts, the same stiff upper-lipped, Londoners who we'd mocked as weaklings just weeks earlier.

I filled the bathtub with hot water and weird bath salts. I spent the better part of an hour playing with my rubber duck and soaking in the bubbles from the foamy bath gel. The water steadily became cool and I noticed that my fingers and toes had transformed into prunes, ageing me by about fifty years. It was time to emerge from the watery womb, back into the world. I was sorely tempted to stay cocooned in the comfort of the tub. I'd taken an emotional battering and was in no mood to go to the Syrian Poets convention. Not many folk were likely to be there anyway. But I knew I had to dig deep and find the strength to attend. My gut told me that it would be worthwhile, and experience had taught me that it was always better to satisfy curiosity than to be left pondering the possibilities. One of Gerry Anderson's puppet shows had put it best. As a kid, every Saturday morning I'd sneak into the living room to tune in that fourteen inch black and white television screen, just to hear that booming introduction, 'Anything can happen in the next half hour!... Stingray! Stingray!"

But it wasn't the action that interested me as much as the intricate and unique personalities of each character, just like real-life. People had always been my drug of choice. It was safe to say that I was a social addict. The good, bad and ugly all caused different reactions in my booze addled brain cells. Fabulously mad optimists with hints of intelligent delusion were like uppers, inducing highs that lasted for days, weeks and sometimes even months. They were the artistic oddballs that bought into the gimmick of false confidence and endless hope. Spending time with the sad and solitary, however, quickly counters those magic moments of mania. Downers: too many of them and you bought yourself a one-way ticket to Introspection Bay and Gloom Central.

I thought about what kind of people I was likely to encounter at this gathering. Were these foreigners prone to the same strange tendencies as us civilised westerners? They were a curious breed of desert people, willing to speak their minds on what they thought and felt. This, said their religious scholars, made them a force of evil. They were corrupting the youth with their notions of self-expression. It was all the fault of the decadent infidels. Perhaps he was right. We certainly weren't in any position to judge. Our own society was falling apart before our very eyes. 'Broken Britain'; that was the buzzword concocted by the government to describe it, as if at some point it had been perfect and then snapped like a toy train. To fix it, our freedoms had to be taken away. It was for our own good. We needed it. It was not, of course, in any way similar to the Arab situation.

I got out of the bath, dried myself and wrapped a towel around my waist, searching frantically for a fresh pair of underwear. Luckily, I found a clean pair of boxer shorts in the chest of drawers in my bedroom. I was still feeling lethargic and the grey skies outside were doing little to boost my energy levels. I closed my eyes and took a deep breath. I pulled on my khaki golf trousers and 'Buffalo County' t-shirt and went into the kitchen. There was a half empty bottle of Southern Comfort sitting on the worktop. I reached into the rickety cupboard above to take out a whiskey glass and filled it with ice. I couldn't understand people who drank anything neat; unless it was a single malt. All liquor, especially blended scotch, always tasted better on the rocks. I'd spent my formative years in high school drinking warm bottles of Buckfast behind garbage sheds and had grown to dislike the forced necessity of forgoing ice-cubes on warm summer days.

The hour was fast approaching. I stuffed a compact Kodak camera in the inside pocket of my black biker jacket. It was too late to take the bus but I had just enough time to call the cab company and get there by taxi. It was never a good idea to show up at any event after the first thirty minutes. The spotlight typically ended up on the latecomer who, after clanging the doors shut, would almost knowingly step on the toes of seated spectators for a brief, twisted thrill. You could always hear the groaning from the irritated crowds. They'd all mastered the art of pre-planning, which naturally made them better than any shambles of a tardy attendee. 'Fuck them', I thought.

The car arrived promptly and the driver honked twice. I ran out and jumped into the back of the cab, instructing the driver to take me to the CCA on Sauchiehall street. The artificial pressure was mounting and I could feel the adrenalin coursing through my veins. This was the boost I needed. I could feel the rusty wheels turning in the machinery of my mind, and I began to look forward to an evening of obscure poetry that I wouldn't understand. But more importantly, there was a bar on the premises, which meant there was sure to be some heavy drinking at the end of it all.

"Step on it!" I said to the man behind the wheel, "Come on man! Is this a car or a horse driven cart?"

"It's a Skoda," he replied. "It can do about a hundred if I push it. But this is a main road and the limits thirty."

"Speed limits are made to be broken," I said. "Besides, they're more like suggestions."

He didn't seem amused.

"Do you want to get out and walk, mate? I can let you out here if you want to be a dick about it."

"No, no. This is fine. Just get me there in your own slow-ass time," I said.

He pulled up to the kerb after a tense ride.

"That's six pound and fifty."

I paid him the money and stepped onto the pavement. He drove off quickly, giving me the finger as I watched him speed away. I turned my attention to the bright lights in the town centre. There was something almost hypnotic about Glasgow at night. I stood there, right outside the entrance to the Centre for Contemporary Arts. A large, colourful banner hung from a lamppost, waving in the wind, welcoming street walkers and students alike into the bosom of culture. Its doors were the golden gates of this Emerald City.

There, standing in the foyer, was Jim; carefully scanning the stairs for familiar faces. He was smartly dressed in his sports coat, jumper and jeans. A blue raincoat was bundled in his arms. I approached him and held out my hand, ready for his usual firm handshake. Instead, he flung his arms around me and gave me a hearty pat on the back. I was a little shaken. He was a slender man, but his six foot frame gave him an advantage over most. His ever growing auburn hair had become fluffed and frizzy from the windy conditions.

"Maxwell! It's bloody good tae see you! How've you been, dood."

Jim was one of Paisley's finest poets and a communist sympathiser with connections to worn out faces in dangerous places. In Hoover's era, he would have been bundled into the back of a van, never to be seen again. He'd fought staunchly against Thatcher's poll tax in the '90's. Those were tough times. Times of mass unemployment, yob culture and deep despair. The whole of society had gone back to the 60's in the hopes of finding some nugget of wisdom. But all they got was a promiscuous, heroin induced orgy of fucking and being fucked over. The youth spawned from the soup of free love found that nothing, not even love, was free. Forced to face this fact, they turned to the arts as a means of escaping the horrible realities of today.

As well as being a champion of an age long gone, Jim was also a rip-roaring drunk; the only man I knew who could drink me under the table. He had the constitution of a bull and the libido of an African rhino. It was obvious he was inebriated. Although not entirely sober myself, I wasn't noticeably intoxicated either. Jim's present condition, however, was easily guessed when he moved toward a slim, freckled redhead wearing glasses and told her that she had shapely legs. His observation couldn't be faulted. She didn't respond and showed no immediate reaction. Jim stood there bemused as she turned toward me.

"Your friend is incredibly rude!" she howled, slapping me firmly across the face.

She grunted and left, with her nose upturned. I was completely dumb-struck. Most women usually responded well to compliments. But it was Jim who'd come onto her, not me. I was thoroughly confused. My cheek suddenly felt hot and began to sting.

"We should probably head to the convention. Where are they doing this thing?" I asked him.

"The Studio Room, I think. Aye, we should go now. That was strange. Very strange indeed," he said. "I've pre-booked seats for us so there's no problems."

The two of us thought about what had just happened as we ascended up the stairs and into the main entrance of the Studio Room. I reached for the door handle and paused.

"What exactly did you say to her, Jim?"

"I just told her that my friend and I thought she had beautiful legs."

"Oh," I said.

"And then I asked her if she had a sister and that I'd pay good money to see them get off with each other."

"Ah," I said. "That would have done it."

On opening the door, we discovered that the room was packed and the show had already started. We hurdled over the seated audience and clambered into the empty chairs with 'reserved' tickets placed on them. Jim fit in perfectly with the rest of the crowd. They were all well-turned out in their Sunday best.

I, on the other hand, looked like a common thug who'd barged in unannounced to gatecrash the event. The only other patron wearing a leather jacket was the inimitable Alvin Biscuit. But his was tailored-to-fit in the form of a suit jacket. There was a gold chain hanging from his waistcoat. He was the only soul I'd met who had a functioning fob watch, and he used it for all practical purposes. He abhorred the internet and the slack-jawed generation who swore by it religiously. Although he was well under forty, he took his style tips from Winston Churchill. In his spare time he was a Scottish nationalist who advocated independence for Scotland. This made him a fun sight to watch in debates against royalists. His better half, Christine McMannus, was sitting beside him in the back row. Alvin was a renowned novelist at the forefront of contemporary Scottish writing, while Christine was well known for her numerous short stories, which had been published in every literary journal this side of the grave.

In front of us, a short, stout young man with a dark complexion was speaking feverishly into a microphone in his native tongue. I could barely see him and I certainly couldn't understand him. This made the whole performance difficult to follow. The wooden pulpit hid his face, with only his forehead remaining visible, glistening from the overhead lights as beads of sweat trickled downwards. When he finished, a tall blonde woman from the first row stood up and glided onto the podium.

"Thankyou very much Ali Ibn Yousef, for that moving piece. I'll now read you a translation in English....

The spring wells in Arabian eyes.

The water burns into oil, into blood.
I cry, I cry.
For my mother, for my father.
My tears run clear.
Dying under the midnight stars.
Dining on ashes in sand and dust.
Lights burning dimly,
Fires dancing in the night sky,
Spirits of the righteous crushed.

Diamonds in the desert,
Hearts yearning for truth,
Beating against the bombs.
Give us life, let us laugh.
Love! Free us from your hands.

Shackle our souls,
Our goal is one,
Dropping mortars of mind.
We are peaceful warriors,
Walking with the angels."

A small ripple of applause built up into a loud wave of unending appreciation. The young man whose poem had just been interpreted smiled gently before both he and the translator sat back down in their allocated chairs.

Several more readers took to the podium, but none had the elegance of the first. That may have been down to their own interpreters. I wished I had the ability to understand the language. Never before had I felt so sorely lacking in knowledge.

By the end of it all, several members of the audience rushed the stage. It was like a rock concert, only with less noise and considerably more boring. What got my attention was that these people had escaped persecution to share their life and word. They were real people with real problems, instead of the self-involved idiots suffering from the self-inflicted pain of a broken heart. Some of them had danced with bullets to make it to the ballot box. In a supposedly civilised age, brutality was still the first spoken language.

Jim and I quickly exited the room and made our way to the bar next door. The drinks were anything but cheap and we spent the better part of an hour nursing our Corona's, planning our next move. There were plenty of bars, clubs and pubs around, but few appealed to our tastes. Most were little more than glorified fuck pits; catering to student troglodytes, who crawled, climbed and drooled over each other to reach the prettiest girls. For refined drinkers like us, this was a pointless exercise. We waited for the girls to come to us. Of course, this was a flawed plan. There was a plethora of fish in the sea, but rarely did we cast our lines in the right oceans, and normally we were stung by jellyfish and met by shell-locked clams.

Then it hit us. The Griffin. One of the finest drinking establishments we'd had the pleasure of frequenting. And so it came to pass that we staggered toward the legendary boozer. There followed several unconnected conversations about Robert Tannahill, Romany gypsies and the importance of pinning one's wallet to their underwear as a theft prevention mechanism.

"How dae yae feel aboot Rasputin?" asked Jim.

"Rasputin?... You mean that crazy mad Russian fella with a fetish for flagellation?"

"Aye, him!"

"Kinky fucker wasn't he? Do you think he got it on with the Queen?"

"He must've done Max. There's no way a sex mad Russian priest would have turned her down."

"Yeah, you're right enough. Still, at least he wasn't part of the priest mob today, what with all the bastard buggery of young kids and that. Those fuckers make me sick. I'd shoot each one of them given the chance!"

We'd been walking for some time down Sauchiehall Street, and I began to question whether we were even going the right direction. When drunk, my inner compass; both moral and geographical; became utterly useless. We came upon Elmbank Street. I was ready to cross the road and carry on walking, but Jim grabbed my arm and pulled me around the corner.

"Where are you going Max? It's doon this way. And I thought I was drunk!"

About half a block down, the bright lights above the sign hit our scarred retinas. The nectar of the gods was sure to flow freely in the infamous saloon. I imagined that heaven, if there was such a place, wouldn't be entirely dissimilar: a pub with a custom built lounge and free cable TV. We stood silently for a moment, adjusting our eyes to the halogen lamps before swaggering in like John Wayne and Paul Newman.

12. Australians Don't Give A Four X:
A Mythical Monster Makes An Appearance

An indiscernible rabble of voices greeted us once we were inside. The mild tones of soft rock blended in with the sound of a thousand conversations. In the far corner, sitting on a barstool, was Evan Mackleson, a successful screenwriter and serial novelist. With him, Roger Van Winkleton, a supposed poet and patron of the arts. I'd never met the man before, but his thick moustache and horn-rimmed glasses had become the stuff of folklore among the bohemian art community. I motioned Jim to join them while I got the drinks in. The barman glared at me like a Doberman, ready to pounce on his unsuspecting prey.

"What'll yae have?" he growled.

"A pint of Guinness and a Speckled hen." I retorted, squinting slightly.

He could see that I was not a man to be trifled with and threw a white dishcloth over his shoulder to signal his surrender. In the arena of hard drinking, every pint pulled was a deadly game of chicken and every bartender was a potential friend or foe. The wrong choice of poison could result in sudden death, or a slow form of social suicide.

Jim hadn't moved, he was still fixed to the same spot next to the door. His eyes were glazed over and he'd adopted a thinking man's pose, with one hand on his chin and the other in his coat pocket.

"That's five eighty mate!" said the barman.

I picked up the two glasses and stumbled back to persuade Jim to join the living.

"Max, whit does that look like tae you?"

"What does what look like?" I asked.

"There, up there, next to the men's room."

"That? Well, that's obviously a big fuck off stain. Probably from damp or a leak or something."

"Look closer. Seriously, just look at it," he said

I did as he asked. It took me a while to register. He was right. There was something emerging from the pattern.

An image finally began to make itself visible and a bearded man with long hair emerged from the piss and water stains on the wall above the entrance to the gent's bathroom.

"Jesus!" I said

"Aye," said Jim.

"Man, that's freaky. That's better than that Turin toast on Ebay."

"No kiddin'. Come on son, we'd better join they two over there before they start wondering why we're staring at the men's toilets."

"Yeah. I only came over to tell you to move your ass; not to stare at trippy religious iconography in a leaky pub."

In the artist's corner, both men got up and shook our hands, greeting us with smiles and small talk. Evan was a short round-faced man with ginger hair and a Ginsberg style beard. He was a true revolutionary. He believed in the power of the people. But he was also a reverse futurist. He believed modern society was doomed to decay; that everything would soon revert back to Dickensian times, with workhouses and prisons taking the place of government supported institutions. According to him, technology was about to meet its demise. It had all reached a saturation point and the tide would turn, rolling back through the years until nothing remained.

I didn't share his bleak vision. If anything *was* going to destroy us, it was likely to be our own emotions and hatred; those were things to which no-one was immune. No ancient bird god or long haired desert preacher could save us from ourselves. But I was hopeful. Evolution had spared us so far and the process itself would perhaps one day lead to the elimination of all our irrational fears.

I drank my pint of Guinness as Jim and Evan tried to discuss Marxist philosophy in coherent sentences. I was already past the point of comprehension and chimed in every so often with an "interesting", or "I see", to avoid seeming out of place. Roger was busy staring at the girl three tables to his right. I could understand why. Her well toned legs and miniskirt left nothing to the imagination.

"So Max... What do you think about this whole free market capitalism thing?" asked Evan

"Eh, well... I guess..."

"Hey Evan, check out the rack on that cute number!" said Roger

I was glad for the interruption. It took the attention off my brain-dead responses.

"Oh she's got it going on awright. But the missus would kill me if she knew I was perving!"

"Don't be daft," I said. "What she doesn't know won't kill her."

"That's true. But she's meeting me in here in ten minutes," he replied.

"Well, unlucky you," said Jim. "I'm gonna have a crack at her. Nothin' tae stop me lads!"

We watched with anticipation as Jim got up and staggered towards the young brunette. She seemed unimpressed and her body language became defensive as he thrust himself into her personal space. It was obvious to everyone but Jim that she was becoming more disinterested by the minute. Ordinarily, when he wasn't quite so drunk, women found him to be charming and amusing. But his decency took a back seat when he'd had a few.

"Get away from me you dirty old man!" screamed the girl.

Jim came back to the corner, sulking like a misbehaved child who'd been caught by the teacher.

"Maxwell," he said, "It's entirely possible I'm a wee bit drunk."

The three of us burst out laughing, unable to stop. At first, Jim didn't see the funny side of it, but the laughter was infectious and he soon found himself joining in. I eventually regained my composure as did the others.

"I guess it's my round," I said.

Evan suddenly became very still and his face lost all expression.

"I've just seen Jason Donovan walk through that

door."

"Who the fuck is Jason Donovan?" asked Roger.

"Jason Donovan?" I said. "Are you sure? What the fuck would Jason Donovan be doing in Glasgow? "

"I'm sure man. It was him. But I could be wrong. We should double check. He's just gone into the lounge."

We all looked at each other with a look of confusion. None of us wanted to meet the man and we weren't quite sure whether the old rule of backing up a friend applied in this situation.

"Come on guys, it's Jason Donovan! He used to be one of Australia's biggest soap stars!"

"I still have no idea who the fuck Jason Donovan is!" said Roger.

"Oh come on guys. Please," said Evan. "He knows Kylie!"

"Oh!" we replied in unison.

"He might have her number," he added.

"I've had a crush on Kylie ever since I can remember," I replied. "This girl I was stuck on; she kind of looked like her."

The others still seemed unsure, but I wasn't going to let them stop a potential romance dead in its tracks. I got up and followed Evan toward the lounge area.

"Listen man, if he doesn't give us the information we need, I say we hit him over the head, tie him up and drag him across town till he spills the beans!"

"Max, I don't want to kill him, I just want to meet him."

"Who said anything about killing him? Just a little mild torture."

"Torture? No, I'm not going to torture one of Australia's best exports for some bint's phone number."

"Fuck you man! You take that back!" I said sternly. "Kylie is not a bint. She's a goddess! Perfection personified! A true vision of beauty!"

"Okay Romeo, take it easy. Let's just find the guy first."

There he was, sitting alone at his table with a 'Sound

of Music' script in his hands and a pint of Australian beer beside him. That's when it hit me. It was the reason he was here. I'd read in some tabloid rag that he was set to star in the musical at a local theatre, though I couldn't remember which one. We hovered nearby, looking for some opportunity to present itself. That script was our ticket in; for Evan to meet one of his twisted heroes, and mine to possibly meet the pop princess of my dreams. His glass was empty before long, and we spotted our chance to go in for the kill.

"Excuse me, Mr Donovan? My esteemed associate and I were wondering if we could buy you a drink," said Evan.

"Actually mate, I'd prefer not to have any company right now. Thanks for the offer though, it's really decent of yah."

"Here's the thing Jason; can I call you Jason? My friend here is a huge fan. God knows why, but he is. Anyway, he's a very talented screenwriter. Done a lot of work down in your neck of the woods. You've probably heard of him, Evan Mackleson."

Evan looked visibly uncomfortable and began to rub the back of his neck. Donovan, on the other hand, seemed appreciative of my forthright manner.

"Oh yeah, Evan. Right. Yeah, I've heard good things mate. Pull up a couple of chairs guys. Please, sit, sit."

"I'll get the beers in," I said.

So far, our improvised Machiavellian designs had worked. I felt hopeful that my own dream would soon become a reality. The odds were in our favour. Evan had already realised his ambitions and I deduced that my own were likely to come to fruition soon. But it was Steinbeck who'd postulated on the best laid plans of mice and men.

When I rejoined the table, I found the two men jabbering away like old friends, sharing stories of high school shame and degradation. I'd missed out on the bonding experience and it became plain that I was now the outsider.

"...So Jason, the Sound of Music... How'd ye get roped into that? And in Glasgow at that?" asked Evan.

"Actually mate, I jumped at the chance. It was a pay-cheque for a stage production, which I loved, and I get to see a bit of Scotland, which is great. After I did Joseph and the Amazing Technicolour Dreamcoat, it left me with a taste for musicals."

"Here you go gents!" I placed the beer glasses on the table and we each scuttled our respective drinks in front of us.

"Cheers dude! You're a top bloke."

Evan raised a toast to his boyhood hero and I joined in, sure that I was now part of an exclusive clique. The subject of discussion remained fixed on the highs and lows of Donovan's career, and he spoke briefly about his work in the great Australian soap opera through which he and Kylie had become household names across the country. In every school playground across the land, kids had pondered the question, 'Will they or won't they?' Just as the focus drew closer on the subject of my desire, he drank down the last of his beer and slammed down the glass.

"Well fellas it's been great chatting, but I've got to get a move on."

He was up like a shot and out the door quicker than a jack rabbit.

"Fucking bastard!" I growled. "He knew we were gonna ask him about Kylie."

"What a great guy," said Evan.

"Great guy? Did you not see what just happened? He shut us down man! No fairytale pop princess, no glass slippers... not a damned thing!"

"Shut *us* down?" Evan was pissed. "No Max, he shut *you* down! You and your fucked up fantasies. Honestly, you're like a hound in heat!"

I was on the verge of swinging for him, but I restrained myself and managed to hold back. It was a dangerous game to destroy the hopes of a battered soul, no matter how delusional his dreams might be. But Evan obviously didn't know that I was barely hanging on to my sanity by an increasingly short and loose thread.

"Let's get back to the rest of the gang," I said, sure that I would be less prone to violent tendencies in the presence of others.

Evan's better half had arrived and was sitting next to Roger, who despite knowing she was unavailable, was doing his best to tempt her toward the dark side. He had always sworn that women responded to him because of his moustache. He said it was a sure sign of his masculine virility. But it was obviously failing in this situation, as her every move showed she was uncomfortable with his advances. Evan approached her and stood squarely behind Roger.

"You hittin' on ma bird?" asked Evan in a stern yet jovial tone.

"Naw. I was just... We were just talking about the Scottish Elections."

"Oh aye? I'd love to hear all about it."

Just as Roger was about to speak the barman hit a large gong and called time on last orders. He'd literally been saved by the bell. We debated for a moment on whether it was worthwhile getting another round in or if it was best to bring the evening to a close. The others all had early mornings, either with work or other errands and it seemed unfair to persuade them to continue on the road to ruin for a night they were sure not to remember.

"Well lads and dear lady, as always, it was a pleasure and an honour to share a pint or four with you. And even if my plans for this evening didn't quite pan out the way I'd hoped they would, it wasn't entirely wasted," I said.

Evans arms were draped over his lady love as she explained where she'd parked the car. She'd stuck to soda and fruit juice, which was wise. The law was particularly strict on such matters and drink driving was dealt with more harshly than most other crimes.

I bid my companions good night, advising them to

take care of Jim before leaving the pub. I knew of his predilection for finding trouble. He was at that point, somewhere between being a fun and pleasant eccentric and being a mean spirited drunk ready to spit blood. I was in no mood to nursemaid him through misplaced attempts of ego masturbation. I had too many problems of my own. The full moon shone across the dusty sky. As far as I was concerned, the night was still young and full of possibilities.

13. Deadly Nightshades –
The Scent of Two Roses

I walked down Sauchiehall Street, toward the heart of the city, hoping to find a vibrant hotspot, a hive of social activity. I needed that kind of energy, I fed off it. There, after about two blocks, was Firewater. It seemed quite ordinary for a bar, full of student types and amateur pool players. Its outward appearance wasn't anything special; unless you counted the bright green lights that flooded the pavement in a radioactive glow. A barrage of disco lighting and musical grooves assaulted the eyes and ears of passersby.

I immediately made my way to the bar and commandeered a high chair next to the wooden panelling. A hefty A4 menu welcomed new and old patrons alike with its colourful drinks list. I flicked through it for a few seconds before ordering a large Cherry Bomber; one of their many inventive cocktails.

"Go easy on the cherries!" I told the girl behind the counter.

"I'll bring it right over!" she said.

The whole place was decked out with red patent leather seats and mahogany tables. I sensed the girl staring at me from behind the bar and felt a burning sensation in the base of my neck. She tapped me on the shoulder and put a full pitcher, complete with bobbing cherries, in front of me. I asked her for a glass to try the alien concoction.

"Thank you Miss... It certainly looks interesting."

She smiled and held her elbows in her hands before flicking back her long, lustrous hair.

"My name's Mandy. I work here through the week. Mostly nights. I don't think I've seen you in here before."

"Nice to meet you Mandy. My name's Max. No, first time in here. I love your hair. It's so... pink... But beautiful!" I said.

"Thanks... I think! You seem like a pretty nice guy."

It was obvious she was attracted to the golf trousers. It was only a matter of time before someone, somewhere, developed this kind of sick fetish for them; and here was that someone. Why this relatively intelligent and good looking woman had developed this fascination was beyond me. I'd once read about a man who'd become obsessed with a bicycle tyre in China, with the full intention of consummating the union. There was also the curious case of the French woman who'd married the Eiffel tower. At least this was slightly less unusual. Men often developed strange tastes for articles of female clothing. Was it so wrong that a woman should want to feel the sensation of golf trousers against her skin?

"You can't have them," I said.

"Can't have what?" she asked.

"Never mind."

She gave me a perplexed look and moved onto serving another customer. I carried on pouring the Cherry Bomber into a tall, thin glass. Concentrated fruit juice mixed with vodka goodness. It tasted like a tub of mouthwash, but I helped myself to two more servings. After all, I'd paid good money for it. I glanced at my watch. In five hours, dusk would turn to daylight and the bustling city lights would wind down like a carnival shutting up shop before going on the road again. I didn't want to waste what was left of those few hours in a bar with few redeeming features, despite the excellent drinks menu. That would have been a sure sign of an alcoholic.

I finished my drink and leapt from the stool, ready to explore greener pastures. As I got closer to Hope Street, my head started to swirl inside and I felt a little woozy. Shadowy images were flashing past and I was sure that time had somehow slowed down, allowing me to move faster than everything, and everyone, else. But this quickly passed and I soon had a clear idea of exactly where I wanted to go.

Twenty minutes later I was in Mitchell Street. It was a long walk, but my legs didn't feel at all heavy or tired. Diamond Dolls was no ordinary watering hole. The name was the brainchild of some hippy generation porn addict who'd seen too many movies about high-class hookers with hearts of gold and had capitalised on the idea. The heat in the night air made standing there unbearable.

Gradually, I made my way through the portal leading into a dimension of depravity. Two large gentlemen, who may as well have had handlebar moustaches, frisked me and ushered me toward the coat check. A hideously obese and unattractive old woman greeted me and took my jacket, giving me what looked like a raffle ticket. The two stout men waved me into the main club hall, but not before issuing a few words of warning.

"No hand contact with the girls."

"Don't worry," I replied. "I won't even touch them with my toes!"

The core chamber of horrors was filled with sweat drenched cannibals pawing at their prey as they garnished them with sticky wads of money. It was an interesting way to get around the rules. It nearly showed a degree of brainpower. The ever changing mood lighting combined well with the suggestive soft music. It was a far cry from Burt Bacharach's greatest hits, which were my own choice in the realms of seduction. A voice whispered into my ear.

"Hi there stranger. Are you going to buy me a drink?"

I turned round to find a pale brunette barely three inches from me. Her face had a beauty comparable to Julia Roberts and, unlike Shakira, her breasts were easily confused with mountains. She was an 'exotic' entertainer, but there was nothing exotic about her; except maybe her fake fingernails – made in Thailand. She seemed nice enough to share a beverage with.

She stared at me deeply with her light brown hazel eyes. What was she searching for? I asked for her choice of poison; a cosmopolitan with a slice of lime. I was impressed with her selection and ordered the same. She guided me to a vacant booth and I followed her willingly, drinks in hand. I noticed the beer stains on the table and wondered why they didn't have coasters. Maybe they'd been used in a bar brawl. Perhaps some poor soul had been arrested for assault with a deadly beer mat.

"I'm Debbie," she said, crossing her legs and heaving out her cleavage.

"Max," I replied.

I was starting to feel dizzy and dehydrated. Things were moving at a fast pace in the vicinity of vice. I gulped down my Cosmo and laughed nervously. I was a deer caught in the headlights of a speeding train. Debbie was completely at ease. She was used to handling all kinds of men, in all kinds of ways. Shy or bold, it didn't really matter. We were all just another pay-day.

"Why don't you and me go to the private lounge. We can relax there and I'll perform for you," she purred.

She rubbed her finger down my thigh and pointed out the mythical palace of pleasure. I was unconvinced until Debbie began nibbling on my earlobe. She got up and I followed closely behind, stopping at the bar for our beverages. I held the door open and she made herself comfortable next to me on the large black leather padded sofa that circled the room. This was where improvised entertainment met with skilful dexterity.

"It's fifty pounds for a dance and a hundred for anything else," she said.

I laid some notes on a small table in near corner and she signalled to someone through the small window in the door. Mellow music filtered through the speakers as she counted the money. She smiled with a smug satisfaction, safe in the knowledge that she'd met her quota for the day. I watched the full hundred and fifty pounds disappear into the small black purse she carried under her arm. She put it on the side table next to our drinks.

The show commenced. Debbie used all her honed agility and grace, creating a smooth and sensuous atmosphere. The air seemed heavy again. Her soft supple body reflected the dim light as she moved with elegance and endearing play. She moved closer and brushed against me. Something caught my eye, a mole maybe. She thrust her breasts into my face. I saw it again, what looked like small punctures on her inner arm. Maybe track marks but I couldn't be sure.

Was she a heroin addict? A thief? A lawbreaking fugitive living in squalor, with an antique dealing pimp called Jaunty? Was he the kind of guy who chewed the bones of golf loving delinquents? My thoughts were scattered and strange visions clouded my brain. It didn't really matter. I gave in to the moment and watched her writhe in ecstasy.

Debbie then straddled me and unbuttoned my trousers. I groaned as she reached in and grappled with my throbbing member. My breathing became faster as her hand moved with a firm intensity, full of purpose. She kissed my cheek and then my lip. Waves of pleasure washed over me and I couldn't hold back.

"Oh God!" I yelled.

Debbie continued, not letting up until I was drained of all my energy. She kissed my forehead and held me against her chest for a few moments. My crotch felt cold and wet as she took her hand away. I wondered if this qualified as breaking the rules. Confusion set in as I watched Debbie riffle through her purse.

"Ah ha!" she said, taking out a handful of tissues.

"Wow, you sure made a real mess!" she giggled, wiping her fingers of any incriminating evidence.

"Yeah. Can I have a couple of those?" I asked, slightly embarrassed by the situation.

"Listen, let me at least make sure you get your money's worth. I'll do a couple more dance numbers for you."

"Sure," I said. "You know, with your dancing skills and your head for numbers, you could make it in any field. Except the one where my beloved Cleo sleeps."

"Cleo?" she asked.

"Yeah, Cleo the cow. Get it? Cows & fields?"

She laughed.

"You're not like most of the guys that come here, excuse the pun."

"You're not like most other dancers," I replied.

"Well, I did a few years at Glasgow Uni. Business Management. When the economy started going tits up, there were only a few jobs that paid as well as this does. Besides, I enjoy it. Mostly."

About an hour later, Debbie's acrobatic display ended in the same fine form it began. My shirt was damp from the salty sweat running down my chest. We'd done every sordid thing known to man and the experience had left me a little shell-shocked. She winked at me as she put on her frilly black suspenders. I was suddenly overcome with the desire to flee and escape the shame of my mortal soul. Thoughts of Kandy were still swirling in my fractured mind. But the ugly cloud of inner pain went away when Debbie's gentle voice broke through the dark horizon.

"Listen... I don't normally do this... I was thinking maybe... I finish work in half an hour. I don't suppose you'd want to go clubbing afterward?"

I nodded.

"Sure, why not!"

We headed back to the main hall, where a young blonde woman stood waiting with folded arms. She embraced Debbie and the two women spent a great length of time talking about hair extensions, eye curlers and something else that was outside my scope of understanding. I stared at the floor tiles for a while before we were properly introduced.

"Sorry, Katrina, this is Max. Max, Katrina. Kat's from the Czech Republic."

"It's a pleasure to meet you dear lady," I said.

"Hello Maxie! It is pleasure to meet you too,"

She spoke with a slight accent.

"Your English is good," I said, trying not to sound condescending.

"Thank you. I have not been here long. But I read many Harry Potter books and learned much English from them."

Katrina's hair flowed down to her waist. Her slim but alluring figure echoed the shy introvert it embodied. Unlike

Debbie, her presence wasn't overstated, catering to those who bought into the illusion of innocence. Her harsh blue eyes showed anything but innocence. They spoke of harsh winters and lonely summers, and a soul sold into bondage for a new country and its currency.

"Katrina, can I get you a small aperitif?" I asked.

"What is that?"

"A drink, dear. He wants to buy you a drink," said Debbie

"Yes, I would like that very much. I will have an orange juice and vodka."

"I'll have the same," said Debbie

I ordered two screwdrivers and an Argentinian beer to keep myself sharp. The women were back to talking about shoes and Cavalli dresses and I was clearly better off out of that whole scene. There wasn't much I could say on that sort of thing, and it would have been rude to change the topic of conversation to football or the latest issue of the Daily Sport. No new punters were coming through the doors and the other dancers spent their shifts persuading unemployed patrons to part with their social security cheques.

I got back to the table and found the ladies giggling like giddy schoolgirls. I assumed the events that took place in the private room had become the subject of discussion and I could feel myself turning red. Katrina's eyes pierced me with a look that would have made butter melt. An awkward silence followed. She was the kind of woman that a man could easily fall in love with. But I wasn't a man. I was a shell; a bestial cockroach that survived the fallout of an emotionally charged nuclear bomb.

When their respective shifts ended, I agreed to meet them both outside. They had to freshen up and change into something less respectable. I still had to go back to the coat check and collect my jacket. I fumbled in my trouser pocket for the ticket stub, hoping that I hadn't dropped it somewhere in the labyrinth of pure pleasure. The redhead with the jowls of a Brazilian boa constrictor scowled at me for a second time, handing me my garment amidst a Jesus based tirade about filth ridden perverts.

I shook my head at the small minded chattering of a fat old lady who had likely not been laid in months; except on special occasions when her pet Labrador consoled her in moments of anguish. I prepared myself for what was going to be a long night, with more twists than Chubby Checker's dance class.

14. The Devil Disco Dances Where Angels Fear To Tread

Droplets of water began falling as I waited outside the flesh pit. The not-so-gruesome twosome certainly took their time. The rain added coolness to the suffocating heat. It was a welcome change from the atmosphere inside. I spotted Debbie and Katrina coming out and called out to them. Debbie slowly strolled toward me. I was stupefied by her new mode of dress. Her full length skirt flowed down to her ankles and her frumpy blouse brought her one step closer to joining a nunnery. Only the high heels stood in her way. Not long ago, this perfect vision of womanhood had been busy waxing my wooden carrot.

Katrina broke the silence and mentioned that she was feeling peckish. I too was becoming aware of my own hunger. I hadn't eaten since breakfast. Sustenance had consisted of a liquid diet and stale peanuts, but my stomach was beginning to growl and hunger pangs were setting in. It was no longer possible to survive without solid food. If we didn't find somewhere to eat soon, I was sure I'd be carted away in a box by dawn. And it would be the cheap kind, the kind built from plywood and rusty nails, probably made earlier by a former children's tv presenter who'd taken up residence in a funeral parlour after being fired because of budget cuts.

The three of us embarked on 'Operation Food Forage'. Off we set, the terrible trio, on an assignment of vital importance. There were plenty of take-outs in Merchant City, but none would be open at this ungodly hour. Fast food had become the cornerstone of our on-the-go society and places like McDonalds, Burger King, Pizza Hut and KFC were second homes to most of us and, on rare occasions, even strains of botulism found somewhere to hang their hats in the wee hours.

"Let's go to McD's on Jamaica Street," said Debbie. "They'll still be open. You're lucky I'm a cheap date Cassanova!"

I flashed her a quick smile.

"It's a pity that Thai place is closed. You'd both have loved it," I said.

"I love Thai!" squealed Katrina.

"I'm more of a breast man," I said glibly.

Katrina laughed. Debbie shook her head at my impotent dry humour. I noticed Katrina's leopard print Gucci shoes shining in the orange street lights as we walked and I complimented her on her excellent taste in designer wear. She blushed a little and thanked me before telling me all about her obsession with all things Gucci.

We reached McDonalds by around twelve-thirty AM and ordered four quarter-pounders, one vegetarian meal and a salad. I was out of hard cash and had to use my American Distress card. In these times of financial instability, a man's best friend wasn't a fluffy puppy called 'Fumbles', but a cheap piece of plastic with his name, rank and card number printed on it.

The whole restaurant was deserted and we picked out a table next to the window. One of the young workers was busy sweeping the floor in preparation for his mopping duties. He was probably an overqualified brain surgeon from Zambia who'd come to Scotland in search of a better life. And here he was, cleaning floors and toilets full of human muck and drug needles. I'd munched my way through two burgers and stolen some of Debbie's fries. Katrina grinned at me, mesmerized by my ability to digest food at an unprecedented rate.

She'd moved onto her salad by the time we got onto the subject of our favourite movie genres. My own proclivities for rom-coms were a matter of public knowledge, but this surprised the girls. Their respective tastes for action and horror were equally shocking. Katrina's personal fascination with vampires and werewolves unnerved me slightly. I'd often noted that in most horror films, the victims of vampire attacks eventually became predators themselves; and this was no exception. Katrina was setting her sights on her newest target: me. I could see she wanted to get her meat hooks into my beef bourguignon. Debbie's phone chimed twice. She flipped it open and read the text message before clicking the buttons at lightning speed to send off a reply.

"That was my friend Tom. If you're still up for a nightcap, there's this great place where the drinks are cheap and the music's live and happening. Tom's doing a set there tonight."

"Yeah. Sounds interesting. I'm in," I replied.

She shot a curious expression at Katrina and the two smirked and stifled their laughter. I'd clearly missed something. This was a unique form of torment. My inquisitive brain found it difficult to accept a sense of not knowing. But my masochistic side won out and I didn't press the matter. I was confident that clarity would prevail and that the joke would be revealed soon enough. I excused myself to use the bathroom. It was a risk in a joint like this, but my bladder was like a swelled up balloon and I didn't want to put the cleaner to further trouble with another puddle to mop up.

There wasn't enough hand sanitizer in the world to wash away the stench of shit smelling foulness. The whole experience killed my appetite. On my return, we all decided that it was best to leave, if we were to make to our next port of call. Going everywhere by foot had numerous advantages. Not only were we cutting our carbon imprint, but also getting our recommended daily dose of exercise. Unfortunately this was not the foremost thought in the minds of my beautiful companions. Shapely feet came at a price and high-heeled designer footwear came at the cost of comfort. But there they were, unwitting eco-warriors, battling the evil of the oil giants and excess oestrogen.

We reached Barrats, blister free and ready to groove. Our mismatched motley crew sauntered into the building. YMCA was blasting across the floorboards and the designated dance floor was littered with well manicured men in tight jeans and an excellent sense of colour co-ordination. The women saw the uncomfortable grimace on my face and burst out in a fit of uncontrollable laughter, heckling like hyenas. I was redder than a radish but the embarrassment passed and I found myself enjoying the sounds of the 70's.

Debbie had disappeared into the thick of the crowd while Katrina and I were left standing there, as out of place as two sausages in an ice-cream factory. She tried to say something, but I couldn't hear her over the music. I stared into the crowd and remarked on the liberal use of mousse and gel, which rivalled the entire inventory of Sally's hair salon. Debbie returned and the two of us breathed a little easier knowing we hadn't lost one of our number.

"I was talking to the P.A. guy. Tom's going to be on next. You're going to love this Max! He's an absolute artist and a real darling. Let me get you both a drink. What'll you both have?"

"A Southern Comfort on the rocks thanks!"

"Vodka and lime juice!" said Katrina.

"You two wait right here and I'll go get them!"

It was always wise to be wary of Greeks bearing gifts in such places. There was no telling who or what was lurking in the shadows, waiting to cop a quick feel. Helen of Troy must have felt safer during the Trojan War than I did at that moment. But the music gave my limbs a life of their own, and I jerked and jived like a choking chimpanzee suffering sciatic spasms.

I could see Debbie trying to get back to where we were, ducking and diving through an armada of athletic men. With a combination of luck, prayer and skill, she made it and hadn't spilled a drop from any glass. To the left, I heard two camp crusaders discussing the virtues of Botox.

"We should cull the ugly and extract their DNA for scientific research!" laughed one.

The thought of a harebrained homicidal rampage made me wince. I was not particularly attractive and I knew that I would be first on a hit-list for the aesthetically deficient. The liquor helped calm my perturbed and nervous disposition.

I began chanting to myself.

"There's no place like home. There's no place like home."

But this only served to get the attention of a hip jiggling youngster who'd barely learned to shave.

"Are you a friend of Dorothy?" he asked, in a seductive tone.

I yelped and clutched my shirt as he twiddled with the buttons.

"I'm not anyone's friend. I'm a vicious, brutish bastard!" I replied.

"Hmm that's just my type!" he retorted, breaking out in a lewd smile.

The speaker system suddenly let out a deafening popping sound and all eyes turned to the MC who was about to introduce the live act. Spot lights flooded the stage area as he tested the microphone.

"And now ladies, lads and gentlemen, please put your hands together for the Queen of queer, the Dame of delight, from the throne of Vesporia, the Countess Verity Von Glitter!"

The audience howled in appreciative applause. I was a little confused. I had expected Debbie's friend. Perhaps he would follow afterwards. Verity stormed the stage with a horde of bare-chested muscular male models, all dressed as firemen. A booming baritone voice reverberated through the bar. I was struggling to connect what my ears were hearing with what my eyes were seeing. The image of a dolled-up feminine guy in a long black wig and toilet roll stuffed down his dress proved too much. Katrina moved closer to me and I could feel her heartbeat against my shoulder. I had an erection, but I wasn't sure which of the two things had caused it.

"Hello guys and gals, its time for me to rock this special place from stem to stern and make *your* special place rock hard. Come on my lovely glitter bugs, let's see if you can put out *my* fire!"

I felt like a hairy caveman in shrinking swim shorts.

Things couldn't have been any worse. Verity screamed out a rendition of 'It's raining men' like a possessed banshee, and the sprinklers went off during the climax of the act. The girls were enjoying themselves as was everyone else. They were like card carrying members of the Tom Jones fan-club, who regularly attended his infamous knicker-throwing concerts.

If there was a supreme deity, he was either ignoring my pleas for help, or on vacation in some remote, wi-fi free hotspot. Out of the blue, Verity pointed at me and honed in like a heat seeking missile aboard a Russian submarine. "Oh, you sad little bunny. Doesn't he look like a terribly sad wittle bunny folks? Why don't you get your cute bum up here and wiggle it for mama!"

My feet were glued to the floor. I couldn't move. Not even to escape this awful nightmare. The crowds parted like the Red Sea and Verity stepped down to where I was standing, grabbing me by the hand, and launched me into the glaring spotlight. Luckily, I'd already finished off the glass of Southern Comfort. The women were in hysterics as they, along with the rest of the audience, watched me get mauled and man-handled in the name of entertainment. Finally the demoralising display ended and the drag queen thanked me for enduring it.

"I hope you didn't mind that bit of bump and grind for these nasty voyeurs."

"It's all in good fun," I said, leaping off the stage and back into the safe womb of anonymity. Debbie took me aside and explained that Verity was in fact Tom's alter-ego. I asked her about the proper terms of address and brought up the delicate question of whether to refer to Verity as he or she.

"When you see a woman, then you address a woman. Just use your common sense and be respectful. Don't worry, I wasn't sure on that front either at first, but you'll get the hang of it."

The physical exertion left me exhausted. Any wasted effort wasn't part of my biological make up. I'd never been one for any sort of manual labour or anything that required a serious use of energy. I needed to sit down. A party of five were about to leave, and the three of us noticed the vacant chairs. We made our dash before others spotted the spare seats.

The night wore on and the live music wound down. Each of the performers were congratulated for their fine sets, which stunned and wowed the masses. By the final act most of the customers had left the premises. There were only a handful of us who were prepared to stay to the bitter end. Verity joined us and Debbie invited her to pull up a chair. I was about to mention something related to fire hazards when I noticed a man gazing menacingly at our rag-tag group. I'd seen him throughout the evening and didn't think much of it. But there was something disconcerting about his demeanour and body language.

"Ladies, I don't mean to worry you all, but why is that guy staring at us?"

They too looked over and were greeted by the sight of a six-foot broad shouldered wild man. A look of recognition rung in Verity's eyes, followed by a heart crushing sigh.

"That's Edward. He's... he was, a friend," she said as disappointment and sadness washed over her face.

The shadowy figure moved closer. His forearms were covered in tattoos, the most prominent of which was a large swastika on his left. An alchemical symbol for fire stood out on his right. His psychopathic tendencies were there for all to see - to fear. And it worked. I was rattled and not at all looking forward to the ugliness that would soon shatter our tranquil, mellow state.

"Verity, I... I... I've missed you."

He could speak. For some reason this surprised me.

"Edward, look, this really isn't the time or the place. Maybe we could talk later."

A voice abruptly said "What's with those fucking tattoos? You know in certain places, you can get thrown in jail for that!"

The drink had given me Dutch courage. I knew I was soon going to meet a violent end.

"Who the fuck are you?" he snarled.

"Never mind who I am. Let's talk about who you are. An overt jackass. But no, that would be an insult to all donkey kind. In this case, yes, I think I will take that risk."

I was aware I was speaking the words, but they were independently coming out of my mouth. Somewhere in the thought process, my brain had disengaged itself entirely and allowed for a level of automatic vocal reaction.

"What did you say ye wee prick?"

"You heard me you Nazi bum bandit!"

Vanity interjected.

"Boys, boys please. Look Ed, please don't make this tougher than it has to be."

"Tom... Verity, I don't want to lose you."

"Fine. If you want to do this here and now, then we fucking will! Ed, you weren't the man I thought you were. I can't be with someone so twisted! You're too messed up. You're a disgusting homophobe of the worst kind! You couldn't even tell those fucking morons you were gay!"

"I'm not gay! Don't talk about me and my friends like that or I'll..."

His hands started shaking as he balled them up into fists.

"They're patriots who care about our country."

"They're not your friends Ed, they're evil! They don't give a fuck about you, this country or anyone else!"

"Were you dropped on your head as a child?" I enquired.

I knew provoking him was not a smart idea. But I had this odd notion that it was better for me to be in the line of fire than a lady; even if she wasn't actually a lady. I wasn't sure if it was a sense of chivalry, stupidity or a mix of both.

"Stay out of this you weird fucker!"

"Look, you're obviously a conflicted man with confusion swirling around that brain. Let me buy you a drink and we'll say no more about it."

He was bemused, but nodded in agreement. I asked him what he was having and made a mental note on the drink orders for each of my companions. A sense of calm was returning to what had become a toxic and volatile situation. I went to the bar and watched the bartender rustle up two glasses of Jack Daniels on the rocks, a vodka and lime, a cosmopolitan and a Singapore sling.

After setting the drinks down, I reached into my pocket and popped two Prozac pills from the blister pack, washing them down with the Tennessee whiskey. Verity seemed on edge. Debbie and Katrina hardly said a word except to thank me for their beverages. The tension finally broke

"What were those pills you just took?" asked Ed. "Can I have a couple?"

15. A Nihilist's Narcotic Nightmare

I was in a prescription drug and drink filled cocoon, nestled in its warm safety. We were all starting to relax that little bit more. The buzz crept into every crevice of my soul, wrapping itself around me like a bespoke blanket. Nothing could touch me. I was invincible.

"You fucking foreigners always know where to get the best drugs," said Ed. "You might be raping our cities and invading our country, but damn, you know your drugs. I bet you could get your hands on the best hash too."

It was true, I could, but I wasn't going to let this sinister bastard have any. He was already high as a kite and out of his Nazi skull on lightweight anti-depressants. Katrina and I looked at each other, shocked at the ignorance of this half-witted excuse for a human being. Neither of us had spawned from the waters of Scotland; but we were solid citizens, tax payers; well one of us was. I'd yet to set eyes on a tax return.

"Ed, I have a question. Why do you hate us foreign folk so much?" I asked.

"Oh, for fuck sake. Do I really have to spell it out for you? This is the problem with you lot! You come over here, barely able to speak English and steal our jobs. You talk funny, you dress funny, you even *smell* funny. You filthy fuckers have probably never even seen a bathtub! And when you talk to each other in that Paki-speak, all you talk about is your plans to take us over!"

"When did you last actually try and get a job?" I asked.

"Well, there's no point, is there? There's none left for people who are proper British."

"I don't think you believe that. I think maybe you've been *told* to believe that. I mean let's be honest. Even you, being in this bar, that's surely a big no-no in the bible of far right commandments."

He looked awkward and ashamed, "Well... It is," he said, becoming quiet. An air of thoughtfulness encompassed him. "They talk about it at the meetings, how homos are filthy and sick in the head. I... I don't know what I am, or why I am the way the way I am But It's just not natural. It's wrong. God made Adam and Eve, not Adam and Steve! Christ! I wish I was normal!"

The brain boggling rhetoric that had been pumped into him was spewing out in an uncontrollable torrent of verbal diarrhoea. It had been a long time since I'd witnessed so much hate bottled up in one person. And it was coupled with a self-loathing I'd never witnessed in anyone; except myself. I'd spent a lifetime cornering the market on being a living fuck-up. I was the black sheep in every flock. Perhaps that was why I felt a certain twisted sense of empathy towards Ed. In his own way, he was as much of a head-case as I was. But he was evil to the bone. It was buried right inside his marrow.

"Well, you obviously didn't listen to the Beatles much when you were growing up. All you need is love. All love is cool. It doesn't matter where it comes from or where you get it. Without it, that coldness you feel deep inside when you wake up will just stay with you till the day you die."

Verity's eyes were fixed firmly on the bottom of her glass. She looked at me and a smile broke out across her heavily made-up face. Debbie was nursing her cosmopolitan and Katrina was stirring her Vodka and lime with two little black straws the barman had been kind enough to give.

I pondered the belief systems that led to the waste of what could have been a valuable and productive member of society. I knew firsthand how tough it was to let go of any long held dogma. You spend most of your years nursing them and nurturing them to adulthood. It doesn't matter that they might be distortions of reality and wholly wrong. And then one day, all you hear are the silent screams emerging from the agony of quiet desperation; a deafening silence. There, on the edge of that comfort zone, between the dawn of a new day and the darkness of old, no-one notices the untamed living. None of us are prepared for it. We're easily frightened by the light. We hope, we pretend, that there's some way back to the blackness of ignorant bliss.

For Ed, that wasn't an option. He was already straddling the chasm, but he wasn't willing to open his eyes to the bright side of life. I had to admit to myself that there was no point in trying to have a logical conversation with him. He was lost, a man choosing to sleep through this lucid dream.

The bar staff were preparing to shut up shop. We each gulped down our drinks and prepared ourselves for leaving. But I was in no fit state to make it to the front door. I forced my weight onto my legs and was just about able to maintain my balance. I weaved through the maze of upturned chairs and pulled open the door, holding it open for my friends, who by this point were also thoroughly drunk. I searched my pockets for my pack of Marlborough cigarettes and light one up. We walked as I smoked. None of us knew quite *where* we were going. There was just a prevailing group mentality, following the herd until it reached the edge of a cliff. Faceless memories and empty streets greeted us at every turn.

We ended up in a violent neighbourhood, somewhere near the Gorbals. Before any of us knew what was happening, we were faced with young thugs in hoodies demanding our money and valuables. The youngest of them, a black teenager with a lisp, waved his knife around threateningly.

"Come on, come on, hand it over! Fucking hand it over now! Quickly bitch! Give us that purse!"

I reached into my pocket slowly to take out my wallet. Ed looked at him in disbelief, while the rest of us did our best to comply, hoping to avoid what was sure to be.

The kid threw himself at Ed, blade first. The steely edge of the shiny blade flashed as he repeatedly opened and retracted it. It was one of those Stanley knives that could easily be bought in any hardware store. He was becoming more agitated by the second and my gut told me he was a reactionary, jittery sort of person who wasn't likely to leave it at a simple robbery

In an effort to help avoid a needless murder, I grabbed the boy by the arm and threw him to the ground, easily wrestling the weapon out of his inexperienced hands. I kicked it away, stumbling back to catch my breath. Ed marched toward him, his eyes reflecting volcanic anger and violent disgust. A relentless barrage of punches flew from the enraged psychotic. The boy could do nothing to defend himself. His comrades had abandoned him, realising the seriousness of the situation. The blood from his bruised and beaten face ran onto my shoes. I remained fixed to the spot, shocked and appalled. Suddenly, a spurt of adrenaline shot through me and I found myself tackling Ed to the ground. The youngster just lay there, not moving in the slightest.

Ed and I were still struggling. There was no way I could have kept him pinned to the ground for long. He was considerably larger than me and stronger than an Ecuadorian elephant. His fist connected to my chin as he raised his hand and delivered a teeth shattering blow.

"You fucking wanker! Get off me!" he yelled.

He was ready to rush me again as I recovered from being hurled to the edge of the pavement. I moved out of his way to check on the condition of the injured assailant. He was still breathing and had a strong pulse. His jersey was stained with drying whispery darkness. He regained consciousness and rose to his feet, disgraced, humiliated and utterly scared. He'd suffered defeat at the hands of a colonial imperialist, which brought its own shame. The boy fled the scene, running as fast as his legs could carry him. Ed stopped in his tracks, realising his worst had been witnessed by everyone, including Verity.

"If you'd killed that kid just now, we'd all be sitting in a police cell explaining this bad trip," I said to him.

Debbie consoled Katrina, who was distressed by the whole affair. Verity closed her eyes and wrapped her arms around her chest. I put my hands on their shoulders and tried to comfort them, telling them that there was nothing to worry about and that the danger was over. Unfortunately, that was far from the truth. We hadn't just dealt with one psychopath, but two. Ed rambled wildly to himself before letting out an almighty anguished roar.

It was at that point that the four of us decided to leave him to his fate. The whole situation had been partly my own fault. I'd allowed the malevolent jackass to integrate himself into our fun loving group. I looked back and saw the sorry sight of the gay white supremacist standing in the street crying a river of tears, mixing with the blood of another. Enoch Powell's poster child was as helpless and alone as a lost kitten. But his vicious pit-bull nature would always be there, hidden in the vacuous space where a soul should have been.

We headed toward the main road and were lucky enough to find a free cab waiting at the taxi ramp. Debbie instructed the driver to take us to her place. None of us seemed in a fit state to be alone. The taxi pulled up at 420 Victoria Road and we piled out in front of the close. The sun would soon be up in the murder capital of Europe.

As we clambered up the stairs to her flat, several residents came out of their homes to tell us to keep it down, but we were too inebriated to pay any attention to those killjoys. Three flights up, inside the flat, a large dishevelled king-size bed awaited us in the bedroom. Each of us collapsed in a drunken haze.

I felt the unusual sensation of silk and skin under my fingertips. Weeping voices; flashes of fuchsia bed-sheets; vivid memories merged with fantasy. Images of loveliness crept into my dreams and I sank happily into the void that presented itself. Lines were being crossed and unseen, unspeakable acts were being visited on my comatose body.

Then came the descent, down into the bowels of hell itself. Nocturnal horrors encompassed me, engulfing my dysphoric brain particles. There it was, the foul monstrosity that vexed mankind, a great engine of evil, like a mighty military machine, crushing the broken bones of whoever got in its way. It was us who had given birth to it centuries ago.

We'd created it to be our Bellerophon, a hero to champion our cause. But it quickly become the infamous Chimera from Greek mythology. It thundered on, in far away lands bearing its teeth and killing mercilessly.

I could see its limbs sprawled across the globe, lying in wait to sink its jaws into all man and womankind. The politics of hate. It had its claws in every pie, stealing food from the mouths of the starving. The preternatural entity knew no bounds. But there was no way to subdue the infernal parasite. It was eternally turning the thumbscrews onus, while our thumbs were nailed firmly to bare tables and empty chairs. The missing. The dead. It devoured them without a thought, venomous and cold.

Morning came, and with it fresh beams of sunshine broke through the curtained window, heralding the dawn of a new day. Katrina was at the foot of the bed wrapped in a sheet next to Tom, no longer in his drag costume. Debbie rolled over and swung her arm around me. They were all sleeping rather soundly. I was the only one awake. I looked at my watch. It was eight o'clock, too early to be up, too late to go back to sleep. I lay there for a while, contemplating the mysteries of the universe before a familiar voice croaked in my ear.

"Hi."

Debbie was awake. She had a wicked grin from ear to ear. She lifted her arm and I could once again roam free. As I became more aware, I realised I wasn't wearing a stitch of clothing. I clung to the duvet as I searched for my Walmart boxer shorts. I eventually found them under the metal frame of the bed, but my shirt and trousers were half way across the room.

"Thank you for last night," she said.

I wasn't sure exactly what she was thanking me for. So much had happened, but I remembered so little of it. Yet her comment brought me a perverse feeling of accomplishment. But there I was, a pilgrim in an unholy land, unsure of where I was or why, like a lost commando in the jungles of Borneo.

"You're quite welcome."

I squeezed her upper arm before fumbling with my underwear.

"I should really get going," I said. "It's already after eight and I got so much to do today."

I didn't. But the need to flee was setting in. I'd never been particularly good with morning afters, especially in these kinds of situations.

By nine fifteen, I was at the cross-section of Alison Street and Victoria Road. Any of the buses passing by would get me into the centre of town. The number forty five just happened to be the first of them. But the fascist bus company that ran the service would only take exact change. Luckily, the money I'd spent on drinks the previous night resulted in my jacket being weighed down by a considerable number of coins. Ninety pence went into the ticket machine and it growled before spitting out the paper. The ride on the bus gave me time to reflect on the events of the past twenty four hours. By the time we reached Glassford Street, my head was empty. The thoughts had frittered away into the ether. I was sure I'd experienced some kind of profound epiphany, but there wasn't a single thread to grapple from whatever train of thought that had crossed those tracks.

The bus stop on Union Street was busy. There was madness on the roads. Rush hour had passed, but still angry motorists were honking, screaming and turning into rage driven lunatics. They all had to get somewhere, to do... something. This sense of urgency had gripped them, turning them into amped up hell-hounds, sneering and snarling at pedestrians who got in their way. I was glad when the twenty three showed up. I didn't want to be in the middle of the incredible ugliness I was seeing.

Ordinarily, I liked sitting near the front of the bus. But I was in no mood to have my peace disturbed. The green polyester upholstery seemed to calm my spirits. The solitude at the back was exactly what I needed. I rested against the window pane and spent a while watching cars, people and the occasional squirrel pass by in a blurred fog of activity. My stop didn't take long to reach and I got off at the stop next to the pub. At last I was home, soundly tucked away in the isolation of my private sanctuary. I crashed out on the couch, still tired from a lack of adequate rest.

16. Samson On Super 8 & Tough Times: Musings On An Overdressed Man

The phone rang sometime in the afternoon. I gasped, swallowing saliva and sputtering as I answered. I was still hacking and coughing when someone on the other end identified themselves. I stopped coughing long enough to hear the voice. It sounded familiar, but I couldn't place it immediately. The hangover from the night before impaired my senses slightly.

"Max? Are you alright?"

"Yeah," I said, clearing my throat.

"Oh okay. Good. You sounded like you were dying there for a minute. And that would be terrible, especially if it happened before you knew the reason for my call."

"Walter? Is that you? Christ, man, this is surprise. It's been a while"

"Yes, since the dangerous gun raving craziness in Cumbernauld. It was only a squirt gun. I don't know why the police treated it so seriously."

"Well I have one of those faces. It's painfully obvious to anyone that criminality runs in my veins. It's the face. It gives it away. I was like 'Jesus, fuck, Mother Mary, they're actually going to arrest me for having a toy gun?' I was shitting bricks man! I damned sure didn't want to end up in prison again. Shower time in Bar L tends to be a group activity," I said.

"That's for sure. But surely the huge camera and the lighting equipment should have given it away! I mean even a four year-old would have known we were filming an amateur movie."

"Maybe. But it *was* Cumbernauld. They breed the intellectually deficient like cosmetic companies breed rats," I said.

"Yeah. You're not wrong there. And of course there was also that insane homeless guy with the dog who'd escaped from a secure psychiatric facility. That didn't make things any easier. He wanted you hung drawn and quartered!"

"That was not our finest moment. Funny as fuck though! And I thought I was a gibbering lunatic!"

"It's that MQB energy. You draw these insane types like a dog attracts fleas. Jeff, the director; you remember him? Anyway he was laughing his ass off over it for three days straight."

"That's true. So anyway, What can I do for you Mr Samson?"

"Well, I've got this project lined up with these cash-strapped students. They're entering the 48 hour Glasgow film short festival. They asked me if I knew any decent actors. I mentioned you. They were intrigued."

"Jesus. I'm flattered. Students are always fun to torture. But Walter, there's just one small thing you seem to have overlooked. I'm *not* an actor."

"Nonsense! You're a great actor. Hell, at the very least, you're a character! I want you involved in this thing. I'm amazed the other entrants haven't asked you!"

"Most of them have no clue I'm back."

"Back? You were away? Anywhere nice?"

"Yeah. I was over in the States catching up with some old friends. It was good. But this thing, I'll do it. I'll read whatever lines you want me to read. But don't expect me to be happy about it. When would you need me?"

"A couple of weeks from today. How's that sit with you? I'll give you the details nearer the date."

"Great. Works for me. Oh, make sure you have plenty of cheap whiskey. You know I never work without it."

"You got it!" he said as he hung up.

I'd met Walter during the colder months of last year. November, I think. Our mutual friend Jeff had invited a few of us down to Cumbernauld village for a couple of pints in a vain attempt at holding off the winter blues. Unfortunately, by then we were already in the middle of a big freeze, which pretty much blew the plan to hell. But we drank all the same in that quaint little pub. The locals had heard of Glasgow, but had never dared to venture outside of their familiar, secluded world. The very thought of travelling to those far reaching ends of the universe and leaving the confines of their homes filled them with dread. It was like a miniature reproduction of the island from 'The Wickerman'. Even the name of their sacred inn sent shivers down my spine; 'The Skull'.

Thankfully, none of us were left permanently scarred from the incident and lived to tell the tale. Walter and I forged a bond, despite his being straight laced, sane and very grounded. He saw things in the same way I did, but he also had a clarity of vision in his approach to camera work and life. That lager fuelled brainstorming session led to the genesis of Jeff's ambitious and highly unusual idea. The commercial success of films like Shaun of the Dead, along with the confirmed Glasgow location for the upcoming big budget Hollywood film World War Z, contributed to the formation of his delusional dream. He too would make a zombie movie. His would be the best one ever filmed; a Scottish standard bearer by which all future films would be defined and measured. However, his discombobulated grey matter had failed to take into account the reality he had to contend with. He had no script, no cast, no crew, no budget and no camera. But after a long, and occasionally brutal negotiation, with his business partner Miranda Finkleton, the pair decided that they would embark on this impossible pursuit.

It was January 15th when I got that call. I remembered it well. I was sitting at my IBM Selectric typewriter struggling with the first line of a short story that had been rattling around the back of my brain, like a ball-bearing trapped inside a child's chew toy.

"MQB? It's Jeff. We've put together a team of highly skilled actors for hire. Walter's doing the camera work, I'll be directing the operation and Kes is running sound. Yours is just a small part. Wouldn't involve much work. Are you in or out?"

Fuck it, I thought. I wasn't having much luck with writing anything. In the last three months, the only thing I'd produced was a three line poem, which met with plenty of acclaim, had been published twice and read on radio. But I knew just like most, it was in actuality, complete and utter horse-shit.

"Sure," I said. "I'm in. You know my rates. Booze and broads."

"You'll get both. I'll make sure of it if I have to hire the hookers myself. Now get your unemployed ass down here on Tuesday at 7pm."

The remainder of that January was filled with train trips to and from the village of the damned. I fondled beautiful women outside of working hours and drank myself into a stupor with the free flowing supply of Southern Comfort and Jaegermeister, the latter of which went quite well with cans of Red-bull; an energy drink more lethal than crack cocaine. In those rare moments, between the madness and brief flashes of clarity, I would read lines from a large printed sheet, stapled to a board or camera stand, mostly mumbling incoherently while I watched Jeff swell up like a toad.

"That's brilliant! Just brilliant darling!" he'd scream. "I've never seen such deliciousness ooze out of a man and into the camera!"

Jeff was supposedly straight and married, but from the start of the filming process, he had the curious habit of wearing his wife's cardigan. This puzzled us all greatly. Undertones of gayness pervaded through the entire production. Most of the cast tried to dismiss this odd behaviour, putting it down to issues of weather and staying warm. But we all knew there were countless jumpers and jerseys designed solely for gentleman that met these requirements. When Jeff grew a long John Holmes style moustache, a flurry of questions arose surrounding his sexuality and frame of mind. Suspicions were banded about like facts and Chinese whispers had blown rumours into the realm of the ridiculous: a guy who knew a guy saw him groping a bearded man in a cotton shirt; that sort of thing.

The sensible ones among us tried to ignore this terrible gossip. We were told we had to be serious actors because we had serious parts; and we had standards to maintain. At the end of the gruelling film shoot, it ended up in post-production hell and no-one, not even Jeff, knew exactly when his project was going to hit a projector screen. This didn't bother me particularly, as I'd already gotten my rocks off and managed to snag seven free cases of whiskey and beer, which lasted until the end of February.

The entire crew had gone on to other endeavours, personally and professionally, which were a direct result of our experiences. Those hard nights of rigorous rehearsals and never ending retakes were a strange but special time. Friendships blossomed, ideas mushroomed and inspiration struck. There was lunacy in every undertaking. But we followed our true spirit paths, doing what we were designed to do from the moment of our conception. We were making art. There was really no way to explain any of it. Being a part of something where every cog turned a wheel was a unique experience. Six months later, the soul of it was still alive and kicking. Our drive and determination had been distilled, bottled and pumped back into us intravenously. One hundred percent pure concentrated coolness flowed through our veins. It didn't matter that our journey hadn't borne fruit. What mattered was that the mountain had been climbed. We'd cut it down to size and shown it who was boss.

I was looking forward to working with Walter again. But I had no clue what this new project of his was. It may have involved shooting high definition candid shots of monkeys masturbating in space. Whatever its nature, it was sure to be interesting and generally intelligent, with just a hint of overall madness. It's that same madness that pushes a kid from Govan to steal stereos and television sets from the homes of the better off. A renegade spirit, refusing to be caged or cajoled with promises of gainful employment and a subservient suburban lifestyle. It revels in the joy of freedom; the freedom to do what it likes, when it likes. But this romanticised notion also makes it as dangerous as it is attractive, especially in the realms of art and crime. Sometimes the two fuse, resulting in violent sociopathic tendencies; the desire to commit the perfect crime artfully, a masterpiece of illegal action. That fine line of unpredictability; between genius and being mentally deranged; between good and evil; had given us the best and the worst of humanity, with most of us straddling the chasm.

A Non-Educated Delinquent; a NED. That's what they'd branded me all those years ago, and it remained invisibly tattooed on my forehead like an emblazoned emblem; my badge of honour. I was a troublemaker, a hoodlum, a reckless refugee from a lost generation. I watched my mother cry as they read out the long litany of my indiscretions and alleged activities. Courts, schools and prison had done nothing to change the nature of my character. No-one had bothered to ask me *why*. They talked a lot. Social workers, teachers, doctors with plenty of fancy certificates and diplomas.

I was misunderstood, they said. They wanted to 'understand' me, like some newly discovered species, dissected with blunt tools in a sealed off lab by men in white coats.

At the age of sixteen, with no home and a family that wouldn't accept me back into its folds, I enrolled in the British Army as a signalman. After a few months of basic training, I found myself in the middle of a war-zone, completely unprepared for the reality of it. Bosnia was my first adult experience of life outside the British bubble. Senseless killing, rape and torture were the norm amidst the devastation. There are no words to convey the true horror and impact such a thing has on the human mind and soul, because the only people that understand it are the ones who have been there.

By nineteen, I'd been honourably discharged on medical grounds after being diagnosed with post-traumatic stress disorder. I was already self-medicating with heavy boozing sessions and a series of bear-knuckle brawls with fat men in bars across Hackney. I had no job, no money and no qualifications. All I had in my wallet was my driving license and all of about five pounds after paying for a rail ticket from Glasgow to London. I'd met Susan not long after boarding that train. She was a svelte redhead with big blue eyes and a petite posterior that caught my attention almost immediately. I bought her a drink and a bag of peanuts from the passing cart and told her that I'd just spent the last of any money I had. We chatted for a while before adjourning to the bathroom for a quick fuck. When we got to London, she offered me a place to stay and I accepted graciously.

I moved into her one bedroom hovel, where space was exceedingly limited, electricity was a privilege and screaming matches were held frequently above and below us. The convenience of sex and the need for companionship suited us both, filling some kind of mutual void. I took up work at a local restaurant as a waiter and got other odd jobs whenever I could, as long as they didn't require too much in the way of reading or writing. I couldn't do either and struggled to put together a coherent sentence most of the time. I remembered how the four-eyed experts with large bank balances had classified me as autistic. They said that was the root cause of all my behaviour; which was utter bullshit, but they may have been right about the cognitive effects it had on my ability to perform well academically.

Weeks later, I found out that Susan suffered from schizophrenia, which in itself was not a major issue for me, save the fact that she hadn't followed her doctor's advice and spent the following months unmedicated. Our arguments began to rival those of our neighbours and things reached a head when, during one of these incidents, she picked up a frying pan and brought it down on my head with almighty clang, which continued to reverberate even after she'd put it down.

A short hospital stay later, Susan and I called it quits and I left for Manchester, where life didn't get any easier. A couple of gangster wannabes, who'd seen too many Guy Richie movies, roped me into helping them in their efforts to take over the turf of a rival racketeer. I had no issues with doing this, as by that point I'd generally lost the will to live, thinking like some that it was better to go out in a blaze of glory. A part of me would continue to feel this way, and a dramatic suicide was never entirely off the cards. Things got extremely heavy when they brought shotguns into the equation. These sorts of things were fairly commonplace, but I'd lost my taste for unnecessary bloodshed and decided to leave before I found myself with another gun in my hands, destined to fire its bullets into the back of another misguided soul's head.

Those early years weren't entirely without merit. I was fortunate enough to run into an old friend who'd established himself as a legitimate computer repair specialist and had expanded his modest empire into a three outlet thriving business. He offered me steady short-term employment as a cleaner and I was desperate enough to do almost anything. His kindness extended beyond that, however. I spoke to him one afternoon about my fondness for the New World. I had some extended family there, hailing from my mother's side. With his help we sorted through the appropriate paperwork for emigration and ticked all the necessary boxes. The process was a complex one but within a year, I was bound for America and the great state of New York.

For the next two years, I made Trenton, New Jersey my home. It was noisy, filthy and frequently subject to drive-by shootings. On a couple of occasions, the sound of a car backfiring startled me and I was tempted to take cover behind garbage cans or unlawfully parked Cadillacs. My distant cousins and other family didn't want to know me. This was not because of my acquired reputation, but because of the fact that my mother had married my father. They disowned her for that. I found it dreadfully ironic.

I held down three jobs and took one day off through the week, which paid the rent. It was on one of these breaks that I discovered the New Jersey public library system. The sheer number of books in that place astounded me. As a boy, I'd never set foot in one. They were used the Dewey decimal system, which boggled the hell out of me. I'd watched a lot of Hammer horror films and especially liked Christopher Lee's overly dramatic acting method when he played Dracula. I knew the whole story had been based on a book, but didn't know much more than that. Thinking that this would be a good place to start, I asked one of the staff where I could find it. I was embarrassed by my own ignorance, but the old lady was good enough to locate it for me and gave me a brief explanation of how to find other books in the text-rich maze of doom. I also checked out a dictionary and spent the next eight months reading Bram Stoker's rather excellent work from cover to cover.

Learning to read was the easy part. I soaked up the words like a sponge, expanding my vocabulary until I was sure I'd used every word in that dictionary at least once in everyday conversations; particularly the offensive and rude ones. And they came in handy on those unkind streets. At night, after finishing work as a toilet attendant, I would spend two hours writing out words one-by-one. It's fair to say that my handwriting was, and to this day remains, atrocious. Books on grammar and punctuation followed, but those were considerably more difficult to understand. There were numerous rules on what went where, how and why. I wrote my first poem at the age of twenty three and it was about as exceptional as Humpty Dumpty sitting on a wall, though I didn't let that deter me. I kept plugging away at it and it was slow progress indeed. Sometimes, I struggled with things like clarity of ideas. Oftentimes, I had a hundred thoughts all inflicting themselves on my already overtaxed brain cells. An abstract thought process allowed me to see words and sentences as a puzzle that simply needed to be solved through the application of logic and a little bit of jiggery-pokery. I honed my instincts and writing skills until they were sharpened to the point where they could split photons. But the innate desire to live on the knife-edge was already ingrained too deeply in my psyche to ever leave.

Looking back at these events, I can't help wonder where things went wrong. Most people say in retrospect, that they wouldn't change anything about their lives; that they wouldn't be the people they became because of their trials and tribulations. I'm not entirely sure I believe that kind of answer. There's no reason why the core of who they are should be any different to what it would be without encountering hardship. If anything, the difficulties of abject poverty, hunger and suffering take away from a person's ability to tap into their fullest potential. My own beginnings in a slum in the Punjab of India certainly tested me.

17. A Scottish History X

In October of 1925, a child was born in a small village in the Punjab on the Indian subcontinent. He was the son of a poor and humble bricklayer during the age of the British Raj. Everyday for eight hours, three hundred and sixty-five days through the year, he toiled in the hot baking sun. He carried concrete blocks and building bricks on his back to cement his future foundations. The going rate for his sought after service was the equivalent of fifty pence an hour in today's money, which was more than what most were earning. The job market was oversaturated with uneducated and unskilled workers, and any prospect of employment depended heavily on the concepts of natural selection; only the fittest survived.

Such was the strength and spirit of this father that he frequently sacrificed his daily bread so his wife and son could eat. He had almost nothing in the way of worldly possessions, little in the way of creature comforts and lived a simple life in a small mud hut. There was however, one item that he always kept by his bedside, a small pamphlet depicting individual letters of the Hindi alphabet, given to him by a childhood friend as a gift when he was about fourteen. With those tattered bits of paper, he taught himself how to read and passed that knowledge on to his son, whose thirst for learning exceeded his own.

This full-time labourer was also the village weightlifting champion. The Schwarzeneggers of modern times have precision made barbells and dumb-bells, conforming to safety checks and health regulations. But back then, in those backward times, they didn't have those sorts of things. Instead they used the heaviest boulders they could find from nearby farmlands, and lifted them above their heads before tossing them as far as possible. By all accounts, a man could easily be crushed underneath one. But the years he'd spent hauling inhuman loads gave him a hide tougher than leather and a will stronger than steel. He was the original Iron Man and he didn't need a suit or a Mr Universe prize to prove it. But eventually ill-health and old age caught up with him and he was left bedridden.

His son was no less a man. By the age of eighteen, he'd educated himself to be fully fluent in his mother tongue and had also learned to write in several other languages, including Hindi, Urdu and Sanskrit. He was the first in the village capable of speaking a few words of broken English; which got him noticed. The people elected him as a kind of spokesperson in a tribal system of politics. By then he was single-handedly carrying the burden of the bricks that his father had carried before him. When the old man finally passed away, he took on the full responsibilities of the former, but continued in his study of the English language by enrolling in formal classes at a school in a nearby town.

There's a story that's often told about this man by his friends: one day when he was in that town he saw a scrawny holy man scavenging for scraps. With his begging bowl in hand, he sought alms from a British soldier, proudly wearing his smart, starched uniform. The soldier kicked the beggar away and mercilessly beat him like a mistreated dog. The little man had all seven shades beaten out of him. The beggar seemed more concerned with picking up the pieces of his broken bowl. It sounds funny that a man should do this, but on thinking about it, it was probably the only thing he owned. Our native moralist, now armed with the basics of the English language, walked up to the soldier, snatched the baton from his hands and said softly, "You knocked him down. Why don't you try knocking me down." Shamed and scared the soldier ran away, presumably into the arms of his mother and cried about how the big bad indigenous man had scared the colonial corporal. That man was my grandfather.

Some years later, news of war came to the village and men were being asked to volunteer for the British Army to fight a most dangerous threat in a far away land. My grandfather was the only educated man residing there and had read the newspaper articles about the Nazis and the heinous wrongs they were visiting upon countless souls. Most were indifferent to what was going on. It was Europe, thousands of miles from their doorstep and they were still busy fighting for their own freedom from British rule. Some were still mourning the atrocity of the massacres at Amritsar, where innocent blood had been shed by a well armed, cruel militia. But my grandfather had met Gandhi and seen him take up the fight against oppression and tyranny in his own homeland. To him, two wrongs didn't make any kind of right. So when the call of duty came, my grandfather answered. His sense of justice and ethics super-seeded his pride. His own conscience wouldn't let him sleep at night unless he did something to oppose the scourge of the Third Reich.

His fiancé didn't understand and rowed with him in what he often called 'her great fit of foolishness'. They'd met during the summer months when he'd worked for her father. My grandfather was not a romantic, though some say he was known for his legendary prowess as a lover. The two were set to be married by the end of that year. I think deep down he knew that she didn't want to see him become another casualty of a bloody war that showed no signs of ending. Nonetheless, he didn't allow his personal feelings to sway him. He put down his bricks and picked up a rifle.

In 1952, after doing his duty and travelling the world, he came back to his beloved India, which by then had been divided into three states, with boundaries of religion, class and creed separating whole families. Mob mentality had taken over at the height of the troubles and the murder of women and children was commonplace. He tried to understand the reasons behind the mass killings. Why had things had gone so hideously wrong between people who had once stood together, even fought together for their motherland, their Bharat? What should have been a simple transfer of sovereign power had descended into angry anarchy. He poured over past newspapers to find answers but found nothing that could answer these burning questions. My grandmother later told me that it was the only time she'd ever seen this powerful man cry.

Some years and two kids later my father was born. He had no patience for education and no stamina for hard work. He spent most of his time playing with chickens and chasing girls. He had some schooling but preferred his own company to sitting with other kids in stuffy classrooms. My grandfather took up work as a desk clerk in the same nearby town where he'd received his formal education and was given living quarters the size of a shoebox by his employer. There was no way his family could stay there and so his wife and children elected to stay in the village. Being the primary wage earner, he spent little time in the family home. The wages were pitiful, but he tried to save as much money as he could, though occasionally he did take trips back to the village.

By 1975 my father had met my mother, a Jewish woman who's family had settled in the neighbouring town before the war. They were completely against the relationship and vowed on everything holy that they wouldn't accept my father because of his Muslim heritage. But this didn't dissuade my parents. At the time they married, India was at war with Pakistan, the cold war had begun and crops were failing throughout the region. My grandfather had spent his savings on the elaborate ceremony and things looked grim. Food prices began to soar, living costs shot up, and work was scarce. When the small firm he worked for closed down, my grandfather took the grave decision to move his family out of the village and into a proper city, the nearest of which was some 100 miles away. He was sure that work could easily be found there and he was right.

Like many others searching for the pot of gold at the end of the rainbow, they ended up living in a small slum, under tin huts with leaky roofs. My grandfather quickly found work, but again it didn't pay particularly well. My father was unsuccessful in finding any gainful employment due to his lack of qualifications. When my mother had me, they were barely eating a meal every three days. It was around then that a close friend of my grandfather's, who'd served with him in the war, had the good fortune of meeting him at a political rally and told him of how he could take reach the magical land of Enoch Powell's England. My grandfather borrowed money from a disreputable loan shark and lodged an application with the British Embassy. The British Empire had robbed his country of its resources and asked him to fight a war on its doorstop. Why, he asked himself, shouldn't he take advantage of this opportunity to get something back; a chance at a decent life for himself and his family?

We arrived in Birmingham some years later, but found it difficult to acclimatise ourselves to another country with completely different cultural norms and terrible weather to boot. Value systems clashed, language barriers stood in the way and racism was rife. But it was still the land of opportunity, where work was plentiful and wages were such that a man could live like a king; or at least his servant. It wasn't long before our nomadic ways took us from Birmingham to Milton Keynes, and finally northwards to Scotland.

By the time I was seven we had settled in the city of Glasgow. I knew little in the way of English and at school I was considered to be a slow child; one of the 'special' children. My younger brother, who'd been born some years previous, had by then been diagnosed with a rare disorder known as Thalassemia. It was similar in nature to sickle-cell anaemia, in that the body can't produce the required red blood cells that carry the oxygen to vital organs necessary for proper functioning. It's generally not a serious problem when a person is afflicted with the minor variant. But when two afflicted people have children, the chances of a child developing the major condition are greatly increased. However, things like this were not widely understood in those days and especially not by the generally uneducated populace from third world countries.

Countless blood-transfusions followed and

appointment after appointment with specialists, GP's, and nurses yielded no long-term solutions to the problem. Finally, a bone-marrow transplant was deemed to be the only option. They took blood samples from each of us and checked them for matches. I was too young to understand most of what was going on, but I got the general gist of it. That was when they laid it on me. I was the only match due to my not having either the minor variant or any other medical issues. They asked me if I understood what that meant, the implications of the whole procedure. I didn't, but I said I did. The only thing that I knew was that I had the chance to save my brother's life. And so I agreed to be the bone-marrow donor. During the early '80's, the transplant methods were nowhere near perfected. The risks were extraordinarily high and Thatcher's government cutbacks meant that funding for the National Health Service was not what it should have been.

My mother and father argued night and day on the pros and cons of the decision and neither seemed completely happy, nor willing to go through with it. Yet, there seemed to be no alternative. The doctors took great pains to explain how, without the operation, my brother would slowly lose all his faculties as he grew older. I would find out in the years to come that this was not entirely true. Many people with the condition lived relatively normal lives with their faculties fully intact, as long as they underwent regular transfusions and were monitored carefully. The procedure itself was later perfected and in modern times, the risk factor was reduced to a minimum.

Sadly, not being hopeful of what the future might bring (most of the country was experiencing a blanket pessimism in those days) my parents chose to take the doctors' advice and we were both admitted into hospital for the operation and anaesthetised before surgery. I remember groggily waking up in the middle of the operating theatre and someone saying "He's awake! Can you increase the dosage?" and I lost consciousness again. When I woke the second time I was in an uncomfortable bed inside a curtained cubicle. I got up and walked around and asked the various orderlies where I could find my family. My brother was in a sealed room with 'Intensive care unit' labelled on the door. Something had gone wrong. There was panic etched on everyone's face. My father sat solemnly outside the room, holding his head in his hands. My mother didn't say anything but cried a great deal.

A man in a surgical mask and overalls came out of the room, crouched down next to me and said "He wants to see you." and patted my shoulder as he guided me into the cleaning area and had me wash my hands and elbows before putting on a similar smaller outfit. The room was white with a plastic feel and the floor stank of bleach. The frail boy opened his eyes and spoke a little, asking for water. The guy in the mask went to fetch it. My brother picked up his metal cereal bowl and threw it at my head with the force of a Japanese sumo wrestler. I could have choked the little bastard then and there, but instead we both burst out laughing, throwing whatever came to hand at each other. We shared the same sick sense of humour, but I can honestly say that he outdid me in every act of misbehaviour. The nurses were not at all pleased at having this feral child on their hands, but he often made them smile and they in turn developed a strong affection for him.

In the spring of 1989, as flowers and lambs were coming to life, his body withered away and eventually he died peacefully in my mother's arms at the end of the season. The crazy lunatic even managed to crack a joke before he went. The funeral service was short and some of the hospital staff even put in an appearance; at least the ones who could make it. The ones who couldn't also sent cards and letters of condolence. My grandfather in particular was grief stricken by the death of a grandchild. He used to call us his 'champions', and I'm sure his friends got tired of hearing about the awesome daily feats of his personal gladiators. He'd tell everyone how we'd stomped on some classroom bully or bitten some gloved dentist who insisted on using archaic torture devices on innocent children. He never seemed to mind our wayward ways, even when our parents scolded us for being 'uncontrollable'.

I personally cried continuously for four days before a sense of melancholy washed over me. A big part of me died along with my brother. The sky seemed a little darker without one of its brightest lights shining his sunny smile on this mortal coil. I never cried again after those days of mourning. My father's temper became more frightening as he struggled to deal with the loss and my mother just stopped speaking, lying in a catatonic state through the passing hours. I didn't mind the beatings and in a way, I looked forward to them as a break from the emptiness that filled the house. I often wished and sometimes daydreamed of what it would be like to live in the school I went to at the time instead of that god-awful home. I even convinced myself that I must surely have been adopted; that my real family was out there somewhere, people that actually loved me. My grandfather spent a month explaining to me that this was not the case.

There was one particular day, nothing otherwise exceptional about it, when I was walking through the park at the end of a long school day. I was stopped by a group of young thugs yelling things like "Paki scum", "Darkie" and "Black bastard". I tried to go around them but before I knew what was happening, I was being punched in the face repeatedly. They spat on me then left me on the wet grass to nurse my wounds. I got home sometime in the late evening and I remember my first thought was to check on my mother. My father was out, I wasn't sure where or why, but I was grateful for the reprieve and the lack of twenty questions. I probably wouldn't have been able to take too much more blunt force trauma that day anyway. My mother glanced over at me with her sunken eyes, bundled in a quilt, covered in the eerie stench of the grim reaper. She hadn't touched her breakfast, which was still lying in the same plate it was in that morning on the small wooden tray next to her bedside. I went to the bathroom and cleaned up with soapy water.

As usual my homework was still lying undone in my backpack. I had no plans on actually doing it. It consisted of composing sentences for words the teacher had scrawled in white chalk across the blackboard. There was no way I could complete the task, but I had something else on my mind as I was scrubbing the mud and spit off my face. There was one word that the kindly old woman had taken great pains to explain as she wrote it for the class. "Hate" in big bold letters as the chalk squealed on the dry board. It may seem strange, but I'd never previously thought of myself as being any different from anyone before these events. But I realised that I was in fact being seen as different; somehow less than people with a lighter skin colour. It's really not the kind of epiphany you would want to have in a supposedly civilised first-world country. I never managed to understand it, either then or now.

I can't say how I managed to get through those testing times, because my memory of the years after that is splintered. What I do know is that my parents divorced not long after my tenth birthday. My own reactions to things were not good and I ended up involved with all kinds of nefarious elements within society that were considered bad influences on a young and impressionable mind.

I didn't see my father again for many years and my mother's general state of health, both mental and physical, declined over a period of time. The worse she got, the more I reacted. I kept hoping that something I would get her attention and that she'd wake from the stupor that kept her in a cloud of depression. Eventually, this tactic worked and after being arrested, charged and taken to juvenile court, she finally got upset enough to throw me out of the house and into the arms of the designated homeless. My grandfather, being the only constant in my life, was a voice of wise counsel and reasoned gentleness, and he persuaded me to try doing something useful with my life.

Whilst walking past a poster and a recruitment officer, I decided to sign up and "be the best". The polished foot-soldier in his full-dress uniform insisted that "It's not just a job, it's an adventure" The fact that I had no formal education, however, posed a problem. But it was easily overcome with a battery of aptitude tests and a whole host of medical check-ups. I was a little stunned when they told me I had a very high level of intelligence, despite my obvious impediments. I was sure they'd confused my results with those of some other recruit. But if it got me three square meals, a bed and a steady income, I wasn't about to complain. There were clearly flaws in my logic, but I was lacking in common sense and maturity.

The years went by faster than a super-sonic jet and at the age of eighty-two, after a good innings, my grandfather passed away unexpectedly in his sleep. He was surrounded by loved ones and the greatest of friends. Unfortunately, I was in New York when it happened, but I flew in for the funeral. I met my father there and we spoke briefly. He was an older and greyer man than I remembered, but he'd aged well otherwise. He seemed more settled and stable than the man I'd known as my dad. He told me that my grandfather had left me a recording which he wanted me to hear after his death, along with some other various nick-knacks, including his war medals and a journal.

I took the cassette with me back to New York and it remained sitting there on a small writing bureau for some months before I eventually found the courage to play the thing. I listened intently as my grandfather's voice spoke to me from beyond the grave. He told some amusing anecdotes and a fart joke. He always liked to keep things light. As the machine played on, his tone became more serious as he described in detail his life and times. I began to notice the parallels between his life and my own and gained a sense of comfort from just hearing the sound of voice. At the end of the tape he told me he was proud of the man I had become and that even his son, my father, was just a man who'd seen too much too soon. "Above all else," he said, "...a man must live like a lion and love like he means it."

That tough Punjabi lion had gone up to the spirit in the sky and left this world in a better state than he'd found it in at the start of his existence. There was something funny in the fact that he'd made Glasgow his adopted home; the city was an asphalt jungle with just as many dangers as undiscovered regions of the Amazon. But its coldness had taught me how live, how to survive and how to eat. The salt on its streets, my streets, was mixed in with my blood. This was our story, my story, and it was to be but one amongst a million; from Generation X to a Scottish History X, consigned to antiquated history books with broken spines and loose leaves.

Once, the past and present had merged at a singular point in the space-time continuum and we saw a slew of participants on the world stage forever changing the course of future events. Nelson Mandela, Gandhi, Martin Luther King Jr, Che Guevarra, Bob Dylan and The Beatles, had all played a part in spawning a new breed of thinkers and revolutionaries. Their ideas crossed oceans, parted the seas and turned the waters of change into the sweet wine of human goodness. 'In Vino Veritas'.

18. Sherwood In The Forest Reads Rabby The Hood

'They've taen a weapon, long and sharp,
And cut him by the knee;
Then ty'd him fast upon a cart,
Like a rogue for forgerie' – Robert Burns, John Barleycorn:
A Ballad

I slithered into my bedroom, still feeling a little drunk and depressed from unearthed memories that were best left buried. But I couldn't sleep. I tossed and turned, desperately trying to get to that mellow zone where the brain can disengage from itself and slip into that warm pool of subconscious slime. The mattress was soft, the pillows were Egyptian cotton and the sheets were silk lined. But it didn't make any difference. I stared at the ceiling, watching peeling plaster curl into weird shapes that seemed to come alive for brief moments in between blinking. The soothing sounds of passing traffic on the main road slowly built to a crescendo of incoherent petrol burning dissonance. I preferred the noise to absolute silence. I'd grown accustomed to it; even found it reassuring in those dreadful moments when you know you're all alone with only your thoughts for company. They begin talking to you, saying things like "Look at you. Why are you even wasting your effort breathing. Let it go. You know you want to. I'm your friend. Your only friend.." That's when just knowing that people were going about their daily business outside helped to drown out the menacing demons inside.

Suddenly, screeching, howling and high-hat drum beats burst through the thin film of comfort. The music crawled up my spine and bit hard into the base of my skull, injecting itself into my brain and pouring out of my ear canals. My upstairs neighbour had just bought Lady Gaga's latest album. I had nothing against the woman, but if she was going to insist on assaulting my senses, did she have to do it with the atrocious auto-tuned ravings of a wailing banshee, raving and screaming like a half-baked hell-hound?

There's nothing quite as intense as being in the throes of a brain bending hangover induced migraine. The last thing you need is an inconsiderate neighbour. Soon the real fun would begin and I'd start gnawing on balls of twine and talking to giant imaginary cockroaches; all in the vain hope that stamping on them when they least expect it will offer some relief.

The state of heartbreak, coupled with temporary insanity, can make a man do curious things. Take for instance, the act of molesting your neighbour's pet hamster with a cooking utensil. Ordinarily this isn't something that would cross one's mind. But in desperate circumstances, one gives serious thought to resorting to such sick and desperate measures.

I crawled out of bed and slipped into my piss-stained slip-on shoes. I was going to have to give the bitch a piece of my mind. I'd put up with this bullshit long enough. Week in, week out for months on end, it was always the same thing. Music blaring at three o'clock on a Monday morning or a Thursday night. Then there were those rare joyous afternoons when my walls would shake like a Las Vegas whorehouse. It was just as much of a full-force fucking over really.

I grabbed the golf club I'd placed next to the door for protection purposes and ascended the stairs. I rang the doorbell with violent abandon and rapped the knocker mercilessly. I could feel spit bubbles forming at the corner of my mouth. I was doubtful that she would answer, but then I heard something smash and an almighty clang. She was wrestling with the deadbolt. The door flew open and there she was, dressed in a yellow Lycra jumpsuit. If I hadn't been foaming at the mouth, I might have been inclined to fuck her.

"Do you know how loud your bastard music is?" I yelled.

"What!?"

She seemed alarmed at the sight of the golf club in

my hand.

A red mist descended and I stormed my way into her home, quickly locating the source of the infernal noise. A succession of well honed blows led to the destruction of the sound system and it ceased squawking immediately. I walked out with the same speed that I'd entered.

"You're going to pay for that! I'm going to call the police!" she screeched.

I spun round to face her, having regained my inner calm.

"No, you won't," I said, before grabbing her waist, tipping her over and kissing her firmly on her pale lips.

She didn't fight it. I was surprised. Perhaps she was too stunned to do anything.

"Send me the repair bill and get another one, but for fuck's sake, keep the volume down. There's a button on it for a reason; use it!"

She smiled as I let her go and I quickly skipped back down the stairs and into my sanctuary of solitude. I was too wired to sleep so I decided to switch on my computer and check my emails. It was a basic junker that I'd gotten for free from a guy called 'Junkie Jack'. I didn't use it very often but it was a handy way of keeping in touch with people in the work sphere, and it added to my otherwise bare living room.

I scrolled through the offers for Viagra and penis extensions that flooded my inbox regularly. Most of these were hustles of one sort or another. I knew one friend who'd been gullible enough to take up the offer of a Russian mail order bride service. Next thing he knew, his credit card had been charged for three large screen televisions, a thousand dollars in jewellery and a hefty number of subscriptions to Asian porn channels, transmitted across directly from the other side of the world. Those sneaky fraudsters always had some kind of hook for what they called 'phishing' scams.

Once most of the garbage was deleted from my account, I came across an email from Matt Sherwood, a lauded and well respected member of the Writer's Foundation for Scotland. I wasn't quite sure how the crafty devil had gotten my email address. I clicked on the message icon and up it popped.

"Hi Max. Find your work very interesting. Could use tweaking.
Don't know if you've heard, Forest Cafe in Edinburgh is set for closure.
This would be a great loss to the Scotland's grass roots counter-culture.
Many fine artists, writers and poets have found a home there and gone
on to greener pastures. Hosting a fund raising event to get a 'Save the Forest'
collection going. Can we rely on you to support it? Would be great if you
could be there to address the audience. Starts tomorrow at 6.30pm.
Many thanks, Matt."

I checked the date on the email. It was sent yesterday. Tomorrow meant today. I glanced at my watch. It was already a half past three. If I got cleaned up and left soon, I might just make it. The train would take at least an hour to get there, and getting from here to Queen Street station would also take around thirty minutes. I went into kitchen and switched on my coffee maker. I was going to need a lot of caffeine to stay alert and awake among that crowd. They were perfectly decent people, but their style of reading aloud was such that doctors ought to have marketed it as the perfect cure for insomnia. On and on they'd droll, searching for some faint acceptance, applause and adoration from the same five people that showed up over and over again, each seeking the same. In some ways it was a grotesque example of the fame and fortune culture that had been cultivated by the privileged, 'Get rich quick!', 'You too can have your fifteen minutes of glory in the spotlight on X-Pop-factor-Idol-Big-Brother!".

I had no time for that sort of thing and under other circumstances, I wouldn't have bothered. But Matt was one of a rare breed; an exceptionally talented lovey of the upper class crumpet munching crowd. This made him a bit of a pompous prick, but I had a profound respect for his writing style, which was balls out and brash. In many ways, he was similar in nature to the great Truman Capote. It often surprised me that he hadn't reached the same heights as the former, but then, one never quite knew what the future held.

My coffee had percolated nicely. I mixed in the sugar and cream and clouds of white appeared, infusing in the mug. Wisps of dairy goodness streaked up to the top like marble tiled patterns of the Venus de Milo. I stirred it slowly as I watched the sun break through the murky grey. The rain had stopped sometime earlier and it looked like summer was finally coming back in force.

I turned the knob on the old radio on the table and the sweet sounds of Anthony Hamilton's motown music grooved through the stuffy air. I cracked open the window a little to let in the fresh breeze as I sat there sipping my cup of coffee. The silky smooth dulcet tones washed over me as I finished off the last remnants in the hot mug. A peculiar scent was wafting in the air. I sniffed out the source of the terrible odour: it was me. I smelled like an Albanian goat herder who had just spent the morning molesting chickens in a henhouse. A shower was definitely necessary if I was to go out in public.

By four o'clock, I emerged fresh as a daisy, wearing a pair of pressed boot-cut jeans and a beige mock turtleneck that clung to me like clingfilm. Outside, the weather was cool and rays of sunshine broke through the branches of the evergreen tree next to the bus stop. As I'd anticipated, it didn't take long for the bus to show. By the time I got to Queen Street, my left leg had a cramp. The walk from Hope Street was too much for my weary self. I had a choice between the automated ticket machine and the manned service counter next to the entrance. I chose the machine. Three of them only took credit cards, with only one taking cash payments. I had no option but to wait in the long queue.

The large board overhead flashed with various departure times and platform numbers. The train leaving for Edinburgh was due to leave at 4.55pm. I figured that gave me a good twenty minutes at least. It took almost all of that time before I got to the front of that god-awful line. I stuffed the two ten pound notes and a five into the slot. Clank. Buzz. Screech. Two laminated tickets fell into the bottom container.

I went through the automated turnstiles and waited patiently at platform one with all the other passengers. The train itself was cramped and people were crammed in like sardines in a tin can. I was lucky enough to find a seat before the deluge of last minute commuters piled on. I was beginning to regret wearing so much cotton heavy clothing. The combined body heat of everyone on board made the temperature soar and the whole carriage felt like parched desert.

I rested my head against the back of the seat and drifted off. At each stop the driver announced the various stations. I vaguely remember Falkirk and Haymarket being mentioned somewhere in the list, but the rest were a blur. The few times I opened my eyes, there was nothing but rows of endless fields and the occasional hill to be seen in the placid and peaceful countryside. The most interesting sight was that of a man with his gloved hand steadfastly probing the hind orifice of a cow. I assumed he was a veterinarian as the alternative explanation seemed too disturbing to even think about.

We arrived at Edinburgh, Waverley at six on the dot. On leaving the train, I walked up the ramp and out onto North Bridge and then towards Cowgate. I'd always thought it strange that they'd given a street such a weird name. I passed by the Cabaret Voltaire. I had fond memories of that place. Between it and the Banshee Labyrinth, Scotland's capital had a stronghold on friendly banter and excellent boozers.

The University grounds next to Chambers Street were astounding. That curious combination where history met modernity was spread throughout the city. Old bell towers next to glass windowed shopping complexes, beautifully crafted stonework next to cruel and unusual apartment blocks. The same thing was happening in Glasgow; except on a greater scale. Tourists in Edinburgh still got the authentic feel of its past. But in Glasgow, most of the old buildings and hallowed churches had been desecrated, with monstrous ivory towers taking their place.

Another point of note was Edinburgh's re-introduction of the old tram system. It had been responsible for the chaotic destruction of the city's many roads. The costs had spiralled out of control, beyond the four hundred million pound mark. Allegations of back-handers being kicked upstairs to higher-ups in local council circles were ever emerging. However, the idea had a certain quaint appeal to history buffs like me. As some in the Scottish Parliament had quite rightly pointed out, it was a clean and efficient form of public transport. But were we really prepared for these kinds of birthing pains required for this transformation?

I turned right then took the second left, zigzagging past the hordes of work-tired passers-by. You could tell they'd put their noses to the grindstone, a hard day's graft. Even the bums wore a look of exacted strain as they begged for their next fix from a can of copper coins. I knew something of the hard life, but that was another time. The rough-sleepers of the modern age had it worse in some ways. They still hadn't caught up with the basics of economics. Increasing inflation meant that the two pence pieces in their foam Costa coffee cups didn't guarantee them a decent meal. They'd soon have to sing and dance for their supper. And the rest of the world didn't give a damn. They were too busy trying to stave off starvation in their own countries, which were one step away from complete decimation.

I pressed a ten pound note into the hand of a dishevelled woman. She wouldn't take it, muttering something about it being too much and then thanked me profusely with strange drugged up blessings worthy of some Sufi sitting on a Persian carpet in the mystic east. I couldn't imagine anything worse than being an invisible member of society. You weren't even a face in the crowd. You were an unheard, unwanted non-existing person of unknown origin, blanked out of vision by those with Passports, birth certificates and National Insurance numbers. Did you even exist? Were you ever really here? Perhaps as that famous song says, 'all we are is dust in the wind'.

I was tempted to stop at the National Museum of Scotland, but with only ten minutes to spare, I thought it best not to tempt fate. I reached the fork where Forrest Road and Bristo Place split, near the Bedlam Theatre. Across from it was the Forest Cafe. There was a small anteroom where people congregated and exchanged looks of recognition, shaking hands with strangers they'd seen once at some stage play or other but couldn't really remember who they were. Besides Matt, no-one knew who I was, at least not by my face, which suited me just fine. They'd never met me and I generally tended to keep it that way. My first thought was to make up some gibberish on the spot when my name was called, say whatever came to mind, then leave as quickly as possible without being held up by these unmasked zealots of the written word.

This all hinged on one thing; being somewhere at the bottom of the list for these proceedings. My plans were soon scampered when Matt decided to announce me as the first act of the evening. There I was, just through the door and I had to deal with this awful situation. I went through to the larger room in the back, where the event was in fill swing. On either side of the entryway were two volunteers with clipboards and collection tins. It was sickening. Their biscuit tins were likely to be overflowing by the end of it all. The middle-classes were often the worst offenders, throwing in money they couldn't afford to burn; but doing it anyway, just so they didn't look out of place. They wanted to be hip, one of the in-crowd. Some of the patrons were still getting settled. Matt waved me over to the middle of the room. I scrambled up the steps and grabbed the microphone. I had no material. Nothing was coming to mind. I tapped the microphone a couple of times to make sure it was working before rocketing into a rant of epic proportions, saying anything that came into my head.

"Sorry for my appearance. Ah, I have a drink fuelled, prescription pill induced headache. It's accompanied by hallucinations of aliens with an unhealthy obsession of probing Earth cattle. Extra terrestrials are real sickos!"

There was nothing. Not even the white of a tooth. I figured I was going down about as well as an uncooked lobster. I continued. "Well, you know you have a serious drinking problem when you've destroyed your neighbour's sound system, thrown your golf clubs at a passing squirrel, and thought out a series of pick-up lines for donkeys in heat. Don't worry about my neighbours; they're all evil Satan worshipping goat fuckers who blast loud music at all hours."

Finally, some of them began loosening up and started cackling like hyenas. I carried on. "Unfortunately, I didn't actually bring anything with me to read. So I'm going to wing it here and riff a little bit on writing itself. To be considered a good writer in any sense, you must first have something to write about - which requires a certain amount of life experience and depth of understanding. Secondly, one must have the capability to transmit that something through the written word. Both of these can generally take years to refine. The number of writers who meet those criteria under the age of forty is tiny. And the competition is certainly brutal. The key, however, isn't how many books you sell, poems you get published or even whether you please the critics. It comes down to whether one can be happy with the quality of their own work, and many young writers that are dismissed today may well become staples of literature in the future."

A hand went up and I nodded at a thin middle-aged gentleman with half-moon glasses perched on his nose and a stripped cardigan draped around his poised torso. He was like a coiled cobra waiting to spring.

"What exactly do you mean when you say that the competition is brutal? I've never seen writing as *brutal*. Isn't it about *expressing* yourself?"

'Oh God,' I thought. 'Here we go with another one of these privileged hacks with a superior sense of entitlement.'

"Well, it is about self-expression. But it's still a brutal field. When one considers the sheer number of books churned out by authors, regardless of quality, it is truly an astounding thing. This forms the basis of what becomes an aspiring writer's competition, because... in order for any writer to become a *success*, he or she has to tackle through those hordes and become noticed. It's like having the loudest voice in a room full of shouting children. That's how great writers like Hemingway, Fitzgerald, Twain and others are born. They keep screaming, keep writing, honing their in-built talent until some poor influential soul pays attention. And they eventually have to, because through the process, they've developed unique and distinctive styles and subjects in their writing. But it also takes luck, skill and plenty of grit-based determination. Anyway, it's been a pleasure talking to you. Thank you Matt for the opportunity."

The roar of applause surprised me. The fact was, I had absolutely no clue what the hell I was talking about. But I managed to get through the ordeal and left quietly before anyone noticed. Matt got up, thanked me for my contribution and read some of Robert Burns' work as a follow up.

19. A Scientologist, An Atheist
& A Page Three Girl With Herpes

It was 7pm by the time I reached South Bridge. The sun was low in the sky and the roads were jam packed with cars, bumper to bumper, all waiting their turn at temporary traffic lights across town while men with jackhammers ripped up the tarmac. I was just glad to be out of the adult jungle-gym where the literary word took the place of monkey bars and well groomed gorillas thumped their chests in a show of verbal virility. The irony was that they lacked the necessary fertile imaginations, which prevented the conception of new ideas within their mindless material. It wasn't their fault. My brain frequently numbed from boredom and banality. I'd subjected myself to too many extremes for prolonged periods of time and, as any good psychologist will tell you, this generally results in desensitisation.

While I was considering the ramifications of this, an unusually happy man came toward me. I'd noticed him earlier in my peripheral vision, standing in a shady doorway where the light couldn't get to him. He extended his arm and grabbed my elbow with his free hand.

"My friend!" he said. "Aren't you sick of the way you're dictated to by the government and the newspapers? I'd love to talk with you about a whole new wave of thinking, the way of the future!"

I didn't know this guy from Adam, yet here he was calling me his 'friend', bandying the word around like it meant nothing; as though friendships were something he juggled around and threw off inconsiderately in his private life. It pissed me off. If that was the case, I preferred to remain his total stranger.

"Actually, I'd much rather not. I have a lot of stuff to do and..."

"Wait just a minute buddy, this'd only take a few minutes of your time. Our Academy offers free IQ tests –

ah, I see you're a literary man."

I was carrying a leaflet from the café detailing its next poetry session. He carried on.

"Did you know we offer lots of literature for free minds like yours?"

He was driving home the hard sell. His car salesman style and clean cut appearance made me wary. But I did have some free time on my hands. My motto had always been 'if it's strange enough, throw yourself in head first'.

"Tell me more," I said, flashing a smile.

He seemed a little shocked, but instantly regained his previous composure.

"I don't mind telling you, you're the first one to take interest this evening. Why don't you come on into the Academy and I'll tell you all about it."

The big colourful monogrammed sign was wedged above the door, hidden in plain sight. I followed him and took a seat in what looked like a cheap imitation classroom, worthy of a porn movie film set. Formica covered desks and plastic moulded chairs were sprawled across the scratched laminate flooring. He swirled round in another seat opposite mine and began to tell me all about the media and its disinformation tactics and how almost every news story was designed to focus on something negative. This was all true of course, but I was all too aware of it beforehand.

It was then that he went on to expound the virtues of L. Ron Hubbard, a sci-fi author who'd written several books, mixing the ideas of Jung, Freud, Nietzsche with pseudo-scientific psycho babble. I'd once been loaned his Dianetics book by a friend. It was interesting and offered some unique ideas on what made human beings tick, but it wasn't a million miles from the ravings of Jim Jones – the preacher man of Kool-aid killing fame. When he realised his slick pitch wasn't working, he switched subject and suggested I take the Academy's version of an IQ test paper.

I scanned through it briefly, scribbling away with the pencil he'd placed on the desk. I wrote like the wind and finished well before the end of the given time. I handed him the completed paper and walked over to the large panelled window. It seemed silly to be wasting my time indoors on a beautiful day. But I was getting a sick thrill from the cat and mouse game that was ensuing in this house of ill repute.

"Wow," he said as he marked the answers. "You're one smart guy!"

"I am?" I said, sounding surprised.

"Yeah, totally! You'd be a perfect candidate for joining us."

"Well I don't know. I'm still not sure on that," I said.

"I have an idea. Why don't I show you some of our videos. I think you'd find them interesting. Then you can have a chat with one of our Auditors."

He escorted me to another room with a couch and an out of date DVD player. I watched the short twenty minute film that explained the freedom that was to be found in their philosophy. They were careful not to call it a religion. I looked at the DVD case. Part of a set that was priced at over a hundred pounds, which you had to pay if you wanted to be 'clear'. A person who was 'clear' was deemed to be free. But before you could be sure you were 'clear', an 'auditor' had to process your progress. These sessions also cost money. But they led to the land of freedom. They also led to being out of pocket.

In came the brown haired 'auditor'. Gone was the smiling face of my previous 'friend'. A serious, piercing set of cold eyes took over, analysing and x-raying my soul with his obviously elevated spiritual state. He recommended immediate induction. There was no time to lose. I was a suffering soul, doomed to an inner hell without the assistance of their program. It was imperative that I did what he told me.

"I'll need to think about it," I said.

"Why do you need to think about it?" he said. "If you were diagnosed with cancer, would you need to *think* about treatment?"

The obvious answer was yes. But this freakish bastard was beginning to make me angrier with his analogy, citing a serious thing like cancer as a close approximate to what he viewed as a lack of spiritual awareness. These were pressure tactics, plain and simple. The thickness of the bullshit was getting heavier and I no longer had any patience for the gibberish that was emanating from this negative kid, who couldn't have been older than twenty five. But here he was, with zero life experience, telling *me* that I was lacking in spiritual sense.

"Listen you little piss ant," I shouted. "I lived and learned more than your morally bankrupt soul will learn in ten lifetimes."

He didn't like that outburst very much and pressed a little green button on the wall. Three suits entered the room, grabbed me by the collar and threw me out. It was inevitable, but I'd hoped to get more of a debate from the fiendish little prick. Still, there was no real harm done and at least they hadn't taken it upon themselves to inflict a serious skull injury on my person. I carried on walking down South Bridge, safe in the knowledge that I'd soon be back on a train destined for Glasgow and I could put this whole terrible experience behind me. But this was not to be. Near the Fruitmarket Gallery, I saw a young woman engaged in a battle of wits with a card-carrying conservative Christian. I recognised her from a newspaper clipping I'd come across last month. She was a page three girl, a glamour model who, as I recalled, had one of the finest female forms I'd seen in a while. Her favourite hobbies were chess and polo.

"Porn empowers people!" she screamed. "It leads to sexual, emotional and intellectual liberation. How dare you people disempower women! It's people like you that can't see the inherent value of another human being. What concern is it of yours what women do with their bodies and sexuality? Why do you reduce them to non-beings, there to simply perform certain tasks? Or to conform to the preconceived notions of men at the top of the food chain? Throw out these old outdated ideas, oust the idiotic lunatics running the asylum and then you'll have real equality, respect and love. Then there'd be no need for feminism, positive discrimination, or any other counter measure we clamber to as a half-baked solution."

She was one clever cat. But so was the "Jesus saves all" banner waving bible thumper.

"What *you* do is morally and socially repugnant! We already live in a pornographic society, and a society which sexualises women and children. Our country is saturated with porn and sexualised advertising and magazines. There is an epidemic of female eating disorders, self esteem issues and insecurity! Porn and page three are a great evil! So are the individuals in it, for the individuals watching it and the society that tolerates it!"

It was then that I interjected.

"Dude, your views are obviously based on personal belief and moral absolutes, which is fine as they're grounded in religion. We don't live in a 'pornographic' society, we live in a society that's comfortable with itself. Eating disorders are *not* down to porn but down to how people see themselves and usually rooted in the 'I hate myself' deep guilt complex that results from *any* dogma that's espoused by the mainstream media, or religious institution! If we teach people to love themselves for who they are, then we cancel out any such negative impacts. And there's no goddamn link between sexualised advertising and the porn. Advertising is a form of consumerist exploitation of the less well off through mental indoctrination! Sexual liberation teaches people to be free in themselves and their thinking. *Brainwashing* tells people *need* something, be it religion, the latest trainers, or a car that will guarantee you hot chicks, in order to feel better about yourself."

"Have you ever spent time in the company of a bunch of lads on the pull?" he retorted. "They've clearly spent their developing years furtively and secretly masturbating to porn and topless models. You should listen to their thoughts on what constitutes a real woman! You're naive and deluded, and should be ashamed of being in favour of an industry so destructive and debasing."

I smiled, knowing that his stupidity meant that Miss June 12th and I had already won the argument.

"Therein lies the key word that your whole argument rests on – 'Ashamed' - Why should she feel 'ashamed' of anything?? But yes, she *should* feel shame shouldn't she? So should *all* the women who have children outside of wedlock, gays, and people who don't put money into the collection plate every Sunday. I'm sorry, but I won't allow you to use these kinds of psychological bullying tactics on people. If anyone's deluded it's a placard sporting indoctrinated freak who believes in an invisible man in the sky who tells him when to brush his teeth and will punish him in the fiery pits of Inferno if he doesn't do as he's told!"

He was silent for a few minutes and we both looked on as his face scrunched up as though he was being fingered by a fat nun. "You're an atheist aren't you? I can tell. I pray for your lost soul. Because when you die, you're going to see that all the science in the world can't save you. It's all made up anyway. You atheists just make up these facts and numbers!"

"Don't go assuming shit. You have no idea what I believe. Don't bother praying for me. You cloak pity wrapped in an insult and expect me to accept that as some twisted form of Christ love? If you want to get into the science versus religion, I'll kick your ignorant ass on that front too!"

"Try your best!" he hissed.

Like the biblical hero that was David, I was about to verbally slay this verbose fool and put the slimy bastard out of his misery for daring to pick on a woman. I cleared my throat and prepared to unleash an unparalleled onslaught.

"Can you prove God doesn't exist? Can't you see his wonders around you?" he asked.

That was when I sprung it on him.

"If you're discussing God as existing in the wonder of life itself and nature at work, then you're being metaphorical. Yet you often forget the harsh brutality of nature in this sense. There are birth defects, pathogens, parasites and so on that you utterly ignore."

"But belief had to originate somewhere? People wouldn't have started believing in God if he didn't exist," he replied.

"Well," I said. "Many stories and legends exist in plenty of cultures. These mainly evolved from exaggerated claims about someone or something they saw in their lifetimes that made them question things. Like the Sun. There were lots of Sun gods in a lot of religions."

He thought about this for a moment before retorting.

"But Christianity is the only religion that gives you the answers to those questions. It helps people make sense of the world by giving them the right moral codes to live by."

"To truly make sense of the world and who we are, it's not within some divine book that we need to look, but outside at the greater picture; that's where the true miracle exists; in the fact that those of us who are happy and healthy have, by the laws of probability, beaten the odds. We should be glad of this and do our best as social animals, to ensure that others, who did not survive the battle unscathed, are looked after better and not preyed upon by charlatans and power mad institutions."

He looked on as he listened to the ravings of a caffeine crazed insomniac whose synapses had fried in a way that allowed for sense to prevail. But it didn't stop him from trying to go against the grain of common sense.

"Yes, but science and rationality can't give people the things religion can. People like you aggressively preach atheism and science as if those can replace the Ten Commandments."

"Science and religion are not and cannot be on the same footing. Religiously motivated types like you seem to say that Science itself is a belief. It isn't. It is the reasoned application of logic and method to a series of hypothesis which can be falsified. That means that science is an open field, where what makes sense and what can be proven are its guiding force. Religion, in any faith base, is absolute in its conclusions. Therefore, when evidence contradicts its ideas and ideals, it tries to adapt, but can't. How science measures things is not simply 'made up'. Though it is true it uses mathematical representations in order to value that which we know. They are tangible properties of our universe. Therefore, we can postulate and calculate other various unknowns from those. It's also the case that we don't know everything, but we're endeavouring to learn more about the world around us."

"You do know that if you die, you're going to hell, don't you?" he said.

"Oh, my dear moronic friend, there is no hell but what we make on this Earth. And if there was, and your God was that unmerciful, then I'd happily go there. I wouldn't want to be blessed by a vengeful god who hears the screams of hungry children in Africa and ignores them."

"It's all a test!" he replied.

"A test?" I asked. "A test for who?"

"For us. For people who can do something about it."

"So, let me get this straight. Your God makes innocents suffer to test your beliefs? That doesn't sound very loving."

"Your souls are damned! Especially this whore's!" he screamed.

"Oh, do shut up you zealot! This is becoming tedious. People like you kill Jesus everyday by preaching this crap. And I can tell you voted for Tony Blair. May God have mercy on your shit-filled brain!"

Miss June 12th stood there open mouthed, obviously not expecting some whacked out stranger to leap to her defence in this way. She blinked a couple of times in amazement. The man with the placard was still standing there, stumped.

"Sinners like you are going to end up with herpes!" he yelled. It was a sure sign of madness. Onlookers shook their heads in disapproval.

"I've already had it!" giggled the girl as she watched me casually trot off back to the beaten track.

She skipped up alongside me in her boob tube and

denim miniskirt, which showed off her stunning figure. Her blonde hair gave her an almost angelic glow.

"Thanks for what you did back there. You didn't have to do it. It was really sweet."

"It was nothing. It's just been one of those days. I'd had enough of dealing with crazy fuckers and their nonsense. I can't stand folk who think they can push people around," I replied.

"My name's Tina. I guess you already know what I do for a living. I'm sorry people had to see that."

"Don't be sorry. What are you gonna do? Let that kind of behaviour slide? Better to call them on it."

"Yeah. You're right," she said. "I never caught your name?"

"My name's Max," I replied. "And I'm broke."

"Where ya from? You don't sound like you're from Edinburgh."

"I'm not. I'm a Weegie. Not born in Glasgow, but definitely bred there. You?"

"I'm from Hamilton originally."

"Ah, Hamilton. The place where sunken souls of the undead beckon Glaswegians with sweet promises of Buckfast and unabashed glue sniffing orgies. No mortal can resist, save the few who know the holy words... 'C'mone then ya bam!'"

She laughed.

"You're a weird and funny guy. I like your style Max. You heading back to Glasgow?"

"Yeah, that was the plan. Got a return train ticket. A mate invited me down to the Forest Café for a fundraiser. "

"Sounds pretty exciting."

"It wasn't."

"Mind if I come with you? I was planning in going into Glasgow anyway. My parents stay there. I could use some good company on the journey down. I'll be on my best behaviour. I promise not to start any more public riots!" she said wryly.

We walked together the rest of the way back to

Waverley. She spoke a lot. I wasn't sure if she was just nervous or hyper. Either way, she seemed like a decent girl. She sat next to me in the last compartment of the train. It was completely empty other than the two of us. Tina talked about her family, her sisters and her parents who had been supportive of her life choices through most of her teenage years. I was a little jealous in some ways. I'd never had that kind of family security, or anywhere I could rest when I was soul weary. I didn't say much. I kept her amused with some funny stories and observational humour. The train rocked back and forth and put us both to sleep. Her head fell onto my shoulder and I let her rest against it. I heard other people getting on, jostling and grumbling while the driver was ever vigilant in his duties of heralding the stops.

20. Nymphet Joyriders From Mars:
The Secret Sex-Tapes Of Wallis Simpson

We pulled into Queen Street station at around 10.45pm. Tina lifted her head from my shoulder. My arm had fallen asleep and the sleeve of my turtleneck was covered in drool. I was mildly irritated, but her soft green eyes made it difficult to be mad at her. There was only one other person riding with us in that carriage and he was busy fiddling with his mobile phone. It had turned dark, but an orange glow hovered over the night sky. Tina fidgeted with her skirt. I could tell she was feeling the chill in the atmosphere, or perhaps some semblance of modesty had infiltrated her unabashed persona.

"Listen, let me give you my number," she said.

"Oh okay. Sure."

"Well... I don't have any business cards on me or anything..."

That much was obvious. It would have been difficult to conceal a stack of cards anywhere in that get-up.

"Do you have a pen?"

I riffled through my trouser pockets and pulled out a miniature pen that doubled as a cigarette lighter. I'd bought it at a gadget store and had only used it once in the four years I'd had it.

"Thanks. Hmm... You don't have any paper do you?"

I checked in case I did. I didn't.

"Afraid not."

"That's okay. Hold out your hand."

She scribbled on my right palm and I watched as the ink dribbled out and branded my skin.

"Now, don't wash it off until you get a chance to write it down! I really do want you to give me a call sometime."

Once the train had come to a complete stop, I got up and shuffled onto the platform. Tina and I walked together to the exit. It hit me that there had been no ticket inspector on board the train. Not even the man at the turnstiles had bothered to ask us for our tickets. Tina had just bagged herself a free ride. The girl was beginning to grow on me. But that quip about herpes made me uneasy. In this age of safe sex, it would be foolish to take risks with that sort of thing.

A row of black cabs always waited directly outside the station. She flagged the first one and I helped her into the back of the taxi, shutting the door firmly before waving her off. I climbed into the one behind and instructed the driver to take me home. A sense of calm began to flow through me. I wasn't sure if it was the drive or just the ego-boosting encounter with a beautiful girl. But I had no plans to actually call her. She'd understand. After all, she was a woman of the world; she knew how the game was played. In the frenetic field of hook-ups, there were players who played for sport and other's who played for keeps. I was guilty of the first but fell firmly in the category of the second. That was probably the thing that hit me in the balls in all my relationships.

I remembered the advice of a friend who'd once said 'all relationships, friendships and other ships go through rough seas. Just look at the Titanic.' I'd come to realise that was indeed an axiom of life in the 21st Century. Nothing was certain. You could rely on no-one. It was ultimately always better to keep your own counsel. Trust no-one; at least, not entirely.

"That's nine quid and sixty mate," said the cab driver.

I'd gotten so lost in thought that I wasn't even aware that I was home. I panicked for a moment, thinking that I'd left my wallet on the train, but I'd only put it in my back pocket. It was squished and bent out of shape because I'd been sitting on it for the better part of ninety minutes. I took out my last twenty and handed it to him, counting the change he returned carefully. When you're facing a financial deficit, every penny matters.

I was glad to be back in my nest again. The landing light wasn't working, which made it hard to find the lock on my door. A surge of warm air greeted me inside. I kicked off my shoes and sank into my couch. The beeping from the answering machine caught my attention. I let out a groan. I didn't want to be disturbed by anything petty. But I got up all the same and clicked the replay button.

"Max? Its Rollie. My PC isn't working. I was wondering if you had a spare laptop I could borrow? Anyway, call me back when you get in."

Rollie was one of my best friends. He was a Welsh/English German Jew by descent. He'd been part of the whole 60's explosion and survived the fall out, living to tell the tale. When the whole hippy movement collapsed, he escaped its madness and moved north, got married and settled in a tranquil unaffected part of Glasgow. That was before his wife left him literally holding the baby. He'd single-handedly fulfilled his paternal responsibilities while also working full-time. He was an oddity in that respect. But he was also a prominent figure in the underground arts community, dabbling in all its various shapes and forms. Aside from that, the man was as unhinged as I was and insanely funny too. It would be true to say that he'd become like a surrogate father figure to me. He'd shacked up with a marvellous broad who generally kept him on the straight and narrow.

I dialled his number on the old telephone on my desk. It rung out for a while before he finally answered. He was clearly sloshed out of his skull.

"Rollie? Yes, it's Max. I got your message."

"Ah yes dear boy, glad you called. The missus and I were just discussing the merits of modern technology."

"I see. What happened with the computer?"

"Well. How can I put this. It took over three minutes to load. So I smashed it to smithereens with that sledgehammer in the tool shed."

"Did that help? They do say that sometimes all you need to do is give it a good thump."

"Well no. It stopped working completely. You know what the sad thing is?"

"What?" I asked

"I was in the middle of downloading that porn

collection for you. You remember we were talking about it?"

"Porn collection? Oh you mean the 'Fat Nymphet Joyriders From Mars' special edition box set!"

"That's the one!" he said.

"That's terrible. Absolutely terrible. You know my life is empty without a bit of voyeuristic alien sex to spice it up. I'm already suffering from withdrawal symptoms man! I'm growing hair on my palms and my vision goes wonky every Saturday night!"

" You may have to resort to calling the Russell Grant's psychic sex line for depraved addicts - approved and funded by the generous contributions of Clegg & Cameron."

"My God! I don't want to have to resort to that kind of lowlife debasement. Isn't there anything you can do?"

"Well. I did find a mint copy of anal boys in leiderhosen. It's a Nazi special starring Himmler and a thousand brown shirts."

"Wow. Is that even... legal? I mean I've heard the stories, but man it's supposedly *so* hardcore that even the Duchess of York squealed after watching it. I must have it!"

"Did you hear? Wallis Simpson is in the last reel. She's the one with the jellyfish...it's yours for two pounds of mackerel and a steel penis enhancer. Viagra isn't doing it for me anymore."

"Blimey! That's just given me the world's biggest erection. Ah, Wallis Simpson. The poor man's answer to Winifred Wagner. And with a jellyfish too eh? yes yes yes! I'm sure I can get a generic enhancer; but the mackerel may be a problem. I already gave three pounds of it to the Tory fund for free enemas."

"The Tories get free enemas? Damn that's news to me!"

"Tell me about it! Shocking isn't it?"

"Max, this conversation has probably gone past any bounds of dignified discourse. The missus is giving me strange looks of disapproval."

"Well, anyway, this computer thing. Yes, you can

have the laptop if you need it. It's fifteen years old and I haven't used it lately so I can't promise that it's working."

"Thanks. It's better than nothing. I just need it to write up some basic stuff and surf the internet a little. Does it have a word processor and wireless capability?"

"Yeah. It should have. I'll drop it by in a couple of days."

"Great. By the way, how was America?"

"It was good. Still where I left it."

"Glad you're back young man. Anyway, thanks again. Take care for now.

Rollie had kept up with all the latest techno fads and was more in tune with them than most young people, which was ironic. As I put down the phone, I contemplated the marvels of the internet age. All information was digitised and even news was being consumed in digital formats. It was an awesome leap of human innovation. No-one in their wildest imaginations had ever dreamed of such things in Rollie's age of inspiration. But it also came with inherent dangers. It was all too easy for some all powerful force to make anything unfavourable vanish by simply pressing the 'delete' button. We were already see the beginnings of this in certain forums like online comment sections and even with things like 'facebook', 'youtube' and 'myspace', which were frequently totted out as being bastions of freedom and self-expression.

We were close to a time when we wouldn't need things like newspapers or paper of any sort. There would be no recorded interviews on 8mm tapes, no written records of any kind, no hardcopy to fall back on. But that would also mean that issues like Iraq's WMD scandal, the death of Dr David Kelly and ongoing foreign invasions couldn't be probed and analysed by an ever vigilant public. Therefore, no unforeseen problems could topple governments or tackle injustice with legitimacy. But it did open doors in the realm of information sharing, even if that information could be suppressed or discredited easily.

I wondered if Orwell's nightmare was coming true.

The future map for the digital age pointed to a path paved with good intentions, great sound bites and free junk content for all; a yellow brick road laden with gold for the toll-masters. But its final destination might be somewhere far too shocking for us to actually contemplate.

The present government had already declared war against what it called 'declining morality'. It didn't have quite the same ring to it as 'the war on terror' but fuck it. Clearly the student protests and recent riots had disturbed the rich fat cats so much that they were prepared to go Clockwork Orange on today's youth. And then they came on the radio, wondering *why* people kept saying they were out of touch. The whole thing disturbed me greatly.

It was almost midnight. On what was technically the 5th of August 2011, I switched on the television and flicked over to the twenty-four hour news channel to catch up on two days worth of headlines. The scrolling ticker at the bottom of the screen '£125billion wiped off shares', followed by 'Value of FTSE100 slumps more than 8%. Yesterday's fall of 3.4% takes FTSE to 12 month low', and it kept rolling, 'more than £1.2trillion erased in share value globally'. How could I have missed this?

World markets were collapsing and I'd been busy living it up, partying like it was 1999. It was probably just as well. There wasn't much else to do, except perhaps storming onto the streets in a fear driven frenzy. But that would accomplish nothing and only result in mass public panic. And governments across the globe knew that. That was why, for three years, they had been reluctant to admit to the actual extent of the problem, and it was spreading like wildfire, infecting every economy. At first it was just a slow down. Then it was stagnation. It was only a matter of months before they had no choice but to use the 'r' word – recession. No-one had yet dared to use the right word that would fit the bill. Depression.

As usual, the people at the top weren't going to be affected. Banks and their top employees were still being paid obscene bonuses, despite having created the problem in the first place. Politicians from all sides were still raking in the dough, while making cuts to the wages of other public servants. 'We have a strategy' they kept telling us. It's a commonly accepted belief that no-one in politics will ever tell the whole truth. And it was out there now, ugly and naked. There was no solution. The brakes had failed, the wheels had come off and what we had to accept was that this was a runaway that was going to crash and burn. Like any out of control locomotive, it presented a threat to anyone crossing the tracks.

But this was no concern of mine, for the simple reason that it we had gone beyond the point of no return. We'd passed that point fifty years ago when banking cartels and government institutions colluded to allow financiers to value all national assets and currency through centralised banking and racked up debts beyond human understanding. Yet it was equally right to say that all was not lost. None of the great disasters in human history had wiped us out as a species. All it would take was a handful of intellectuals who could think outside the box. If it was examined logically, people would quickly realise that just as we'd created the entire system out of thin air, we could make it vanish out of existence through collective acceptance that it *was* all an illusion from start to finish.

However, this is not an easy thing for your average sane person to accept. Sane people could only handle digesting increments of spoon-fed information. No rational human being would *want* to think for themselves. It would take up too much valuable time and effort. As we'd all been harshly brainwashed into believing, time was money. That was why the internet provided pan-handled bite sized chunks of content, fast geared spokes turning in a computerised domain. The birth of social networking sites offered Joe Public the opportunity to say whatever he or she wanted across the limitless void of cyberspace. Thoughts were wired from nation to nation and the best we could do with it, was to transmit recipes for dip across continents.

I switched channels on the television as the repetitive scrolling and breaking news screens were becoming tedious. I caught the end of a Jeremy Kyle Show rerun. The central topic was alcoholism, which kept being referred to as a 'disease'. Cancer was a disease, Chlamydia was a disease. Alcoholism was a desire; a need that burned through your liver and into the soft squishy part of your brain. You lusted for it; ached for it; until you felt it coursing through your every vein and artery.

Viewing trash TV made me thirsty. I scooped out some ice-cubes from the freezer tray in the kitchen and popped them into a small tumbler, pouring Southern Comfort over them. I could hear the cracking as the ice soaked up the liquor. It had been an eventful but tiring day. I gulped down the sweet liquid in the glass and reloaded it. I flicked through the newspaper I bought the previous day. The most interesting story, aside from the phone hacking scandal, was about President Barrack Obama turning fifty. Jennifer Hudson was signed up and set to sing at the Aragon Ballroom for his birthday bash. He was said to be looking forward to the festivities despite having just dodged the bullet on the agreement to raise the debt ceiling, which could have led to the first default in American history.

The plight of hungry children in Sudan was given little more than a small caption at the bottom of the eighth page. The war torn region of Darfur was being ripped apart by armed conflict, kids were losing their upper limbs and legs and the biggest thing that we had to worry about in the west was whether or not we'd be able to keep paying our debts and taxes; which went toward waging further wars and purchasing more arms. You couldn't make it up. It was an utterly abhorrent state of affairs. The more you saw of it, the sicker it made you. If you started out mentally balanced, the chances were that you'd end up bat-shit crazy by the end of your term on this upside-down rock. In all the millennia that we'd spent on our planet, we hadn't outgrown our capacity to kill each other. Here we were floating through the cosmos, fucking up almost everything we got our grubby human hands on.

By three o'clock the bottle was empty. I was sufficiently drunk enough not to be pained by the awfulness of the truth and with any luck, the slew of world events would be erased from the memory centres of my mind. I swayed around the carpeted floor in the living room for a while as the room started spinning. I heard a distant voice shrieking and sobbing in fits of uncontrollable rage. No doubt another desperate refugee escaping the earthly confines of a self-effacing existence.

21. Keys To The Kingdom - United We Fall

It was an encouraging sign that after 48 hours of intravenously injecting a Southern Comfort into my system, I was still alive. They say you should treat your body like a temple and I did, regularly cleansing it with alcohol. But I was going to need a bucket full of Aspirin, a defibrillator and a possible brain transplant to zap me out of my comatose state. My head was pressed firmly against the velvet softness of the carpet. I didn't want to get up, figuring it to be a lazy Saturday. But my throat was dry and an unhealthy cough erupted from my lungs. Catarrh shot up like froth inside a cappuccino maker. I spent the next twelve or so minutes hacking violently in the bathroom and another ten shitting a never-ending stream of liquidised crap in between bouts of freakish flatulence.

Finally, having regained control of my bowels and my lucidity, I turned the tap on for the showerhead. A steam spewing jet-stream spurted out, gushing down the drain with a sort crackling, sloshing sound. I stepped in and watched the warm water bounce off my skin. The advantages of being follically challenged were many, one of which was the fortune I saved on shampoo. The soap had congealed on the shelf next to a small bottle of Old Spice aftershave and it took all my sapped strength to lift it out. I gave myself a quick once over and rinsed before stepping onto the bathmat to dry off.

My stomach was growling like a wild wolf in the wilderness. I thought about making some toast; but I remembered that I no longer had a toaster and that my fridge was virtually empty, except for three oranges, a brown banana and a red apple. A fruit salad seemed the best option. I put on a clean pair of chinos and a blue t-shirt, throwing the previously worn clothing into the washing machine. It was an old model and both its feet were damaged. It danced around the kitchen, jumping off the linoleum like James Brown. Fortunately, the hoses that connected at the back were long enough to avoid causing any flooding from leaks. The lady downstairs frequently complained about it, but I didn't have the money to replace it, besides which it made laundry day all the more exciting. A previous girlfriend once had the idea of having sex on it, but that would have been as dangerous as trying to ride a bronco in a Texas rodeo. Given the likelihood of serious injury, I discouraged her from attempting such a thing and instead suggested making love on top of an old fifty-six inch television set. The hotter it got, the more it hummed and the more she got off on it.

I raided the fridge and grabbed a small knife from the cutlery drawer. The banana and apple were easy to cut up, but the logistics of trying to chop an orange into solid chunks proved difficult, so I carved each one into eight even slices, as a sort of accompaniment to the bowl of fruit. If a nutritious breakfast was the cornerstone of a healthy lifestyle, then I was surely a picture of perfect health, a poster-child for a balanced diet.

After eating, I took a handful of small coins from the small change tin next to the front door and went to the shop across the road. I had just enough for a pack of cigarettes, chewing gum and a newspaper. The pot-bellied rotund man who ran the store was always grateful for my custom and he greeted me in his usual cheery manner. We spoke for a short while about the dreadful state of the economy. He seemed confident that it would pass quickly and that it was little more than a storm in a tea-cup, whipped into a whirlwind by the media. I was not so sure. I paid him and left before the subject got heavy. The last thing I wanted to do was impact on his inspiring world view.

Back in my flat, I glanced at the front page and let out a whimper after reading the headline. On the evening of Saturday the 6th of August mass riots took place across London. It started in Brixton after police officers had shot and killed Mark Duggan on the 4th of that foul month. I'd heard something mentioned about it on the 24 hour rolling news station, but I didn't really pay it all that much attention.

Little normally came of these kinds of things. The police were often responsible for a raft of violations, most of them legal. Stop and search powers had been increased to disproportionate levels since the Terrorism Act had been passed, the right to protest had been curbed and even when things took a turn outside of the realms of moral decency, they somehow managed to cover each others backs. They were beyond reproach. The death of Ian Tomlinson had already demonstrated that. We, the people, had to like it or lump it. But *something* had changed.

I read on. The police had released statements implying that Mr Duggan had fired shots at the officers in question, which the family had adamantly maintained was outside the boy's character. On the 6th, they held what started out as a peaceful protest, asking only for justice and honesty from the police. As the evening wore on, around two-hundred people gathered to join them in their quest, demanding to speak directly to an appropriate senior officer who could answer their questions. But their demands were not met. The situation intensified and escalated when more people joined the cause. A few had weapons and violence inevitably broke out. Rioting and looting soon took hold and random acts of destruction became the language of an unheard crowd. Arson and intimidation were the verbs they used to get their anarchic point across. The public at large found themselves becoming victims, caught in the crossfire.

Eventually it all descended into complete chaos and any message there was got pulped and sifted amidst the angry masses baying for blood. But just who or what they were attacking remained unclear. What was becoming more obvious by the minute was that they were now running loose, untamed and feral, like a pack of jackals, searching for nothing more than devastation as an end in itself.

Fear was a dangerous thing. People did a lot of stupid things out of fear; or didn't do the things they should. Courage and strength were what made life worth living. No-one should settle for less. But in this case, the police were afraid, the rioters were afraid and neither side was prepared for the consequences of their respective actions.

That evening, I watched the carnage unfold as live pictures and video footage were transmitted to a frightened nation. The leaders of the country were nowhere to be found, sunning themselves on sandy beaches on their all expenses paid vacations, funded by the average taxpayer. The riots had spread beyond London's city limits. Birmingham, Nottingham, Leicester, West Bromwich, Wolverhampton, Bury, Liverpool, Manchester, Rochdale, Salford, Sefton and even Wirral were all ablaze in the fires of disenchanted youth.

The looting, pillaging and thuggery reminded me of all the fun times of my own formative years. The sad truth was that when young people had no future to look forward to, and no other outlet for their frustrations, they descended to the level of dumb brutes. I knew this all too well from my own experiences. All they *really* needed, was to have their heads stomped on, adults who give a fuck about where they were at 2am on a school night, and a decent chance at an education that could lead to a constructive life. These were things that were being taken away from them through the austerity measures being implemented in many countries. Parents couldn't focus on their children because they were busy breaking their backs for bread, teachers in classrooms couldn't teach because their resources were shrinking and the jobs market was saturated with overqualified applicants from previous generations, who were also struggling with unemployment.

When statements were finally made by some talking heads in the government, they said it was imperative that the state come down hard on those responsible for this loutish behaviour. It was 'terrorising' the good people of the United Kingdom. They would outlaw this 'criminality'. Their own, particularly during the expenses scandal was of no consequence. These bastard youth had to be caught and caged. To me, this seemed a reasonable course of action. After all, no sane human being would advocate this kind of heinous perversion. They were turning entire cities upside down.

Justice had become a joke. We all knew that the course of the great lady would change from that day forth. She'd been stripped of her blindfold and whored to overlords who could afford her. She was lost to those who used to hold her in their hearts; no longer fit for worship. By Vatican standards, she was an unclean harlot. This was the British Nightmare in all its glory. Divided we stood; united we'd fall: one nation under law enforcement.

There was only so much of it a man could see before it shattered his soul and made him into a permanent vegetable. In all the noise and panic, people had entirely forgotten about the real victims, who'd lost their son to a sequence of miscalculated judgement calls and exaggerated half-truths. The relatives of Mark Duggan were set to feel the pain of their loss for the remainder of their natural lives.

A great civil rights leader had once said "I have no mercy or compassion in me for a system that will crush people and penalise them for not being able to stand up under the weight." It was as true today as it was in his day. The Duggan family had come under the wheels of a rigid system allowing for disgraceful deceit. The sheer amount of skull-fuckery in this world knew no bounds. Birds did it, bees did it, authorities did it and even the occasional prime minister did it. I wondered if there was any room left for straight-talking men of moral character.

I switched off the scenes of public disorder on the television and sat quietly in contemplation. I couldn't get the images out of my mind; they were stuck there, like a love-child borne from the loins of Tony Blair and Barbara Bush. You know you don't want it to be real; you keep hoping that you'll wake up and find out that it was all just a horrible dream. But sadly, the reality was sometimes worse than any morphine induced hallucination, and you simply had no choice but to deal with it. This was not something our trusted leaders did well. They were not used to seeing things as they were; they were used to seeing things that never were and convincing themselves of their reality was true. They'd never been faced with a problem of this magnitude.

Meanwhile, the very fabric of our society was disintegrating. Something had to be done. But no-one could say what that was. No half-measures were going to work. The only sure way to fix the machine of normality was to rip out its guts, re-invent it and replace every rusty cog that had clogged it up with sticky-fingered thievery and candy coated promises. Everywhere you looked the cloak of darkness was draped around an infernal figure, crooked as the u-bend of a blocked toilet and just as eager to erupt their sewage over the unstained general population.

My cerebral cortex was overloaded with dismal undertones that pierced my inner bubble of calmness. I was too rattled and hung-over to cope with the full extent of the events that had transpired. Below the belt punches where coming from all directions, with a speed not seen since the Boxing bouts of Muhammad Ali, and the whole country was feeling it. We just weren't ready for the kind of demented activity that was sweeping the land.

I couldn't sit there lamenting the state of the nation. It was too far gone to be saved. No method of CPR could bring it back from the brink. It was taking its last dying breaths. The unique thing about the death of a country is that it conforms to the Buddhist ideas relating to the circle of life. By that philosophy, dying was simply a precursor to rebirth, and with a country, this process could be witnessed firsthand through the decades.

The computer bag in the corner caught my eye. It was stuffed next to the television. I had told Rollie I'd bring it over and that moment seemed as good a time as any. I didn't really feel like spending another day by myself. Especially with everything that was going on. He'd be home by now and I was sure that he wouldn't turn away a friend bearing a gift; or at least the loan of a laptop. I opened up the bag and examined the contents carefully. The computer whirred as I hit the power button and it went through the motions, loading up the installed software and displaying the welcome screen proudly across its 14inch monitor. It was in working condition alright. I scrolled through the menu with the touch-pad and clicked on the shut-down option. When it finally clicked off, I packed it away again.

It was 8pm and the minutes had just frittered away on that particular Sunday evening. It was a curious phenomenon. There were some days that seemed unending; there was always something that needed doing and never quite got done. Then there were some that passed so fast, you barely recall where they started. Sometimes even weeks merged from one to the next, but those were rare.

The buses were all running a Sunday service and there was no assurance that they would be as reliable as they were through the rest of the working week. I called my usual cab company and told them I needed a taxi to Bearsden. The lady on the other end of the phone made idle conversation while she radioed it through. Had I heard the news she asked. Wasn't it just awful what was happening down in England.

"Yes, it's terrible," I said. She sensed that I didn't want to talk about it and said that a car was on its way.

When I got to Rollie's two large garbage bins were blocking the entrance. They were empty, having just been collected that morning, so it easy to move them to the side of the close. I rang the buzzer for his flat in the rhythmic tone of 'help me Rhonda'.

"What!" screamed the voice on the intercom.

"Rollie you old bastard, open the damned door you degenerate! It's me."

"Max? Yes of course. Come on up!"

Rollie lived three stories up and I never looked forward to tackling that never-ending series of staircase. He'd chosen to live there on purpose, thinking that it would help keep his heart healthy and increase his fertility. I was always surprised by his ability to leap over small steps in a single bound. He was fitter than I was and he had the arteries of a twelve year old. My own on the other hand, were clogged with stale cigarettes and thick buttered rolls.

There on his sofa sat Trisha Patterson. Trisha was a curvaceous and beautiful young woman, as full bodied as any corkscrewed red wine. I drank in her image while she rolled a joint on a Rolling Stones vinyl LP cover. Her strawberry blonde hair stopped just past her shoulders. Curiously, with Trisha, I'd never managed to muster the words or the courage to ask her out. The furthest I'd gotten was some lame line about how great she looked in red.

I handed Rollie the laptop and we spent a few moments going through the various bits and bobs inside the bag. He was in no rush to test it and offered me a glass of Glenmorangie. The TV was on in the background but Rollie had the sound turned right down. Rollie's other half Gina came through from the study. They had been going steady for a while and everyone talked about how the two seemed made for each other. I was glad for Rollie, but a part of me felt a sense of sadness at never having experienced that sort of love. I'd long ago come to the conclusion that a man like me was destined never to find it. But Rollie always said that it often arrived when you least expected it. Maybe he was right.

The whiskey went down smoothly and I helped myself to another dram while live coverage of the riots continued to be broadcast on TV. We all lowered our heads, unwittingly synchronous, unable to bring ourselves to say anything. Rollie was never lost for words, but even he knew that on this occasion, there was nothing to be said that would take away from the unbelievable horror that we were faced with. There was only one thing to do; deny it was actually happening. Trisha was the first to speak.

"They shouldn'ae huv shot that wee boy in the first place. That was a pure shame how he died. He didn'ae need tae."

She was right. There was no reason why this vile chain of dangerous negativity had to begin. All it would have taken was some rational thought from the authorities and they would have realised that, like they often espoused to the general public, honesty was the best policy. But the sad truth was, we'd become so accustomed to being dishonest that it was really the only thing we expected anymore.

"Trish, you know better than anyone that life is less than fair. Good people die, bad people prosper. There's no method in the madness. Aren't you the one that talks all the time about how animals get slaughtered by the billions for the sake of corporate greed? It's no different when it comes to our own kind really. We suck as a species," I said.

Trisha was a child of the eighties, raised by hippy generation parents stuck in the 60's. She was an avid environmentalist, vegan and a noted poetess with a big heart and a bigger mind. She'd seen a lot in her life, coped with most of it, hurt from some of it and generally managed to come out the other end wiser and stronger for it. She was about the most normal human being I knew. Normal, but not boring. She had a lot to say on a whole lot of things. We'd argued many a time over opposing views on a range of things, including my man-crush on Hemingway (who she felt was a misogynist) to my daily meat-eating orgies. It was safe to say I liked her a lot but never had the guts to tell her. After all, why would any decent girl take any kind of interest in a certifiable lunatic like me.

"Yeah. I know, but don't ye just wish sometimes that life would cut us all some slack? I mean naene ae us asked tae be here, or tae be intelligent lifeforms like. Since we are, ye'd think we'd all be given the same smarts tae know naw tae kill each other."

"That's true," said Gina. "Rollie and I were talking about this just yesterday. All the wars and that. There's been so many for no good reason. World War I, World War II, Korea, Vietnam, Iraq, Afghanistan and now Libya."

Rollie added his two cents worth. "Yes, but darling, you're forgetting one thing. There's a very good reason behind them all: profit. We, and when I say 'we' I mean the

British Government, make a lot of money selling arms to both sides of any conflict. Then of course there's the construction contracts and oil contracts and all sorts of deliciously devious things that bring in the dough."

I couldn't fault his logic. He was right about the wars. Except this was different. This wasn't about war or making money. This was full throttle lawlessness brought about by errors in judgement. There was nothing to be gained from any of it on either side.

"But these riots Rollie, they're not profiting anyone. I think it boils down to our inherent nature to kill and destroy ourselves," I replied.

"Are you sure about that Max?" he said. "The looting *is* about money, the lack of it at least; the haves being targeted by the have nots."

22. The Terrifying Formless Shape of Tomorrow's Child

"Well, they're certainly sowing the seeds of their own demise. Do you remember the student protests last year? That kid on a wheelchair got dragged across the street and beaten by the cops. Every time they step over the mark, they keep expecting nothing to happen. This time something happened."

"Yeah. I almost wish I was with them," said Rollie.

"We're too old for that sort of thing. It's a game for cocky young roosters with Ipods who've stared at the jowls of Theresa May's bile addled face and lived to tell the tale. None of that horror for us matey. You won't catch us stealing toilet seats and Alba TVs," I said.

"If things don't cool off, they'll mobilise every policeman in Britain and they'll come down on them like a ton of bricks!" added Gina.

"Aye. We're in a right sorry state. Thank goodness nuffin' like 'ats happened up here in Scotland," said Trisha.

"Never say never," I said. "All that trouble could easily head up here if someone stirred us up. Let's just pray that doesn't happen"

Trisha lit up the spliff and passed it around. I took a good few puffs to calm my rattled nerves. Rollie switched off the TV and picked up the Rolling Stones album sitting on the arm of the couch.

"Shall I put this on? Better than watching that mind numbing drivel on the news about how awful those kids are."

We all nodded. Unlike me, when Rollie got angry over something, he'd become very quiet and stand there squinting at some unseen force in the ether, squeezing his fist until all the blood drained from his knuckles. I could tell he was quickly reaching this point when I saw his fingers curl into his hand. It wouldn't take much to send Rollie over the edge. He was one of those hardcore believers who didn't just dangle their legs over the precipice; they threw themselves down the cliff with all the intensity and power of a 747 jumbo jet.

He lined up the LP on the record player and set the needle onto the first track, 'Sympathy for the Devil'. Mick Jagger's vocals screeched at us in tin plated tones as we sang along. It wasn't really singing, it was more of a rabble, the combined out of tune attempts at trying to drown out the negative vibrations that had infiltrated our spirits. We were in a freefall of musical notes bouncing off the walls. Trisha's aura turned wild, fiery red and her arms were up in the air, saluting the Mongolian sky god Tengri. Gina got up and danced against Rollie in a riled sexual manner, not wanting to waste the potent angry energy that had been mustered earlier.

I swayed my head to the beat for a while before giving up on any hope of getting up. I was too mellow and didn't particularly want to change that. I opened a bottle of rum I'd stolen from Rollie's fridge and drank some more. Trisha was making eyes at me from across the room. The Hi-Fi scratched and crackled as it hit the end of the record. The three took a break from their exhilarating partying session and plopped down onto the beige sofa. Rollie and Gina cooed to each other in a sickening display of affection.

"Pass us the bucket!" said Trisha jokingly.

"I'll second that!" I said.

"What do you think missus? Shall we continue torturing these silly sausages?" said Rollie to Gina.

"Well guys, I'll let you two love birds get an early night," I said.

"No, stay my friend. We're not at all sleepy and we do so enjoy your company," said Rollie.

"Who said anything about sleep?" I said winking at Gina. "Enjoy yourselves you crazy kids!"

"How will you get home at this hour?" asked Gina. She had a point. It was eleven thirty and there was no hope of catching a bus on a Sunday night at this hour.

"I'll cab it as usual," I said.

"Listen, you're welcome to crash here Max. I'll share

a secret. This couch isn't just a couch. It's a sofa-bed!" said Rollie.

"That's very James Bond of you!" I replied. "But I really should get home. Besides, isn't Trish crashing here too? There's not enough space here for you to have two guests staying over."

"We can both take the sofa-bed. It's not a good idea for you to be alone when you're this drunk," said Trisha.

She seemed genuinely concerned about my well-being. But I wasn't overly inebriated and I'd in much worse shape many a time. Still, I felt rather comfortable at Rollie's and I didn't really fancy going back to an empty flat on a day like this.

"Well, alright," I said. "I'll take that offer. I appreciate it man."

"No problem young man. It's our pleasure to have you over. Now if you'll excuse us, me and the missus are going to retire for the evening. You and Trish make yourselves at home. There's blankets and bedding in the airing cupboard."

With Trisha's help I folded out the sofa-bed and grabbed a couple of pillows and some sheets from the cupboard.

"You prefer a side?" I asked Trisha.

"I don't mind. You?"

"I'll take the right. I prefer being next to the window. Probably sounds silly but I like being able to see the sky," I said.

She smirked and fired a pillow at my chest. I caught it before it hit the ground and placed it at the head of the spongy mattress. I laid down on the outer edge and Trisha took the left side, with an imaginary boundary line dividing us according to ancient rules of Victorian propriety. The truth was I was ill at ease in the company of a beautiful woman who I harboured deep and twisted feelings for at some subconscious level. Whether the horror of the day's events added to my anxiety, or whether it was the awful gut-wrenching pain of what I'd gone through with Kandy, I couldn't say. But whatever it was, I'd no sooner drifted off than I found Trisha shaking me awake and hovering over me with a look of genuine concern.

"Max! Max!"

"Jesus! God Almighty! What the hell is it woman?" I shouted.

"Oh my God, you worried the hell out of me. You were talking and crying in your sleep. Thank God you're okay."

"I was?" I said, noticing the cold sweat dripping down my back. "Sorry. It happens sometimes. I hope it didn't scare you too much."

"Nightmare?" she asked.

"Night-terrors," I replied.

"Oh," she said. "You should see someone about that."

"Yeah," I said. "Haven't had them since I was a child."

Her voice calmed my shaky disposition and her soothing gentleness eased my troubled soul. She held me tightly in her arms and my hand reached out to meet hers. It was as if Mother Mary had descended from heaven itself to answer my silent prayers. That was the closest I'd ever come to feeling loved. My inner animal was tamed; dormant; unable to claw its way out of the barren wasteland it had thrived in for so long. It didn't want to feed. It didn't want to fuck. It was rendered useless in the presence of this beautiful creature. Her head rested on my chest.

"I can feel your heart-beat," she said, as we both lost ourselves in a mist of dreams, happy and high.

I got up sometime around noon. Trisha was nowhere to be seen. Rollie had made brunch; French toast, poached eggs and salmon, along with a cup of Earl Grey. The plate on the coffee table was still warm. I performed my ablutions and stacked away the bedding back in the airing cupboard and folded up the sofa-bed. Gina strolled in, clad in a pink dressing gown.

"Glad to see you're up," she said. "Rollie's in the

study putting the finishing touches on his latest painting. I know he'd love your opinion on it."

"Oh okay," I replied. "Did Trish leave?"

"Yeah. She's rehearsing for that new play. Ah, the glamorous life of an actor!" she chuckled.

I was slightly disappointed, but also glad in a way. With daylight came a self-confidence that was not to be found in the darkness of night. I hurriedly ate breakfast and scoffed down the contents on Rollie's best china. I couldn't wait to see his artwork and the excitement showed. Gina switched on the TV. On the extended one o'clock news bulletin, they were discussing the aftermath of the recent wave of 'criminality'. There was that word again. There were no reported deaths, just a great deal of vandalism. I was sure that the powers that be were secretly conducting nightly rituals, sacrificing virgins to giant statues of Moloch, hoping that they could pin a few murder raps on some of the offenders. That would have given them a blank check for a blanket ban on chaos of any kind.

I took my tea with me to Rollie's study and knocked on the door three times in a coded sequence that only retired 33rd degree Freemasons could understand. "Abandon all hope if you're going to enter!" roared the voice on the other end. On entering, I stared at the startlingly fine crafted brushwork on the canvas for a few moments. Flaming embers of red danced around burning buildings and large batons next to bullet-proof shields. A blurred shapeless face stood smack-bang in the middle of it all, bound and gagged with a Union Jack flag.

"Well? What do you think?" asked Rollie.

"It's... Interesting," I said.

"Interesting? Just interesting?" he screeched, "I spent three weeks on this thing!"

"I mean its bloody fantastic!"

"But?"

"But I'm not entirely sure the world of British art is ready for this sort of thing," I replied.

"Not ready? Not bloody ready? They sodding well

should be! Pictures may still be worth a thousand words, but those words don't speak the truth anymore. They've had long enough to appreciate the work of cheap hacks like Picasso. Now they're must experience the full throttle excellence of Rollie Erlichman!" he said, waving his brush frantically.

"Yes I suppose so. I like it," I said as I watched him put the brush down next to the colour palette.

"So. You and Trish seemed rather cosy this morning," he said.

"It wasn't what it looked like. I mean there was nothing..."

"Relax Maxwell, I was just pulling your leg. Trish told me about your little episode last night."

I felt a little embarrassed. I wasn't sure why.

"You really should see someone about those night-terrors."

"Yeah. Trish said the same thing. It wasn't too bad last night. There have been worse. Like the time I sleepwalked into the middle of a road," I said.

"Holy Moses!" replied Rollie. "You've never told me about that."

"There doesn't seem much point in grudging up bad stuff, you know?"

"Yeah. I know what you mean. I've never spoken to anyone about Korea. Not the ex-wife, not even Gina. Some things are best left undisturbed."

"You served in Korea?"

"No. Vacation. It was terrible," he said.

I almost choked on my tea. Rollie had the gift of great timing with his jokes.

"Seriously though, yeah, I was a medic. Some of what I saw, the wounded on the battlefield. I don't think even hell itself could compare to it."

"Yeah. Well like you said, best left undisturbed," I said.

"You know, you and Trish would fit well together I think."

"Come on, knock it off Rollie. Quit playin' matchmaker. Besides, she deserves better than someone like me."

"Well, I'm just saying."

"Yeah. Well, listen, thanks for your hospitality and everything man. I really should get going though."

"Not a problem young man. I have to get over to the allotment myself later. Those tomatoes should be ripe enough to be plucked from the vines."

"Nothing better than a home grown red tomatoes," I added.

"Well they're not red. They're green. You know if you leave them in front of the window after picking them, they'll naturally turn red. Makes them juicier too."

"That I did not know," I replied

"Are you good for bus fare?"

"Yeah," I said. "I've got plenty of change."

I delved into my trouser pocket to make sure this was the case. I'd been caught short a few times on buses and found myself without he necessary money or a even a ticket. Twice the driver had taken pity on me and let me on free of charge, once he'd grabbed me by the scruff of my collar to throw me off. It took me three hours to walk home that day and by the end of it, my legs were like jelly. I didn't want to take that risk again.

Gina and Rollie saw me to the door, bid me goodbye and thanked me again for loaning them the computer. I hopped down the stairs, re-energised with a new-found sense of optimism and sprung into street like a Canadian jack-rabbit with laser light speed, ready to run from a pack of cannibal aardvarks. The bus stop was just at the corner at the end of the road. The double decker was twenty minutes late, which irked me. It wasn't like I had anywhere to be or any kind of important deadline, but I was buzzing with impatient energy and I just wanted to get back to familiar territory.

I grabbed a copy of the free newspaper from the secure bundle next to the drivers cabin. The troubles in

London were making front page news, with grainy images of offenders splashed across almost every page. The headline read 'Olympic Ambassador Accused of Riot Attack'. The story continued on page two,

'A Teenage girl who is an Olympics ambassador hurled bricks at police during rioting in London this week, a court was told yesterday. The teenager, described as a 'talented sportswoman' was caught on camera by the BBC allegedly throwing bricks at a police car during disturbances in Enfield, north London. The girl is one of the Olympic volunteers who put themselves forward to help out at the Games next summer. She has met the London Mayor Boris Johnson, Olympics chief Sebastian Coe and visited the House of Commons to celebrate a football project run by a local community sports program. Her mother spotted her daughter on a television broadcast and immediately called the police. She said the decision to report her daughter was 'gut-wrenching', adding 'I had to do what was right'. The teenager was refused bail and will appear in magistrates' court in five days time.'

23. The Lion, The Witch & The Warthog

I got off at the stop on Paisley Road West near Cessnock underground station. The wind was beginning to pick up and I shivered a little from the cooler air. A few heavy clouds were blocking out the sun, with no breaks so I could warm myself in its heat. I wasn't sure if it was going to rain or remain relatively dry. It was impossible to tell which way the weather was going to go on a day like this. I'd seen all four seasons in the space of three hours on similar days the previous year.

The newspaper was wedged under my arm. I hadn't gotten to the funny pages and was looking forward to seeing the daily antics of my favourite cartoon caricatures that were all too real and visible in every walk of life. From the post man delivering mail, to the lollipop lady helping children cross the road; all hollow husks trying desperately to recapture the faded glory of their prime. I wondered which straw broke the camel's back. What had made them into such willing and woeful servants of the state? Muddling through, getting by, eating more, drinking less; like good sheepdogs obeying the whistle of the punch-clock. Every so often, for a brief moment, you saw a spark - a funny joke, a kind word, some sense of righteous indignation - and then lost again. Did you imagine it? Did it really happen?

Yesterday's news quickly became today's chip paper, smeared on garbage cans; the sickly smell of glazed sauce and rotting fish. I could see the stains from dried puke-ridden take-out trays, propped up against a lamp post on the blood-spattered pavement. The inevitable result of drunken arguments, multiple stab wounds and an endless barrage of belligerent grown-ups defeated in the challenge of making it from dusk till dawn; unable to live, unwilling to die. Along came the street sweeping machine, wiping away the muck and sucking up the guts of local hard men who thought they'd have a go at spinning the wheel of fortune; try their luck. Their number was up. Old lottery tickets littered shop doorways - too small to be hoovered into the bowels of the green guzzler.

I turned a corner and plodded along until I came upon Brand Street. There was a small delicatessen a few blocks to the left that served excellent coffee and terrific sandwiches, not that I was hungry. But I thought it only sensible to buy a few eats and treats for later. The man behind the counter was dressed in a white apron, gloves, a pork pie hat and a pair of goggles. I wasn't sure why, but I assumed it had something to do with hygiene rules. The health and safety fad had stemmed from an imported American compensation culture. People were suing for anything they could get away with; from hair in their hamburgers to lewd remarks by antiquated misogynists.

In the eighties, during the Regan/Thatcher era, it'd been drilled into us, 'Greed Is Good'. There was no mention of the price of it all. No talk of the pitfalls. The human cost had been completely ignored. The yuppies had been bred for financial warfare and were armed with trouser braces and a filofax. But here we were, in 21st Century Britain, where privatised utility companies could charge record prices for our energy needs. There was no adequate competition like we'd been told. Whoever controlled wholesale prices controlled the world. The old and infirm were hit hard each winter, unable to afford to pay the extortionately high bills, and many opted to avoid incurring the wrath of the merciless greed oriented companies by going without heating in the harsh cold. The ever increasing number of fatalities from these circumstances should have concerned us as a society. But the rest of us were too busy trying to keep the wolf from our own doors. Straw houses for straw men and women, easily blown down by the huffing, puffing big suits in sheep's clothing. In the past, we'd gotten through tough times by tightening our belts, wearing hand-me-downs, and huddling with entire families in one room. But the children of the modern age had been weaned on the tit of avarice. They weren't used to these sorts of traumatising scenes. They were used to five meal days with excess enough to throw away. They'd come to expect the finest designer threads.

And why not? Thanks to us, seriously wealthy executives could afford to fly around in private jets and sail in luxury yachts with their wives and mistresses. But they didn't get to have all the fun. For the better part of twenty years, it had become customary for the fat cats to offer drippings to the poor. And we put them to good use. Nike and Lacoste were our answer to their Versace and D&G. Where they drank the finest sixty year old single malts, we made do with supermarket brand poly blends. Where they hired expensive hookers with supermodel looks, we were happy with regular streetwalkers who gave every customer a dose of the clap free of charge. It was safe to say that we got the better end of that deal. We didn't have to worry about the market value of our stock portfolios; or think about being caught with our pants down in the middle of a secretarial fuck session. We were already being bummed silly by the rich and powerful. Our pants were firmly lodged around our ankles and we knew damned well we had no hope of ever pulling them back up.

"Do you want mayonnaise on this chicken sandwich?" asked the guy behind the counter.

"Huh? Oh yeah. Can you add in some onions, tomatoes and lettuce?" I replied.

"Sure. Anything else?"

"Oh yeah, a cup of coffee to go too please."

"What kind?"

"Just a regular coffee. Lots of cream, lots of sugar."

"No problem. That'll be three fifty."

I took out a crisp five pound note from my wallet, feeling the porous paper between my fingertips. It seemed a shame to have to spend it. Crisp notes were a rarity, especially ones issues from the Bank of England. The queen's face stared up at me disapprovingly as I handed him the money. He counted out the change into my palm and gave me the sandwich, wrapped in several sheets of greaseproof paper. The coffee caddy spluttered before letting out a stream of coffee and steam. I watched him pour in the cream and seal the polystyrene cup. He threw some sachets of sugar over the glass counter and I gathered them into a bundle before stuffing them into my back pocket. I thanked him and left, heading back toward Cessnock.

The underground was the logical option. There was no sense in waiting for another bus when I could just as easily catch one on the other side. I paid the cashier behind the screen and she passed me a printed ticket. I went through the turnstiles and down escalator. A few minutes later, a gust of air hit me and I saw two bright lights emerging from the dark tunnel. I stepped into the middle compartment and sat down next to the sealed pneumatic doors. The train jutted forward and gathered speed, whooshing along the track. Three stops later, I arrived at Govan.

There was a bus stop directly outside the station. I didn't feel much like walking home and I'd only have to wait ten minutes before the next twenty-six service would grace me with its presence. Several people were already gathered there, also intent on catching the same bus. I realised I was almost out of change when it arrived. The driver was clearly annoyed by my fumbling for money. I paid him and scrambled toward the middle of the bus, taking the seat next to the emergency exit. I didn't like holding up the line of other passengers, but I was sure they understood that it wasn't intentional. Luckily, I had the advantage of sitting next to that special lever, in case the urge to escape took hold. We got under way and I relaxed my grip on the handle.

A fat old woman with tanned leather skin hobbled aboard and spoke curtly to the driver. Another younger, fair-haired lass had already climbed on and was struggling to find space for her belongings. I heard a few familiar words. Evidently the elder woman was of Arab origin. She seemed agitated and jostled past the other passengers before plopping down opposite the young girl; who I deduced was a music student because of the cello case she had with her. The formidable prune faced woman snorted and spewed forth a slew of verbose utterances, which I assumed were not polite because of her demeanour and tone. The girl seemed deeply offended, especially at the few sparse words of English being thrown at her. "British" and "prostitute" stood out and were enough to light the fuse on an already volatile situation. The girl exploded with an angry tirade of her own, laced with shocking profanity in true Glaswegian form. This dual between dialects continued for the better part of ten minutes. I could understand the girl's frustrations. She was dealing with a sort of reverse racism. The rest of us quietly watched the spectacle of a bloated warthog crushing a weaker piglet, who by then was on the verge of crying.

It was a most unfair situation, to be sure, but I'd witnessed similar scenes before. When I was about thirteen, an acquaintance of my father's visited our home and persuaded me to attend a presentation by a Muslim preacher at a local mosque. He felt it would 'cleanse my soul of its impurity'. I'd always been prone to the delights of wine, women and song and these were all strictly forbidden by Islamic law. I went along to the supposed seminar to learn a little about my father's belief system. Instead what I got was a treatise on the evils of Jews. I promptly left; disgusted by the debased teachings of what should have been the bedrock that sprang great poets like Bulleh Shah and Nusrat Fateh Ali Khan. The implication of their ethos meant that I, by default, had to hate my own mother because she was Jewish, and this contradicted one of the fundamental tenants of both faiths; honour thy father and thy mother. I was more than aware that I was not personally living up to that with my wayward behaviour, but to be told by power mad preachers that you should pray for the destruction of all Jews because 'God willed it' seemed stupid; even to my young and impressionable mind. But this sort of poison was being injected into the brains of countless kids on many fronts. Israeli children were being taught to hate Palestinians and extremist Christians were teaching their progeny to hate Muslims, Jews and atheists.

But this was not a problem exclusive to foreign lands. Across Glasgow, Rangers fans frequently told their bairns that Celtic fans were the enemy and vice versa. Their dispute wasn't down to skin tone or religion per say, but down to the Catholic, Protestant divide, which coloured the football field red with the blood of numerous fans, orange and green alike. Wearing the wrong scarf or t-shirt in the wrong part of town would ensure you got spat on and perhaps even 'chibbed' by some glue sniffing moron, who had about as much respect for the beautiful game as the Nazis did for art: they stole it for their own vile ends instead of appreciating the form and talent behind it.

The two women were still bickering on the bus and in all the excitement, I missed my stop. I thought about getting off at the next one, but I remembered that we would be passing by the shopping centre on this route and I needed a new pair of shoes, so I stayed on. My red converse sneakers were worn out and liable to come apart at some inopportune moment. This would not have been good. Running around the city barefoot was not a smart thing to do. Broken glass bottles were laying in wait at every corner and outside every pub. Once, I'd stepped on a shard by accident when, in a drunken frenzy, I ran across a road without any footwear; all for the sake of a dare. The twenty pounds I won was no compensation for the three weeks I spent limping, shot up with every drug known to man. Then there was the battery of tests, tetanus shots and indestructible titanium crutches that followed. I felt like Lee Majors; the Six Million Rupee Man.

By the time we reached the mall, the cello sporting girl had gathered her stuff and was ready to flee. She'd turned bright pink and I could almost see the steam coming out of her ears. I was worried that her head might pop off her shoulders in a David Cronenberg styled display of animated intensity. I hung back until she was some way down the pathway before I too left the toxic atmosphere aboard the bus.

I could see the car park, full of large automobiles. People were rushing from all directions, going... somewhere. I bopped up to the big glass revolving door and breezed through to the air-conditioned sanctum of consumerism. 'Sale' signs were plastered across windows and even inside the stores. At the end of the walk of death, stood the mega chain that produced cheaply priced clothing and footwear. Sweatshop child labour was giving us bargain basement deals on quality goods. I wasn't going to complain about it; necessity took precedence over moral outrage. Hanging up, next to a pair of Batman pyjamas, were a pair of black converse trainers, at the reasonable discounted price of five pounds. That five pounds would go toward the $500trillion dollar debt we'd racked up on the national credit card. I was single-handedly saving the economy and it felt great.

The cashier rung it up on the till machine and put the shoes into a large brown paper bag, lettered with the company logo across its width. The workers here didn't appear to be any more content with their day jobs than their counterparts in central Asia. Living corpses with robotic responses. Most were students, stuck in dead-end no-brain positions to pay for that prized education. That was the toll they had to pay to get into the fast lane, next to Easy Street, where greased up geese laid five figure golden eggs. But these were pie-in-the-sky notions that would see them churning out till receipts for the rest of their natural lives, like Burmese whores past retirement age, turning tricks for six quid an hour. Overpopulation and rising birth rates meant that they were already beyond help. Move over Jack, there's new kids on the block; come on old timer, make room for the next batch of snot-nosed gremlins. I looked up at the pimple faced boy and he stared back at me with empty eyes; motionless, like a dolls eyes.

"Your change, sir. Next!" he shouted.

I walked away, not completely satisfied, but I'd gotten what I wanted. Wham, bam, thank you ma'am. The security guard was hovering over the men's clothing section like a squirrel guarding its nuts from thieves in the night. I adjusted my belt buckle and passed through the tag detectors. I had nothing to fear. I was, after all, a paying customer. But sometimes those damned detectors went off for no good reason and it was all too easy for an innocent bystander to end up in a holding cell for shoplifters. This didn't happen and I was glad to be spared from going through that kind of trial. Courts across the country were releasing the guilty with little more than a slap on the wrist and maybe, at worst, a little prison time. Behind bars you were given access to a colour television, three square meals and a warm dry cell with an en-suite bathroom. Corporations were not so humane. In the eyes of their fine-lens cameras, you were guilty until you proved your innocence.

The banking system was the absolute embodiment of this. Ethereal entities that could deny you the right to your life-savings at the stroke of a pen. By their will, you were penalised for small transgressions. If you had a mortgage, they could take away your house and banish you to the lower rungs of the economic ladder. They had proclaimed themselves as gods in the place of Nietzsche's 'superman'. The laws of man couldn't change the commandments that came from up on high. It didn't matter that they held shares in the morally ambiguous territory of the arms trade, or that they laundered money for foreign governments intent on exporting real terrorism. They were beyond reproach. If Christ were alive, he'd have struggled to toss today's money changing temple tables. The face of El Diablo was on billboards and commercials everywhere; no longer hidden or possible to exorcise. These god-heads demanded our worship and our money, making Dick Turpin seem like a decent guy.

On leaving the store, I was greeted by a man holding a bucket and a badge. He was a friendly enough soul, but he was intent on getting a small donation from my cash-strapped self. I explained to him that I was one step away from chronic alcoholism and had no money to waste on charitable acts. I was tempted to quote a line from Dickens on work houses and orphanages, but instead I said, "Look man, stop pestering decent people. Rob the rich if you must, but don't feed on the poor."

This startled him as he was not used to this manner of direct speech. These kinds of fuckers were used to guilt-tripping ordinary working folk with pictures of poverty stricken children suffering from malnutrition in the third world. But I'd *lived* it. It wasn't anyone's fault except for the economic powers and despotic dictators, who had created the vile problem in the first place. In theory, they should have been the ones to put it right. Of course, since they had no intentions of doing so, it fell to us, the regular citizens to do something about it. Yet harassing the regular rag-tag team of shopping addicts wasn't really the answer. Folk like this bearded do-gooder meant well, but I couldn't help feeling that their focus was misdirected.

I'm sure in his mind, I was Satan incarnate for fobbing him off that way. He probably even wished that I'd be struck down by some preternatural karmic force. It took a lot of guts to do something about the horrors of this world and I admired him for that. I personally had never felt the obligation to do so. What I'd seen of human beings was nothing short of stomach churning vice and wretchedness. I'd often wished that we as a species would be obliterated by some passing comet or other. The only other thing in nature that took delight in the destruction and pain of others for the sake of its own survival was the single-celled microbial virus.

I left him to ponder these matters and continued on my way. The jewellery shops in the middle of the shopping centre had obscenely priced trinkets on display. Wedding rings, pendants and earrings, all waiting for the avaricious masses to scoop them up for the sole purpose of plundering their dearly beloveds most private recesses. This was how love was bought and sold in the world of the modern age. But hadn't it always been that way? Lust and gluttony disguised in the purity of romance. 'Unconditional' love with terms and conditions in the small print of the sales brochure; the marriage certificate. Couplings made and broken in an instant for pastures new, where the grass was greener, the field fuller. All for the magpie love of shiny slivers of gold and silver.

"Would you like some help sir?" asked a woman behind me.

Her svelte figure and bunched brunette hair made her a desirable choice of saleswoman. I was tempted to ask her to show me her wares, but I couldn't have afforded her expensive services. Although a quick glimpse wouldn't have been out of the question. The richer the woman, the more exotic her tastes.

"I was just looking," I replied. "Actually, perhaps you *can* help me... When do you knock off for lunch? "

"Well I was normally take it around now. Why?"

"I was hoping you might want to grab something to eat."

"I have a boyfriend."

"So? It's just lunch"

"I really shouldn't..." she said. "Okay. You're buying?"

"Always." I replied.

24. Melt Through My Fingers -
Baby, I'm A Man; Not Your Mister

The food court was packed to the rafters. The strong smell of greasy meat wafted through the air and the sound of sizzling deep fat fryers bounced off the hollow walls. Toddlers and their siblings squealed and shrieked as they played their childish games; much to the chagrin of the grown-ups. Meanwhile, beads of sweat poured from the brows of the hard working staff behind each service point. The queues were growing ever longer while customers expected them to put the 'fast' into fast-food. By the time my lady friend and I got to the front, the girl taking orders looked as though she'd been savaged in a house of ill-repute. The manager in the white shirt busied himself watching the fries crackle in the hot oil, twitching nervously like a man close to embarking on a shooting spree because his chips were undercooked.

I asked my companion what she wanted, making sure to ask if she was a vegetarian. She couldn't make up her mind, so I ordered a quarter-pounder with cheese on her behalf, along with a helping of orange soda and fries. We sat down and I watched her scoff the lot down in a matter of minutes. I'd barely unwrapped my sandwich by the time she'd finished. What was left of my coffee was stone cold, but I drank it anyway. This was not the most romantic of settings, but we weren't here to cultivate the affair of the decade. My plans revolved around some fast love to go with the fast-food. It was possible that she wasn't aware of my intentions, though this seemed unlikely given her willingness to spend her lunch hour in my company.

"So, what got you into the jewellery trade?" I asked her.

"I saw an ad for a sales-assistant and I applied. I love being surrounded by pretty sparkly things."

She didn't seem like a stuck up rich bitch. In fact, she came across as a thoroughly decent, down to earth sort of woman, who'd perhaps learned to mimic the traits of a high society girl, prim and proper; not a single hair out of place. Posh chicks turned me on. I found them to be the most debauched due to their sexually repressed upbringing. But this one was a mystery. She could go either way; an easily excitable damsel of devilish delight, or a mouthy maiden who swore like a sailor in heat. The only question that remained was the where.

"You know, you have the most delectable lips. I'll bet they taste like peach ice-cream. Would you let me have a little lick?"

"You shouldn't say things like that. I've told you already, I'm with someone,"

She didn't seem cross, nor did she leave in disgust. My instincts were proving to be correct.

"Of course you are dear-heart. But is it so terrible to explore the realms of possibility?"

"I can't believe I'm even doing this!"

"Doing what? Having lunch?"

"You know fine well! I don't even know your name. Mine is..."

"No. No names. Why spoil something special?"

By this point we were both feeling the electric lightening between our thighs. She squeezed my shoulder and stood up. I did likewise and I watched her take a step toward me. I circled around her and caressed her shoulder, kissed the nape of her neck and whispered into her ear.

We were all too aware that a public display of our wicked perversions would have been extremely indiscreet. She took me by the arm and guided me to an elevator used specifically by centre staff for transporting stock between floors. We stepped in and she pressed the button marked 'G2'. The doors closed and it began to ascend. Without warning, she pulled the emergency stop and latched onto my waist, peppering my chest with kisses. I responded in kind, almost ripping the clothes from her slim body. In a matter of moments, I was penetrating her slick venal entrance as she panted heavily in-between screaming obscenities that would have made Hugh Hefner blush.

Soon the two of us were engulfed in orgasmic pleasure and become lost in the rush of heart-pounding delectation. She composed herself and got dressed again while I zipped up my fly. She pushed the 'emergency' button again and the metal cage continued its journey up the elevator shaft.

When the doors re-opened, we found ourselves faced with three store clerks standing next to a pallet truck bound for the clothing shop on the lower level. Had we been caught 'In flagrante delecto? It was difficult to say, but we went our separate ways so as not to arouse suspicion and she dared not look at me for fear of recognising our morally reprehensible actions. Power was indeed an aphrodisiac. The whole time that she thought we were strangers, I'd read her name tag and knew more about her than she did of me. Knowledge was power and power corrupted. The supposed commitment to her relationship, her protestations of having a boyfriend, all came to nothing. Her desires melted through my fingers and when she'd objected, I allayed her fears, telling her that I was just a man; a ship passing through the night; not her 'mister'. He needn't know a thing about it.

Sated and calmed, I leaned against the railing across from the hand-made soap store and changed into the black converse sneakers in the brown carrier bag. They still had that pleasant, rubbery new shoe smell. I threw the old ones in a nearby trash can and walked out of the shopping mall. It occurred to me at that moment that there might have been a camera in the lift. I'd seen news segments a few times that showed how wired up technology had become. There were numerous occasions where people's indiscretions had been caught on camera in similar situations. If that were the case, then we'd provided some overweight doughnut munching security guard with some decent jerk-off material, destined for his bulging private collection.

As I walked out of the glass greenhouse, I realised that right across from the main complex was the largest computer and electrical goods store in the city. They sold everything from hard drives and miscellaneous components to whole built machines with processor speeds that boggled the mind. I thought it would be a good idea to take a look and report back to Rollie on any bargains that were to be had. The laptop I'd lent to him was an old decrepit thing, a relic of twentieth century engineering. He'd be needing something as a proper replacement, a contemporary feat of invention, with a processor speed that would make Einstein look like an amateur high school physics student.

The place made you feel like you'd walked through a portal into the future. Giant wall mounted LCD television screens looped non-stop ads for their products and services and fancy glass cabinets showcased the newest high-tech fads, stretched out as far as the eye could see, each aisle dedicated to a specific line. The extent to which superfluous items were being brought to market was shocking. Most were absolutely unnecessary but came with such a steep price tag that it made my head spin. They were the ultimate in spinal crackers; ridiculously useless things, deemed fashionable must haves for the ordinary worker, who bent over backwards to purchase them. Where there was a high supply, advertising created an artificial demand. It was a beautiful but deadly cycle for a nation of addicted shopaholics. There was no escape. The exits weren't clearly marked and even the check-out desks were blocked with automated bars. You *had* to buy something; anything. That was the price of freedom. But I didn't *need* any of it. This was considerably worse than the bucket wielding charity man.

I spent the remainder of my incarceration roaming the various sectioned rows. Nothing worthwhile caught my attention. For all the dazzling sights and sounds, it was just never ending rows of sameness. Some computers has see through cases for the geek voyeurs who were into that sort of thing, others had less memory, more memory, bigger buffer sizes, smaller storage capabilities and so on. There was no definitive model that was better than another. What would Rollie make if it all? How would he choose? Why was

I even attempting to gather information on these hideously complicated things? 'Best leave it to him,' I thought. Then again, it was entirely possible that at his age, he would have had a mental breakdown from this kind of sensory overload.

One fellow, kitted out in company uniform, came over to me and offered his help. He was an old dude with nicotine stained fingers and bad breath. Despite this handicap, I asked him to tell me which of these hundred or so machines was the most souped-up, top of the range, undisputed king of the technological jungle.

"Well sir," he said. "I don't think there is any computer in here that's necessarily *better* than the others. I could show you the latest one that just came in today. It's at the high end of the spectrum in terms of speed, power and reliability. It's a newer model from the one you were just looking at. Would you like to see it?"

"Sure," I said. "But do you have one that would do everything it does for less?"

"Ah, you're a shrewd customer aren't you sir!" he said. "But before I answer your question, can I ask, what would you be using it for primarily? Also, if I might also enquire, what sort of budget are we working with?"

We? *We* weren't working with any budget. What was he going to do, offer half his pay-check toward the cost?

"Well, I'm not actually looking to buy today. I was in the mall and thought I'd pop in and take a gander for a friend. His computer went the way of the dodo."

"Oh," he said, clearly disappointed by my response. "Well if you just wait here one moment, I'll get someone who'll be able to help you with that."

'Rude bastard!' I thought. It was obvious what had happened. He wasn't going to get his bonus from a fat sale today and he'd decided to pawn me off to one of his colleagues. It all came down to pounds and pennies. First, they'd persuade you to get the most expensive item they could sell you, and then they'd try to slide in the 'optional' insurance policy that had more holes in it than a tree infested with woodworm.

I waited a good fifteen minutes, but no-one else had bothered to show up, so I made a beeline toward the exit, which I had now worked out was just behind the cashier's desk. Sure that no-one was looking; I made my dash into the open air. Free at last! I went at a gentle pace in my not-quite broken in shoes. There was a travel information booth not too far away which had a dedicated phone for local taxis.

I watched a cavalcade of cars circling the car park, the drivers all praying to the parking-space angel in humbled mantras for an empty slot for their immaculately washed automobiles. It was at times like this that I was thankful I didn't have one. Not only was there the ever rising cost of tax discs and petrol to grapple with, but there was also never any guarantee that you wouldn't have to wedge it into a no parking zone, only to be towed away by some bitter old spinster of a traffic warden, who'd chosen your car in a fit of jealousy after sensing its sexually magnetic properties.

The lady in the information booth was twiddling her hoop earrings while she jabbered away with her boss, who was a portly fellow with a white moustache and little hair. I thought about taking a cab to Govan and picked up taxi hotline to ask their rates. They were cheap enough, but in a moment of absent mindedness, I forgot that I hadn't enough money on my person. I quickly hung up just as she was about to ask me for the address. I didn't want to be rude, it was just an impulsive reaction and I regretted it after setting the receiver down. It would have been better to thank her and politely say I didn't need one after all. The woman in the booth was no longer busy so I quizzed her on bus routes and timetables. She chewed on her gum while her eyes scrolled down the screen in front of her. The overhead halogen lamps shone off her skin. She'd applied too much make up that morning and her face looked more like a lipstick smeared prosthetic mask than flesh.

"There's two buses that pass by the stop just outside

this building. They'll take you where you need to go. There's the twenty-three and a wee local twenty one, but that terminates at Govan bus station. They come by every ten minutes or so."

"Thanks," I said, flashing a quick grin at her.

I waited at the bus shelter as she'd instructed me and stared out at nothing in particular. Voracious shoppers came and went and a few sat down next to me with bags full of goodies. I could see the clouds gathering in the horizon and the sky was getting darker. It was set to rain again. A young man who was also waiting for the same bus asked me for the time. I told him it was fast approaching four o'clock before sorting through my pockets to for the necessary bus-fare.

By 4.15pm the local bus had showed up and five other people queued up as the driver allowed them in. I let them go before me as I wasn't in any rush and they seemed overly burdened with their newly bought belongings, which would now help them feel that they did indeed belong. They were hip, part of the greater galaxy, the in-crowd. Generation Y was conforming to the preconceived edicts of old. Eat, drink and be merry. Fuck everyone else, shag them silly, dance the merry jig round the mulberry bush. Why fight the future brother? Flow with it, go with it, get loose, live big, die hard.

The rain splattered in thick specks against the Perspex window of the bus. It was more of a van really, but it did have the attraction of bolted down seats inside the battered up banger. It took all of about seven minutes of bumpy driving before I was standing across the road from my humble abode. I lit up a cigarette and smoked it under the cover of a tree. An old man and his dog strode past and stopped in front of me. The owner was busy reading his newspaper while his pet poodle grabbed a few stolen moments of whorish leg-humping with my left shin. I looked up at him, but he seemed unconcerned. I was sure that he knew exactly what his four legged friend was up to, he just didn't want to accept the ugly truth of it; or maybe he did, maybe he even encouraged it. But why was the dog fucking my lower leg? Did it on some level sense the mongrel mutt in me? I was, after all, a combined entity of so many parts that no singular segment defined the whole; half animal, half man.

The man and his scrotal scratching pet left as quickly as they'd arrived. I stubbed out my cigarette butt while the embers continued to flick off the ash and strolled toward my flat. I was glad to be out of the rain. Once inside, I kicked off my sneakers and noticed a plain post-marked envelope wedged into the letterbox. The postman must have been doing his rounds earlier. With the lack of mail in recent days, I had begun to wonder if he'd taken a brief sabbatical from his duties.

There was nothing on the back of it, no return address. I felt a strange sensation in the pit of my stomach and knew that its contents were not likely to be harbingers of anything good. I didn't typically receive letters like this. Most were official, bills or pay-cheques. I tore it open slowly, breathing in deeply to prepare for bad news. It was from Kandy.

"Dear Max,

Writing this letter has been the hardest thing I've had to do for a long time. I don't quite know how to tell you this, so I'll just come out and say it. I've met someone. Someone wonderful who makes me laugh and sing with joy. You were special. I mean that. Please don't call or write. I'm happy now. Luv Kandy."

I felt a blow to my chest. It hit hard. I couldn't breathe. I was dizzy, light-headed. It took me a few moments to regain my strength. The incredible pain was still there. Little did I know it would remain there. My throat was suddenly dry and I was struggling to think straight, to unscramble my thoughts. It wasn't like her and I were even together in any actual sense of the word. So why was I hurting? I moved into the living room and lay down on the couch. The bottle of Southern Comfort was still sitting on top of the table. Either I reached out for it, or it reached out for me, but in my hour of need, I took a swig and it consoled my troubled mind.

Those who tell you that it is better to have loved and lost have never really loved at all; at least not with their whole heart and soul. The loss of love is no less bitter a pill to swallow than the loss of a loved one to the always open arms of death. 'They' also say that time heals all wounds, but they never mention how slowly the second hand ticks for self-inflicted wounds of passion.

The remainder of August and the better part of September went by in a drunken mist, barely eating, never quite sleeping, and not truly waking. Each time one bottle was spent, another magically appeared to take its place. Every week the empties gathered for a nightly dance in the trash bin before being whisked away on garbage day.

Messages were left, cards sent enquiring about me and even house calls made by well-meaning friends, turned away by a door firmly closed shut. I'd missed Walter's filming session and I was sorry for that. I'd let him down. Most of all, I'd let myself down. There was no escaping the horrendous emptiness. But just as night washes over the world in the wee hours, the sun also rises again.

26. Golden Balls, Crazy Cats & a Handful of Hope

I cracked open my eye-lids and looked down at my overgrown toenails. I had become a throwback from the caveman era. I forced myself to my feet and went to the kitchen sink to splash my face with water. It was cold and bracing and I gasped as the icy droplets hit my skin. The mirror in the hallway scared me half to death. *Who* was that staring back at me? My facial hair had turned into a self sustaining forest, and my clothes reeked of weeks worth of body odour. Had it really come to this? Had I actually debased myself beyond all imaginable levels? It seemed so.

My stomach was doing yo-yo tricks around my ankles, so I thought it best to avoid breakfast at all costs. I tried to find my nail clippers, but they were nowhere to be found. They wouldn't have been up to the challenge anyway. I grabbed a pair of kitchen scissors, lying there amidst the empty pizza boxes and stale leftover crusts. I started with my beard, snapping away the steel-jawed blades until it was left neatly trimmed, like a prize-winning hedge. I moved on to my fingers and toes, which took greater effort than I'd initially anticipated.

My hygiene standards had suffered dramatically as a result of the depression, and the flat looked like it had been invaded by storm troopers who'd used it as an unceremonious dumping ground for raw sewage. After doing some modest cleaning, I took a warm bath and fell asleep next to a bucket of household bleach and various cleaning products. My nap only lasted for a short twenty minutes, but I felt refreshed and more like my old self.

I checked the messages on my answering machine. I thought about checking them on my cellphone too; but I'd lost the damned thing at some point during all the madness. The machine beeped as I skipped through the cold calling sales patter from double glazing companies and assorted personal injury compensation experts. Finally I came to a voice I recognised.

"Hey buddy. Haven't heard from you since you got back. Hope you got there okay. Anyway, give me a buzz when you can."

I dialled the Rabbi's number: 001-555-818-2260. It would be about morning there, and he was a typically an early riser. If I was lucky, I'd catch him before he left for the gym. The phone kept ringing out, so I thought of leaving a viciously indecent message on his voicemail. But I reneged when I heard a click on the other end.

"Glassman residence."

"Avi?"

"Max! Where've you been dude? I was shitting bricks thinking something terrible had happened to you."

"It did. I was kidnapped by a group of mountain dwellers who tortured me until I revealed the location of that secret stash of yak's milk."

"You didn't tell them, did you?"

"No. But they may come looking for you. They *knew* I was going to send it to you!"

"Oh God! Why Lord, why?"

I could hear that was struggling to keep a straight face.

"I guess they had intelligence. The CIA must have been in on it! Why, they're probably listening to us right now."

"Don't say things like that man. I'm already peeing my jogging pants."

"Sorry. I would've called sooner, but I was on a despicable downer."

"The girl?"

"Yeah."

"Damn. I'm sorry man. If it makes you feel any better, things are rough here too."

"How so?"

"Well my accountant finally decided to file a Chapter 11."

"A Chapter 11?"

"Yeah. Bankruptcy. It was the only option. Not sure

what's going to happen with the house yet."

"Damn. I'm sorry to hear that."

"Don't be. It's for the best I think. The Lord's way of telling me to be one of my flock and focus on my destiny."

"Well, I'm a great believer in looking at the bright side."

"Listen, I don't want to cut this short, but I have to pack the little man's lunch and do the school run this morning."

"No problemo. I'll catch you when I catch you. Take it easy Avi"

I felt bad for the Rabbi. There he was, in the middle of losing everything, and I'd been moaning about some slut. All things considered, I wasn't doing too badly. But I still needed some fresh air and the company of those afflicted with a similar dreadful melancholy.   By mid afternoon I was safely ensconced in the Scotia Bar on Stockwell Street. It was a pub I visited infrequently. In a way, it was like a second home. It made me feel like I was back in the womb, within the familiar folds of a dysfunctional family. Maybe it was the rustic charm of the panelled woodwork; maybe it was the large selection of in-house ales. It didn't matter which. As I got closer to the pumps, Colin greeted me in his typical warm manner. Colin was one of the bar-staff, a real stand up individual who'd perhaps spent too much of his time listening to me whine on certain Saturday nights before inevitably hideous Sunday mornings.

"You're usual?" he asked.

"No. I think I'll have a Guinness today."

"Coming right up."

He pulled the pint and left it to settle on the drainer. There was nothing worse than taking a gulp from an unsettled pint of Guinness. I'd done that once when I was served in a Belgian bar by a man who knew nothing about running a proper pub. I glanced over at the suit next to me who had his eyes glued to his latest gadget. He was toying that ipad like it was his girlfriend's cunt, scrolling up, down, side to side and then stopping because his fingers got too tired. He was probably a clerk in the Sheriff Court from further down the road. He had that look about him; of a jaded man who'd wasted his precious hours in the company of contemptible villains. I glanced over his shoulder as he trawled the Google news links on the touchscreen in his hand. The Bank of England was revising its forecasts for the future, the dollar was being downgraded below its triple A rating, and the Euro was hurtling towards an imminent collapse. All those doughnuts cooked in black oil in American bakeries, ready for export to nations far and wide, were going to cost that little bit more. But I couldn't bring myself to truly give a fuck about it. Not one single, solitary raccoon's ass of a fuck. We'd all rolled the dice once too often. Snake eyes had to come up sometime. Every sensible gambler knows that you have to learn to lose when you play to win. It was time to let it go. We weren't the first to spring up on this godforsaken rock, but we appeared to be doing everything possible to make sure we'd be the last. Humanity was eating itself. We'd forgotten how to stay smart, hang loose and be free. We could never break the terrible constraints of moral addiction and liberate ourselves from the dismal undercurrents of control, poverty and pain.

The barfly at the other end of the bar slammed down his pint.

"This's been such a fucked up year hasn't it?" he shouted.

"Yeah," I said.

"You couldn't make any of this bollocks up! It's just a complete shit storm."

"The suit moved away, unwilling to engage in any kind of discourse with the likes of us. We'd probably offended him with our presence.

"Posh git," muttered the barfly.

Colin brought over my Guinness and I sipped on it, nursing it for as long as I could. He added the cost to my running tab. We'd gotten into the habit of me racking it up as high as it would go and then paying it at the end of the year. It had become a sort of ritual.

Maggie, the kindly landlady who ran the joint, brought over a plate of food for me, and I ravenously devoured the steak and chips while she sat there staring at me. She put on her glasses and folded her arms, sitting back slightly as if she were examining me like some medical doctor.

"You look a little green around the gills. Is everything alright?" she asked.

"Yeah. Everything's fine. I've just been a little under the weather."

"I like the beard," she said. "It suits you."

She went back to help Colin and I looked through the leaflets sitting in bundles beside the wet coasters. There was one in particular that got my attention. It was for a gig later in the evening. I put in my pocket and decided to take it easy on the drinking front. I ordered a tall glass of Coca-cola and watched the football on the flat-screen television mounted on the wall bracket.

This was an Old Firm match that the commentators often referred to as the Glasgow Derby. It was a clash between titans. Rangers FC pitted against their greatest adversaries in the known galaxy; Celtic FC. Rangers had previously won three Scottish Premier League titles in succession, and they held a four point advantage over their arch rivals. But in the last season, Celtic had cleaned up pretty well, picking up the majority of points in the Old Firm league games; though they did not win the championship. In the opening first half, there were no easy chances taken or given by either side. Three precision targeted attempts at securing victory yielded results, and with each goal came the cacophony of celebratory screaming. It took Rangers midfielder and striker Steven Naismith to break the initial deadlock, and he delivered his first successful attack, after returning Kevin Wilson's clearance with terminal intensity. Striker Gary Hooper, an Emboldened Englishman with an equally unstoppable hard-on for scoring on and off the pitch, restored parity for Celtic. But there was another harsh sting in the tail awaiting Rangers. Allan McGregor, goalkeeper and resident half-wit of the day, allowed the ball to slip right out from his hands, following a long shot Hail Mary volley from Moroccan born Left Back, Badr El Kaddouri. Rangers' manager Ali McCoist however, made it a personal point at half-time to praise McGregor for his performance throughout the last season. But it had clearly escaped his attention that *this* was not last season.

The second half did not start well. Rangers Forward Kyle Lafferty 'equalised', only to have his efforts discounted as offside. He then threw away two opportunities to make up for his initial disappointment. This caused some panic in the trenches. Celtic Centre Back, Glenn Looves, kept his cool and went deep behind enemy lines with the intention of shooting his arsenal of explosive footwork into the back of the net. But his well played header met with an immovable goal post, thwarting him and sending him deep into despair. Lafferty still managed to prove his worth after firing the inflated missile of a football past the goalposts and securing the lead for Rangers in this testosterone fuelled frenzy. The fans in both stands went wild, cheering, hissing, booing and baying for blood. This was all out war, two tribes slugging it out for the win. Celtic's aspirations were laid to rest after Brown's injury and a red card send off for Mulgrew put another nail in the coffin. The final seal on the death of the SPL dream came when Naismith swooped down with great vengeance and again delivered a fantastic end score for McCoists team. It was a brutal defeat. But every player had given it their all. Rangers fans celebrated their 4-2 success, while their Celtic counterparts sat in pubs across Glasgow, intent on drowning in their sadness - before punching out some nervous 'Hun' making his way home with his Rangers scarf draped proudly over his neck. Of course, Rangers fans were equally riddled with hooligans. Some were not dignified victors, insisting on battering every 'Tim' they came across, just because they'd dared to challenge them on the pitch. Orange and Green littered onto the streets, outside the stadiums and yelled drunken slogans at no-one in particular.

I decided to wait it out until the trouble died down. The Scotia had no ties to either team and was considered neutral ground; akin to holy ground in the film Highlander. A stack of bundled newspapers lay on the table behind me. I thumbed through one from the top of the pile. There was nothing of great interest. After recent weeks even the generally fascinating, which used to pique my curiosity, no longer got my attention. But around page twelve, a small caption caught my eye. It was a story about the Occupy Wall Street protests in New York. There was a police crackdown on yet another peaceful demonstration, in another part of the world. The barbarity of the beatings and tear gas attacks on people exorcising their constitutional rights was revolting. It left no difference between America, Syria, Libya, or Iran. It roused in me a deep fury that I was sure was going to boil over and make me into a font of misplaced rage. The photographs were abysmally heinous, showing savagery beyond any jungle standards. Women and children were being mauled in ways that not even a Bengal tiger would have. When several of the protesters walked into a branch of a local bank to demand their money, they were either ejected or locked in, and experienced the full wrath of hired goons and plain clothes detectives, conspiring to create mass mayhem, and hoping that their efforts would force the hippy bastards to evacuate the makeshift camps they'd set up.

This kind of crazed badness was enough to send anyone to the local looney bin. I entertained the idea of cryogenics; freezing myself and becoming an immortal human icicle - at least until the gloom was overcome with sensible strategies and decent politics. But I knew that this was not likely. Besides which, there was a serious drawback to the plan. It would quite probably hamper my sex-life, and that did not make it an appealing prospect. I dismissed the notion as quickly as it had entered my mind. I finished off my coke and grabbed my leather jacket. It was 8pm and I felt a desperate need to escape. I remembered the leaflet that I'd stuffed into my pocket earlier. The gig started at 9pm, and I had a little time to kill so I went outside, lit up a cigarette and took a walk around the block. As I stood there enjoying my smoke, I looked out onto the reflective glass-cased St Enoch Shopping Centre. The sun bounced off it's windows and right into the eyes of anyone who looked in its direction.

'Fuck it!' I thought. 'No sense in hanging around here.'

I walked up to Trongate then turned left onto Argyle Street, which was mobbed with football freaks and uncouth sons of a thousand bitches, spitting and spewing over every one who crossed their path. There was no avoiding them. But my demeanour must have shown them that I wasn't prepared to put up with their level of infantile bullshit. They avoided me like the plague after I glared at them like a Rottweiler, ready to tear chunks out of its prospective victim. The no good scum among them terrorised the streets as if *they* owned them. They all headed down into the guts of the Subway system, whooping and screeching like owls on a twilight hunt. I was rid of them. But I spared a thought for the decent people who'd have to put up with them. I carried on down towards Union Street and finally hit Hope Street, where I turned right at the traffic lights. There was a world of difference between Oswald Street and Hope Street; and they were only a road apart. The former looked like Beirut in its worst moments, while the latter was trendy, upper-class and catered to loaded rich men and women of international mystery.

I took a left onto Waterloo street and right on the corner was Pivo Pivo, a sort of bar, restaurant and club, merged into one in a hideous underground bunker, serving imported beers with strange names and stranger patrons who frequented this hideout. I suspected that it had originally been built as some kind of nuclear fallout shelter. The bouncer nodded as I went in and I went downstairs where a large sandwich board announced the designated performer. "Tina Taylor, for one night only: her music makes manly men weep with ecstasy.'

I ordered a bottle of Argentinian suds and sat down near the stage. A nasal speaking no-hoper at the next table leaned over and said something. I couldn't quite make it out at first.

"Awright pal. Yoo waint sum ae this?" he flashed a baggie.

"No, I'm good," I replied.

The freak of nature had just offered me Smack. But I wasn't inclined to trust the gaunt-faced fucker. There was no telling what he or his own supplier may have done with it. It could have been cut with anything; rat poison even. And there was another factor to consider. Heroin was not a recreational drug that I was inclined to use. Its morphine like effects meant that it jacked itself into your system faster than spyware on a Russian horse porn website. The bouncer from outside walked toward me, and at first I was concerned that I was about to be thrown out. But instead, he grabbed the junkie dealer.

"I know you're dealing in here you little prick! Get the fuck out before I call the cops."

I watched the jaundiced druggie run like the wind. It was a shame he couldn't get clean. He may have done well in the upcoming London Olympics.

Tina Taylor came on stage sooner than had been billed on the board. Her jet black hair flowed down past her shoulders, stopping just where her waist started. Her round face and brown almond eyes made her irresistibly attractive. She performed a sound check as the DJ behind the mixing booth turned off the hypnotising melodies that had been playing in the background. Her drummer laid down a 'phat' beat on the skins as she began strumming her guitar and serenading the microphone with the sweetest voice I'd ever heard. I could sense the promise of passion making its way into midnight hours.

For the game of life there was only one rule: take the risk, forget the fall.

END

Proof

10722438R00134

Made in the USA
Charleston, SC
27 December 2011